主　编

李昌银

副主编

黄　瑛　彭庆华

General Editor

Li Changyin

Professor of English Yunnan Normal University

Associate General Editors

Huang Ying

Professor of English Yunnan Normal University

Peng Qinghua

Professor of English Yunnan Normal University

云南少数民族经典作品英译文库
Classics of Yunnan Ethnic Groups in English Translation

主编 李昌银 General Editor Li Changyin
副主编 黄瑛 彭庆华 Associate General Editors Huang Ying & Peng Qinghua

The Gold Flute

金 笛

搜集整理◎刘德荣
张鸿鑫
陶永华
英译◎尹绍东
译校◎[美]包琼

Collected & Edited by Liu Derong,
Zhang Hongxin & Tao Yonghua
Translated by Yin Shaodong
Revised by Joan Cecile Boulerice

云南出版集团
云南人民出版社

图书在版编目（CIP）数据

金笛：汉、英 / 刘德荣，张鸿鑫，陶永华搜集整理；尹绍东英译. -- 昆明：云南人民出版社，2018.12

（云南少数民族经典作品英译文库 / 李昌银主编）

ISBN 978-7-222-17500-6

Ⅰ. ①金… Ⅱ. ①刘… ②张… ③陶… ④尹… Ⅲ. ①苗族－叙事诗－中国－汉、英 Ⅳ. ①I222.7

中国版本图书馆CIP数据核字(2018)第277438号

出 品 人 李 维 赵石定
项目统筹 周 祥 殷筱钊
项目组稿 郭木玉
责任编辑 郭木玉 任建红 李东华
设计制作 马 滨 三人禾
责任校对 张齐英 崔苡菡 付芳侠 周桉吉
责任印制 陆卫华 代隆参

云南少数民族经典作品英译文库
Classics of Yunnan Ethnic Groups in English Translation

金 笛
The Gold Flute

搜集整理◎刘德荣 张鸿鑫 陶永华
英译◎尹绍东
译校◎[美]包琼

Collected & Edited by Liu Derong,
Zhang Hongxin & Tao Yonghua
Translated by Yin Shaodong
Revised by Joan Cecile Boulerice

出 版 云南出版集团 云南人民出版社
发 行 云南人民出版社
社 址 昆明市环城西路609号
邮 编 650034
网 址 www.ynpph.com.cn
E-mail ynrms@sina.com
开 本 787mm×1092mm 1/16
印 张 17.25
字 数 280千
版 次 2018年12月第1版第1次印刷
印 刷 云南出版印刷（集团）有限责任公司 云南新华印刷一厂
书 号 ISBN 978-7-222-17500-6
定 价 98.00元

云南人民出版社
公众微信号

序　一

◎李正栓

民族典籍英译是传播中国文化、文学和文明的重要途径，是中华文化走出去的重要组成部分。文化与文学的传播，是一个国家提高文化软实力的重要方式，在文化交流和文明建设中起着不可或缺的作用，对提高国家对外话语权、构建国家对外话语体系以及对建设世界文学都有积极意义。

中国各少数民族拥有许多优秀的典籍，具有很高的文物价值、文学价值和文化价值。各民族的先人们通过口头流传或用文字记述了他们各具特色的文化。各少数民族几乎都有自己民族的创世史、史诗和神话传说。

中国民族典籍独具特色，不可替代。重视民族典籍的翻译和研究工作，对于挖掘各民族优秀文化，保护各民族文明，增强各民族之间的沟通和了解，进一步向世界其他地区传播各少数民族优秀文化，乃至提高我国文化软实力都有着重要意义。不少少数民族聚居地处于祖国边疆，有的处在“一带一路”建设关键部位，有的处在与周边国家进行各种交流的重要位置。

中国民族典籍是世界多元文化的有机组成部分，与其他文化共同造就了世界文化的绚丽多姿。世界正因为其文化多样性才变得缤纷多彩。我国各民族典籍中包含的文化多样性极大地丰富了世界多元、特色鲜明的文化。人们对多样性形成全新的认识角度和思维方式。多样性开阔了人们的视野，丰富了人们思考问题的角度。挖掘这些典籍中所蕴含的教育价值和文化价值，对世界其他民族都有指导和借鉴意义，并且有助于建设我国的文化自信。

民族典籍本身蕴含的特殊价值对加强民族文化了解、促进中外文化交流具有重大意义。民族典籍英译具有文学翻译和文化传递之功能，有对外宣传作用，还是一种文学外交。因此，民族典籍翻译和研究对于维护祖国统一、促进民族团结、稳定边疆以及增强国内各民族和中外文化之间的交流都起着极为重要的作用。

中华人民共和国成立以后，中央政府一直十分重视民族典籍翻译和研究工作，提供了强有力的政策支持，并采取了一系列有效措施，加快了各少数民族典籍的抢救、整理、翻译和研究的进程。中央政府多次召开西藏工作会议和新疆工作会议。近年来，国际和国内对于多元文化高度关注，少数民族文学典籍的翻译已然成为业内研究的热点。

近年来，民族典籍翻译和研究迅猛发展，势头良好。国家大力支持，发放国家社科基金课题，教育部和国家民委也发放课题，扶持了一大批研究者。很多民族典籍翻译课题得以立项并顺利开展；为数不少的民族典籍被翻译成汉语、英语和其他语言并出版发行；越来越多的业界人士致力于这个满富生机的学术领域。

在中国文化走出去的国家战略下，全国少数民族典籍英译学术研讨会陆续召开，已经召开三次。

云南是中国民族最多的省份。人口在5000人以上的少数民族有25个，其中有15个民族为云南所特有，分别是：白族、哈尼族、傣族、傈僳族、佤族、拉祜族、纳西族、景颇族、布朗族、普米族、阿昌族、基诺族、怒族、德昂族、独龙族。其中除白族人口占全国白族人口总数的84%以上外，其他14个民族95%居住在云南。

云南还是我国跨境民族最多的省份。在云南的25个少数民族中，有16个民族跨境而居，分别是：傣族、壮族、苗族、景颇族、瑶族、哈尼族、德昂族、佤族、拉祜族、彝族、阿昌族、傈僳族、布依族、怒族、布朗族、独龙族。

云南少数民族创造了辉煌的文化。据不完全统计，云南少数民族文字文献古籍蕴藏量达10万余册（卷），口传古籍4万余种。云南省民委少数民族古籍整理出版规划办公室为了挽救和保护这些古籍，计划在5年内编纂出版100卷《云南少数民族古籍珍本集成》。这是一个令人瞩目的庞大计划。将这些古籍中的珍品翻译介绍给世界，不仅能够弘扬云南省丰富多彩的民族文化，而且有助于增进与南亚东南亚国家的理解与交流，为“一带一路”倡议的实施做出贡献。

云南师范大学外国语学院很重视这一领域的工作。在外国语学院领导支持下，李昌银教授带领一个由教授和中青年学者组成的团队对精选出来的17部云南少数民族经典作品进行英译，计划在5年内（“十三五”期间）翻译出版。这是一项十分有意义的宏大工程。

这17部民族典籍，内容全部为各民族的英雄史诗或神话传说，具有很高的历史意义和文学价值。这些作品涉及阿昌族、白族、傣族、德昂族、哈尼族、景颇族、拉祜族、苗族、纳西族、普米族、彝族等 11 个少数民族。

云南师范大学这支翻译队伍实力强大，主要由一些多年从事翻译教学、研究和实践的教授和副教授组成，他们是李昌银、黄瑛、彭庆华、孙兴文、吴相如、刘德周、杨慧芳、郜菊、陈萍、包琼（Joan Boulerice）等国内外专家学者。他们在云南翻译界都是风云人物。

在民族典籍英译中，这支队伍异军突起，为我国民族典籍英译壮大了声势，必将为中国民族典籍走向世界而成为世界文学的一部分做出新贡献。

民族典籍翻译与研究事业关乎国家的稳定统一，关乎民族关系的和谐发展，关乎世界多元文化的实现。在中国，民族典籍资源极为丰富，有待进一步挖掘、翻译。因此，民族典籍英译前景光明。同时，我们也应意识到，仍有许多濒临消失的少数民族典籍亟待拯救，民族典籍翻译与研究工作任重而道远。

（李正栓，中国英汉语比较研究会典籍英译专业委员会常务副会长兼秘书长）

Foreword by Li Zhengshuan

The translation of Chinese ethnic classics is an important approach in spreading Chinese culture, literature and civilization. It is a crucial component of Chinese culture going global. The spreading of Chinese culture and literature is a national policy and an important way to improve the cultural soft power of China. It plays an indispensable role in the cultural exchange between China and other countries and the development of world literature.

The ethnic groups in China have countless excellent classics with high anthropological, literary and cultural value. The ancestors of each ethnic group have passed down their distinctive culture orally or in writing. Almost all the ethnic groups have their own story of creation, epics, myths and legends.

Chinese ethnic classics are unique and irreplaceable. It is imperative to attach importance to the translation and research of ethnic classics; to explore the excellent ethnic cultures; to protect the civilization of ethnic groups; to enhance the communication and understanding among ethnic groups; to further spread the outstanding culture of ethnic groups to other parts of the world; and to build the cultural strength of China. Many ethnic groups live in the border areas and thus play an important role in the cultural and economic cooperation between China and its neighbors in the context of the Belt and Road Initiative.

Chinese ethnic classics are an important component of the magnificence and diversity of world culture. It is diversity that makes the world so colorful. The cultural diversity of Chinese ethnic classics has greatly enriched the world's pluralism and its distinctive features. People around the world have formed a new understanding of diversity. This diversity has expanded people's horizon and enriched their way of thinking. Digging out the educational and cultural value in these classics can contribute to the construction of China's self-confidence in culture.

The special value of the ethnic classics itself is of great significance to the strengthening of national culture and intercultural communication between China and foreign countries. The translation of ethnic classics is not just a literary exchange, but also a form of cultural communication. It is diplomacy through literature in that it consolidates the cultural ties between China and other countries.

After the founding of the People's Republic of China, the central government attached great importance to the translation and research of ethnic classics, provided the a great deal of policy support, and adopted a series of effective measures to speed up the process of rescuing, collating, translating and studying ethnic classics. The central government has convened several working conferences on Tibet and Xinjiang. In recent years, both China and other countries have paid close attention to multiculture. The translation of ethnic classics has become a hot topic.

In recent years, the translation and research of ethnic classics have progressed rapidly and have shown good prospects. The government strongly supports and grants the research projects of the national social science fund. The Ministry of Education and the State Ethnic Affairs Commission are also issuing research projects and giving funding to a large number of researchers. Many research projects on ethnic classics have been approved and carried out. Many ethnic classics have been translated into Chinese, English and other languages and published. More and more professionals have dedicated themselves to this new sphere of learning.

In this context, the academic conferences on translation of ethnic classics are held one after another all around the country. And up to now three have been held.

Yunnan is the province which has the most ethnic groups in China. Besides Han people, there are 25 ethnic groups, each with a population of more than 5,000. Among them, 15 ethnic groups are unique to Yunnan, which are the Bai, the Hani, the Dai, the Lisu, the Wa, the Lahu, the Naxi, the Jingpo, the Bulang, the Pumi, the Achang, the Jinuo, the Nu, the De'ang and the Dulong. Among these, 84% of the total number of the Bai people in China and 95% of the other 14 ethnic groups are living in Yunnan.

Yunnan is also the province which has the most cross-border ethnic groups. Of the 25 ethnic groups, 16 live across the border, namely: the Dai, the Zhuang, the Miao, the Jingpo, the Yao, the Hani, the De'ang, the Wa, the Lahu, the Yi, the Achang, the Lisu, the Buyi, the Nu, the Bulang and the Dulong.

The ethnic groups in Yunnan have created splendid cultures. According to statistics, the number of classics of Yunnan ethnic groups is more than 100 thousand volumes and classics in oral tradition are more than 40 thousand. In order to save and protect these ancient books, the Office of Classics Collation and Publishing of Yunnan Ethnic Groups Affairs Commission planned to compile and publish 100 volumes of *A Collection of Yunnan Ethnic Group Rare Books* in five years, which is an ambitious plan. The introduction of the ancient classics via translation can not only promote and develop the colorful ethnic cultures of Yunnan, but also contribute to the understanding and exchange between China and countries in South Asia and Southeast Asia and to the implementation of the Belt and Road Initiative as well.

The School of Foreign Languages and Literature of Yunnan Normal University is paying close attention to this field. With the support of the School and the University, Professor Li Changyin is leading a group of professors and young scholars to do the project of "*Classics of Yunnan Ethnic Groups in English Translation*", which includes 17 ethnic classics selected carefully from Yunnan's bountiful ethnic classics. These books are the heroic epics or myths and legends of each ethnic groups with great historical significance and literary value. They will finish the translation in five years (during "the thirteenth five-year plan"). After that, all the works will be published by Yunnan People's Publishing House.

The 17 works cover 11 ethnic groups: the Achang, the Bai, the Dai, the De'ang, the Hani, the Jingpo, the Lahu, the Miao, the Naxi, the Pumi and the Yi. All of these groups except the Miao and the Yi are unique to Yunnan.

The translation team of Yunnan Normal University is full of strength and vitality, composed of professors and associate professors who have been occupied in translation teaching, research, and practice for a long time. They are Li Changyin, Huang Ying, Peng Qinghua, Sun Xingwen, Wu Xiangru, Liu Dezhou, Yang Huifang, Gao Ju, Chen Ping, Joan Boulerice and other experts and scholars who are representative figures in the translation field in Yunnan province.

This team is a new force that has suddenly arisen in terms of translating ethnic classics. It is expanding the momentum of ethnic classics translation in China and has made a new contribution for China's ethnic classics to go global and become a part of world literature.

The translation and research of ethnic classics are related to the development of Chinese culture and the realization of multiculturalism in the world. In China, ethnic classics are extremely rich in resources, which require us to make further exploration and research and translate them into other languages. Therefore, the future of translating ethnic classics is bright. At the same time, we should also realize that there are still many ethnic works which are close to extinction and urgently need to be rescued. We still have a long way to go in the fields of translation and research in ethnic classics.

(Li Zhengshuan, Standing Vice Chairman and Secretary General, Classics Translation Committee of CACSEC)

序　二

◎王　宏

好友云南师范大学外国语学院李昌银教授来电嘱托我为“云南少数民族经典作品英译文库”的出版写一序言，并随即发来该文库的背景资料，让我“不着急，慢慢写”。我本人从事中国典籍英译及研究，深知少数民族典籍对外传译的重要性，但又是少数民族典籍翻译的门外汉。因此，我是怀着虚心学习的态度来写此序言的。近年来，在中国文化“走出去”战略工程大背景下，在中央和地方各级政府的大力支持下，我国少数民族典籍的对外传译及研究工作顺利开展，取得了很大的进步。请看以下数据：

2008 年，广西百色学院韩家权教授获批国家社科基金项目《布洛陀史诗》（壮汉英对照）。该项目已顺利结项，并于 2013 年 12 月获得中国民间文艺最高奖“山花奖”。

2012 年，广西百色学院外语系翻译团队翻译的国家级非物质文化遗产《壮族嘹歌》（英文版）由广西师范大学出版社正式出版。

2012 年，东北大学秦皇岛分校吴松林教授主编的《蒙古族系列：江格尔（汉英对照）》（上下册）由吉林大学出版社出版。

2013 年，河北师范大学李正栓教授英译《藏族格言诗》

由长春出版社出版发行。

2013 年，云南财经大学崔晓霞教授撰写的《〈阿诗玛〉英译研究》收入由王宏印教授主编、民族出版社出版的“民族典籍翻译研究丛书”。

2014 年，东北大学秦皇岛分校吴松林教授撰写的《满族档案文献研究》申请到国家社科后期资助，他英译的《英雄格斯尔可汗》由吉林大学出版社出版。

2014 年，中南民族大学张立玉教授主持的“土家族主要典籍英译及研究”获批国家社科基金项目。

2015 年，西安外国语大学梁真惠副教授撰写的《〈玛纳斯〉翻译传播研究》收入由王宏印教授主编、民族出版社出版的“民族典籍翻译研究丛书”。

与此同时，第一届和第二届全国少数民族典籍英译学术研讨会分别于 2012 年和 2014 年在广西民族大学和大连民族学院举行，参加会议的院校分布之广、与会代表数量之众、提交论文数量之多和涉及研究话题之细，十分可喜。2016 年还将在中南民族大学举行第三届全国少数民族典籍英译学术研讨会。

为什么少数民族典籍的对外传译及研究工作在短短几年就受到译界的青睐，取得众多成果？我认为，这在很大程度上归于典籍翻译界乃至翻译界同仁对“中国典籍”的重新思考和认识。中国典籍浩如烟海，卷帙浩繁，举世瞩目，是全人类共同的精神财富。但对于中国典籍的理解，我们以前较多限于汉民族的重要文献和书籍，而对少数民族多有忽略。在讨论中国典籍时，也较多关注古代文学作品。其实，中国典籍指“中国清代末年1911年以前的重要文献和书籍”，这就要求我们从事典籍翻译时，不但要翻译古代文学典籍作品，还要翻译古代哲学、科技、法律、医学、经济、军事、天文、地理等诸多方面的典籍作品，不但要翻译汉民族的典籍作品，也要翻译各少数民族的典籍作品。

民族典籍具有该民族的原型符号的特质，蕴藏着能够“遗传”并不断“再生”的文化基因。民族典籍是中华传统文化的内核，同时还是中华传统文化的符号构成规则。中国是具有56个民族的多民族国家，少数民族典籍是我国少数民族勤劳与智慧的结晶，是中华文明、也是世界文明不可或缺的一部分。少数民族典籍对外传译具有跨文化交流的作用，它不但有助于更多的人了解少数民族的独特文化，而且还有助于保护少数民族文化的独特性、维持少数民族文化多样性、促进各民族团结、提升中华文化软实力等。

中国少数民族典籍涉及宗教、文学、历史、语言、医学、天文历算等领域，内容丰富，版本多样，载体特殊，传承奇特。仅以《中国少数民族古籍总目提要》为例，该书于1997年正式立项，全书总体设计约60卷、110册，目前已出版23个民族卷共20册：纳西族卷、白族卷、东乡族卷·裕固族卷·保安族卷、土族卷·撒拉族卷、锡伯族卷、哈尼族卷、回族卷·铭刻、柯尔克孜族卷、羌族卷、毛南族卷·京族卷、仫佬族卷、达斡尔族卷、土家族卷、鄂温克族卷、鄂伦春族卷、赫哲族卷、苗族卷、侗族卷、黎族卷、朝鲜族卷。该书真实地反映了我国各少数民族古籍赋存的全面情况，充实了中国的历史和文化内容，为后人探索各种文化形式的源流、揭示中国社会文化发展的轨迹提供了极为珍贵的资料，为我国乃至世界各国人文科学研究提供了一套新颖而全面的资料，对于弘扬中华民族传统文化具有深远的历史意义和现实意义。

少数民族典籍的对外传译是一项艰巨的工作，涉及将少数民族语言译成汉语、少数民族语言之间的互译和少数民族语言译成外语（主要是英语）。前两类翻译历史源远流长，最早可追溯到春秋战国时代《越人歌》的翻译，即汉、壮语之间的翻译。少数民族典籍译成外语的时间则要晚一些。据考证，维吾尔族古典长诗《福乐智慧》成书于 1069 年或 1070 年，目前尚未发现完整的原稿，只存留下来三个抄本，分别为赫拉特抄本、费尔干纳抄本与埃及抄本，其中费尔干纳抄本于 12~13 世纪用阿拉伯文纳斯赫体抄写，1914 年发现于今中亚乌孜别克斯坦纳曼干城，现存于该共和国科学院东方研究所。这是少数民族典籍译介到国外的最早纪录。少数民族典籍外译在现代有了较快发展。一些少数民族典籍，如藏族的《格萨尔王传》、蒙古族的《江格尔》和柯尔克孜族的《玛纳斯》等英雄史诗，云南彝族的《阿诗玛》、维吾尔族的《艾里甫和赛乃姆》等民间叙事长诗已先后被翻译成英语及其他外国文字，为世人所知。这对传承少数民族经典，推动中外文化交流起到了不可替代的作用。然而，还有大量的中国少数民族典籍等待我们去翻译和研究。

云南省少数民族典籍资源十分丰富。据不完全统计，云南少数民族文字文献古籍蕴藏量达 10 万余册（卷），口传古籍 4 万余种。“云南少数民族经典作品英译文库”正是依托云南省丰富的少数民族典籍资源，借助云南师范大学外国语学院强大的翻译师资队伍，在云南人民出版社的有力支持下，首次将云南少数民族经典作品成系列对外译介的大力举措。云南师范大学外国语学院对“云南少数民族经典作品英译文库”十分重视，他们首先邀请省内外少数民族语言文化研究专家对云南民族典籍和民族文化经典作品进行筛选，做到“好中选好，优中选优”，同时调配最强的翻译力量承担文库的翻译任务。我粗略看了该文库的选题，发现选题面广，覆盖范围宽，收入了云南省阿昌族、白族、傣族、纳西族、德昂族、哈尼族、景颇族、拉祜族、苗族、普米族和彝族等民族的典籍作品。云南共有25个少数民族，其中11个少数民族的典籍作品都覆盖到了，不少作品还是首次译成英文。这将彻底改变云南少数民族典籍由于对外译介数量较少，不为世界了解的尴尬局面。

对于云南师范大学外国语学院而言，把少数民族典籍英译作为翻译专业的优势特色进行建设，这将对该院的学科建设起到助推作用。“云南少数民族经典作品英译文库”所产生的翻译成果和研究成果将培养出一批优秀的典籍翻译和研究团队，凸显该院在全国的学术特色和学术影响，同时还能将翻译能力和研究能力转化为教学能力，提高云南师范大学外国语学院翻译专业研究生的培养质量，为社会输送高水平的翻译人才，有力地支撑学院翻译专业学科的建设和发展。我对云南师范大学外国语学院的翻译师资队伍较为熟悉。作为云南省唯一获得省级高校优势特色学科建设项目的外国语学院，该院具有雄厚的翻译师资力量，在云南省各高校中当属第一。多年来，该院翻译与跨文化研究团队一直承担着对外交流与合作的各种口笔译项目及任务。由外国语学院精心挑选和确定的“云南少数民族经典作品英译文库”翻译人员绝大多数都是云南省翻译领域里的知名教授或专家，有国外留学经历，且具有扎实的英汉双语语言功底，曾翻译出版多部译著和翻译作品，并且主持和参与过多项翻译项目的研究。我阅读李昌银教授发来的文库翻译人员名单，发现多名我所熟悉的知名教授、博士也在其中，感到格外放心。

“云南少数民族经典作品英译文库”的出版发行是云南省翻译界的一件大事，也是我国少数民族典籍翻译传来的又一佳音。想当年，我和《大中华文库》总协调人李林老师曾在参加全国典籍英译学术研讨会之余一起找到李昌银教授，敦促李教授向学校和同事呼吁，少数民族典籍翻译及研究是富矿，值得快挖、深挖，能早出成果，出大成果。今天，我们当年的心愿变成了美好的现实，心里感到特别高兴。再次热烈祝贺“云南少数民族经典作品英译文库”的顺利出版！

（王宏，中国典籍翻译研究会副会长、苏州大学博士生导师）

Foreword by Wang Hong

My friend Professor Li Changyin of Yunnan Normal University asked me to write a few words for the publication of *Classics of Yunnan Ethnic Groups in English Translation*. I am more than delighted to do it. As I have been doing research in the English translation of Chinese classics, I know how important his work is. In recent years, substantial progress has been made in translating Chinese ethnic classics into English and other foreign languages. Books published in this respect include *The Liao Songs of the Zhuang Nationality* (Nanning: Guangxi Normal University Press, 2008, English Edition), *Mongolian Series: Jianggeer* (Changchun: Jilin University Press, 2012, Bilingual Edition), *Tibetan Gnomic Verses Translated into English* (Changchun: Changchun Press, 2013), and *Geser Khan: a Hero* (Changchun: Jilin University Press, 2014). Several projects in the English translation of ethnic classics have received funding from the National Planning Office of Philosophy and Social Science and, as a result, a number of monographs and PhD dissertations have been published.

Meanwhile, it is encouraging to see that the first conferences on English translation of ethnic classics in China have been held in Guangxi Nationalities University and

Dalian Nationalities Institute respectively. Participants were both many and enthusiastic. Many papers were presented and a lot of topics discussed. The third conference will be hosted by South Central Nationalities University in 2016.

Why, then, has this field attracted so much attention from translators and scholars alike and accomplished so much in just a few years? The answer, I believe, lies in a rethinking of what constitutes Chinese classics as an indispensable part of human heritage. We used to see Chinese classics as more or less equal to the classics of the Han people, excluding works by other ethnic groups. Moreover, when we talk about Chinese classics, we focus too much on the literary works of ancient times. Yet Chinese classics actually refer to "important works and books before 1911, the year when the Qing dynasty fell, bringing an end to imperial rule." This definition requires us to pay attention not just to literary works, but also writings in other subjects, such as philosophy, science, law, medicine, economics, military affairs, astronomy, and geography, not only Han works, but writings by other ethnic groups as well.

The classical works of a nation are its archetypal symbols, the major carriers of its cultural genes. Chinese classics make up the core of Chinese tradition. The Chinese nation consists of 56 ethnic groups. Ethnic classics are an important part of not only Chinese traditional culture, but also of world civilization. The translation of these works into other languages is important in that it helps to promote cross-cultural communications between China and other countries and to protect and preserve the uniqueness and diversity of ethnic cultures by making them accessible to foreign readers.

Chinese ethnic classics cover a variety of areas, such as religion, literature, history, language, medicine, astrology, and calendar, with numerous editions, special media and unique ways of transmission from generation to generation. Take, for example, *An Anthology of Chinese Ethnic Classics*, a colossal project that includes 110 volumes, 20 of which, from 23 ethnic groups, have been published. The anthology reflects the variety and quantity of China's ethnic classics and provides valuable material and resources for studying, understanding and developing Chinese culture and history in a more comprehensive and sustainable way.

The translation of Chinese ethnic classics into foreign languages is a very demanding job, involving rendering from ethnic languages to Chinese, between ethnic languages, and from ethnic languages (often via Chinese) to foreign languages. The first two types of translation can be traced back to the Spring and Autumn Period, when *The Song of the Yue People* was translated from their mother tongue into Chinese. The earliest translation of ethnic classics into a foreign language is *Wisdom of Royal Glory*, a long poem of the Uygurs, which was rendered from the source language into Arabic and is now in the Oriental Institute of Uzbekistan at Namangan. But it was not until modern times that the translation of ethnic classics into foreign languages accelerated. Noticeably, ethnic epics, such as *The Story of Prince Geser* of the Tibetans, *The Story of Jianggeer* of the Mongolians, *Manas* of the Kyrgyz, and narrative poems such as *Ashima* of the Yi people, *Alip and Salam* of the Uygurs, etc., have been published. These translations have contributed to acquainting the world with Chinese ethnic classics, but many remain to be translated.

Yunnan is rich in ethnic classics, boasting more than 100 thousand volumes of written classics and over 40 thousand pieces of oral literature. Relying on such bountiful resources, as a collective endeavor of the translation team of the School of Foreign Languages and Literature, Yunnan Normal University and with the help of Yunnan People's Publishing House, *Classics of Yunnan Ethnic Groups in English Translation* is the first project to translate Yunnan ethnic classics into English on a large scale. The School adheres to a professional spirit and academic standard in carrying out the project by selecting the most authoritative texts in the source language (Chinese) and recruiting the best translators from its huge faculty. The selection of the works, covering eleven of the twenty-five ethnic groups of the province, indicates expertise and insight. The implementation of the project will change the embarrassing obscurity of Yunnan ethnic classics by making them known to the world, many of them for the first time.

In light of disciplinary development, the project is of

great importance, too. Participating in the translation will strengthen the academic foundation of the teachers, enrich their experience and enhance their translation skills and research ability. This in turn will help them become better teachers and thus able to educate students with higher quality. The publication of the books will add greatly to the faculty accomplishments of the School and raise the academic standing of Yunnan Normal University by taking the first step in this direction among the universities of Yunnan province.

This publication project is a great event not only for Yunnan itself, but also for China. Looking back, I remember that Professor Li Changyin, our friend Li Lin, editor of the *Library of Chinese Classics*, and I talked enthusiastically about initiating something like this in Yunnan when we attended a conference on the translation of ethnic classics in Soochow. Lin and I strongly suggested that Professor Li do it as soon as possible. Now I am very pleased to see our talk becoming reality. Again, my congratulations on the publication of *Classics of Yunnan Ethnic Groups in English Translation*!

(Wang Hong, PhD supervisor at Soochow University, Vice Chairman of Classics Translation Committee of CACSEC)

General Introduction

This publication project, Classics of *Yunnan Ethnic Groups in English Translation*, aims at introducing Yunnan ethnic classical works to the world by making them available to native speakers of English who might be interested in them. With the publication of the *Library of Chinese Classics*, which consists only of books written by Han authors in classical Chinese, attention now is being turned to the English translation and publication of ethnic classics, books produced by ethnic writers about their history and culture. Universities in provinces such as Guangxi, Guizhou, Liaoning, Xinjiang, and Xizang, have taken the initiative. We in Yunnan must do something, because Yunnan has the largest number of ethnic groups in China. 15 of the 25 ethnic groups in the province, the Bai, the Dai, the Hani, the Lisu, the Wa, the Lahu, the Naxi, the Jingpo, the Bulang, the Pumi, the Achang, the Jinuo, the Nu, the De'ang, and the Dulong, live in no other place but Yunnan. The classics of these people, either in their own languages or in Chinese translations, are a great treasure house, which should be accessible to English readers and scholars. But what works should be translated first?

All the 25 ethnic groups in Yunnan have their classics, epics, mythology, creation stories, folksongs, folk drama, mountain songs, and funeral lament lyrics, most of which exist in different versions in different places. According to one estimation, there are more than 100 thousand volumes of them, excluding those in oral form. After a thorough survey and extensive consultations with experts of ethnic studies, we concluded that priority must be given to epics and mythologies, as they reflect an ethnic people's philosophy, history and culture more than anything else by narrating the stories of where and how they think they came from. From many epics and mythologies, we selected 17 of the most authoritative and popular classics representing 11 Yunnan ethnic groups, the Yi, the Bai, the Miao, the Hani, the Lahu, the Naxi, the Jingpo, the Pumi, the Achang, the Dai, and the De'ang. These works are all in Chinese, translated from the original by bilingual scholars whose mother tongue is their own ethnic language and who are fluent and proficient in Chinese. Some were recorded from their oral form at rituals and performances. We did not choose texts written in the ethnic language, not least because it is very hard to find a translator who is skilled in both the ethnic language and English. Moreover, some of the classics in the ethnic language were circulated in various oral forms and fragments. The published Chinese versions have been carefully edited and translated, hence they are more reliable. The next question is: how to translate them?

It happens that all of the 17 works except one are in

verse form, with lines more or less the same length and loose rhymes, but no regular meter. A poem must be rendered into a poem; anything less is unacceptable. So here are the general rules we follow when doing the translation.

One. If the original is verse, the translated text must be verse, too.

Two. Reproduce the ideas and the images of the original as completely as possible.

Three. Reproduce the figures of speech of the original as much as possible.

Four. Do not change the number of lines in a stanza unless absolutely necessary.

Five. Do not use standard meters in English, because the Chinese original does not follow any regular meter. Use the natural rhythm of English instead, but most of the lines should look more or less the same length.

Six. Do not use rhyme unless it comes naturally and is faithful to the content of the original.

What we try to do is, to use Susan Bassnett's words, "transplant the seed", not the tree itself. As for the various aspects of form, particularly meter and end rhyme, we reproduce them when it is possible and abandon them when it is necessary.

Who will do the translations? As this is a collective project of the School of Foreign Languages and Literature of Yunnan Normal University, our team consists of a dozen faculty members and two students from our MA translation program who are already teachers in other universities. All the translators have been teaching translation and doing translation research for a long time. They have published not just academic articles on translation, but also translated books from English to Chinese or vice versa.

Traditionally, people translate into their mother tongue, not into a foreign language. But the situation is changing. Many translators today are translating from their mother tongue into a foreign language. The quality can be good, as Nike K. Pokorn and Stuart Campbell prove in *Challenging the Traditional Axioms: Translation into a non–mother tongue* (Amsterdam: John Benjamins Publishing Company, 2005) and *Translation into the Second Language* (New York: Routledge, 2013) respectively. The case of China provides further evidence for their argument. The translation of Chinese classics into English was initiated by James Legge and Herbert Allen Giles in the 19th century and carried on in the 20th century by Arthur Waley, David Hawkes, Burton Watson, John Minford, Stephen Owen and others. It is noticeable that these English and American sinologists were soon joined by Chinese scholars residing in the West, such as Hongming (Tomson) Gu and Lin Yutang, among others. They took up the job because they thought it was their obligation to give English readers more faithful translations than Western sinologists could, who, as their target language is their mother tongue, often misinterpret the original text and misrepresent Chinese culture. Since the 1950s, there has been an increasingly powerful trend for Mainland Chinese translators to render or re-render Chinese classics into foreign languages, English in particular. In our time, this work is gathering momentum, enthusiastically advocated and actively practiced by such well-known translation experts as Yang Xianyi of Beijing Foreign Language Press, Xu Yuanchong of Beijing University, Wang Rongpei of Dalian Foreign Language Institute, Wang Hongyin of Nankai University, Wang Hong of Soochow University, Li Zhengshuan of Hebei Normal University, and many more. These professors are not just translators, but also scholars in translation studies. More importantly, some of them, Xu Yuanchong, Wang Hong and Li Zhengshuan, for example, have had their translations published by Western publishers, which suggests that their English meets the international standard.

In the case of our project, we request that the translators do their best to produce good translations. When they submit them to us, they should represent the highest level that they can attain. Then the general editors appointed by the School read the translated texts and remove inaccurate renderings and grammar mistakes if there are any. On top of that, we've taken an indispensable measure to ensure that our English is readable. We asked Ms. Joan Cecile Boulerice, an American teacher who has been teaching English in our school since

2009, to read every text that we've translated and improve the English by making it more natural and idiomatic. This is the best we can do. Of course any problems that still remain in the translations are ours. They have nothing to do with our American teacher.

As the project is well under way, we would like to thank all those who have helped to make it possible. Ms Guo Muyu, director of the South and Southeast Asia Editorial Department, Yunnan People's Publishing House, has been most helpful in our cooperation. In addition, she has added importance to the project by turning it into a national publication project. Yunnan Normal University has supported us by paying the publication fees so that the translators won't have to be burdened with the financial responsibilities for this project. Professor Li Zhengshuan and Professor Wang Hong not only have always encouraged us to go on but have also written the forewords for the project, putting it in a global perspective. Ms Joan Boulerice's revision has ensured the fluency of the translated texts. Finally, special thanks must be given to Professor Wang Hong, again, and Mr Li Lin of Hunan People's Press for their suggestion that has helped us conceive the project from the very beginning.

(The General Editors, School of Foreign Languages & Literature, Yunnan Normal University, Kunming)

A Brief Introduction to *The Gold Flute*

The Gold Flute is a narrative epic loved and shared by the Hmong (Miao) people in Sichuan, Guizhou and Yunnan provinces in China, and in countries like Vietnam, Laos, Thailand, the United States and France. The plot twists and turns, full of changes, legends and rich ethnic characteristics. Up to now, it is the only epic widely circulated among the Hmong people worldwide and the reason of its wide circulation lies in their cross-border migration.

The epic mainly tells the story of two young lovers, Zhadong Piran and Mengshi Caizou, and their happiness and sufferings. It highlights the two lovers' unyielding spirit, perseverance and bravery demonstrated in their fighting with monster tigers. Mengshi Caizou was kidnapped by monster tigers, and in order to save his sweetheart from danger, Zhadong Piran went through countless hardships. Finally, he killed the tigers, rid people of the evils and reunited with his sweetheart.

The story of the two lovers, told through a gold flute and leaf music, reflects the Hmong people's pursuit and ideals. In terms of literary, artistic and aesthetic value, *The Gold Flute* is undoubtedly an encyclopedia of the history and culture of the Hmong people. The epic covers a wide range of cultural fields like clothes, music, festivals, marriage customs, funeral traditions and psychology of the Hmong people in the south and southeast of Yunnan.

The Translator

目录

Contents

第一章 夜梦

Canto 1 Night Dream

一

夺戈底①地方，
是蒙诗②的故乡。
从古到今多少年，
有支口才歌③在传唱。
口才歌唱的是什么？
一对恋人的悲欢离合；
口才歌唱的是哪样？
一支金笛奇妙无双。
这金笛呀，
能吹出心中的欢乐；
这金笛呀，
能奏出满腹的忧伤。
这对恋人呀，
就靠金笛传情意；
这对恋人呀，
就凭金笛诉衷肠。

I

The place named Duogedi①
Is the homeland of the Mengshi②.
From ancient times till now, for thousands of years,
An epic has been passed on for generations.
What is the epic about?
Two lovers' joys and sorrows, partings and reunions;
What is the subject?
The marvelous story of a matchless gold flute.
O, this gold flute
Could express the joys of the heart;
O, this gold flute
Could express the sorrows of the whole chest.
O, this couple of sweethearts,
Through the gold flute, conveyed the love of their hearts;
O, this couple of sweethearts,
Through the gold flute, poured out the longings of their hearts.

---

① 夺戈底：苗语，苗族祖先居住的地方。
② 蒙诗：花苗的自称。
③ 口才歌：即叙事歌。

① Duogedi: (Hmong language) the place where Hmong people's ancestors lived.
② Mengshi: (Hmong language) the name Flower Hmong people call themselves.

二　　II

夺戈底的山很高很高，	The mountains in Duogedi were very high;
抬头望不见峰顶；	Looking up, you saw no peaks in the sky.
夺戈底的树很密很密，	The forests in Duogedi were very dense;
透不过一线阳光；	Of a vestige of sunlight there was no trace.
夺戈底的河流宽无边啊，	The widths of the rivers in Duogedi knew no bounds;
水手也不敢把波涛闯。	Even sailors dared not swim against their tides.
在那宽宽的大河旁，	Near the wide river,
在那高高的山顶上，	On the highest peak ever,
在那密密的树林里，	In the dense forest,
住着蒙诗的夫妻俩。	There a Mengshi couple dwelt.
他们未生小咪朵[①]，	They had neither borne any sons,
也没怀过小咪彩[②]，	Nor gotten pregnant with any daughters;
夫妻各满五十岁，	Both in their fifties,
孤零相依度时光。	Lonely, they relied on each other to pass their days.
阿支[③]勤劳又诚恳，	Pop was sincere and industrious;

①咪朵：小儿子。
②咪彩：小姑娘。
③阿支：阿爹。

阿奈①贤惠又善良。
日子虽然苦，
心中却欢畅。

Mom was kind and virtuous.
Though life was hard and difficult,
They lived together in delight.

一天清晨，
阿支在楼下打长刀，
一只蜜蜂飞到他身旁。
忽前忽后围着转，
一边飞舞一边唱：
“你打长刀打大点，
打出大刀有用场。
拿在手上有分量，
好砍山地好开荒。”

Early one morning,
Downstairs, a machete Pop was forging
When a bee flew swiftly to his side.
Before and behind him, it hovered around;
While dancing in the air, the bee was singing:
“Make it larger, the machete you are forging,
And a larger one will be needed soon.
One feels it heavy when holding it in his hand;
It works well when one opens up the wild mountain.”

阿支听了叹口气：
“长刀打大了，
年老抬不动。
我无儿又无女，
大事小事没人帮。
谁替我使刀砍山呀，
谁帮我种地开荒？”

Hearing that, a sigh Pop heaved:
“If a larger machete is made,
I being old, it'll be beyond my power.
I don't have a son or a daughter;
Affairs big or small, no one offers help.
Who'll use the machete to help cut bushes down?
Who'll help open up the wilderness and have farm work done?”

① 阿奈：阿妈。

蜜蜂说：	The bee said:
“大刀打好有人使，	“The machete will be used when forged;
欢你莫着急；	You needn’t be anxious.
开荒种地有人帮，	Someone will help do the farm work and open up the wilderness;
劝你别忧伤！”	You needn’t wear a long face!”
蜜蜂的话很蹊跷，	What the bee said was quite odd;
话中有话费思量。	In its words, there was something hard to understand.
阿支眨眼正想问，	Blinking his eyes, Pop was about to ask the bee
蜜蜂早已不知飞何方。	When it flew away and disappeared completely.
阿支拉风箱，	The bellows Pop worked,
风箱呼呼响；	And it whistled and whistled;
阿支舞铁锤，	An iron hammer Pop wielded,
铁锤响叮当。	And “ding-dong, ding-dong”, it sounded.
打了三天又三夜，	After three days and three nights, the machete was forged;
大刀打得九十九寸长。	One hundred and thirty inches long it measured.
一称足有九十斤，	Forty-five kilograms weighed the machete;
从头到尾明晃晃。	From the point to the heel, it shone bright.
阿支老了使不动，	Pop was too old to put it to use,
把它挂在篱笆上。	So he hung it up on the fence.
这把大刀到底谁来使？	Who on earth would use the machete?
阿支天天在思量。	Pop was considering this in his heart daily.

一天傍晚，
阿奈在楼上织麻布，
一只凤凰飞到她身旁。
忽左忽右围着转，
一边飞舞一边唱：
“你织麻布织长点，
织出麻布有用场。
左裁右剪随你意，
好做裙子和衣裳。”

One evening,
Upstairs, linen cloth Mom was weaving;
To her side a phoenix came flying.
Left and right, it was hovering;
While dancing in the air, the phoenix was singing:
“Make it longer, the linen cloth you are weaving;
With the weaving done, you will soon be working on it.
From the left or the right, you are free to cut clothes out;
It’s favorable to sew a skirt and a coat.”

阿奈听了叹口气：
“麻布织长了，
年老用不完，
我无儿又无女，
大事小事没人帮，
织出麻布谁来帮我染？
做出衣裙留给哪个穿？”

Hearing that, Mom sighed in a voice bitter:
“If the cloth is woven longer,
I am too old to use them up for clothes.
I have no sons or daughters;
Affairs big or small, no one offers help.
With linen cloth woven, who’ll help soak them in dyes?
Who’ll put them on, coats, skirts and all the other clothes?”

凤凰说：
“织出麻布有人染，
劝你莫着急；
衣裙缝好有人穿，
劝你别忧伤！”

The phoenix said:
“It’ll be dyed, the linen cloth woven;
You needn’t worry and just calm down.
Coats and skirts made, someone will put them on;
You needn’t feel down!”

凤凰的话很奇怪，
话语之中有名堂。
阿奈瘪嘴正想问，
凤凰早已不知飞何方。

The phoenix's words were really so odd;
There was something more to it than what was said.
Her mouth curling inwards, Mom was about to ask
When the phoenix flew away and disappeared in a blink.

阿奈理麻线，
麻线长又长；
阿奈使飞梭，
梭穿如燕忙。
织了三月零三天，
麻布织得九十九 拏[1]长，

Mom was putting straight the linen threads doubtfully;
They stretched endlessly.
The flying shuttle Mom was using;
It was as busy as a swallow flying.
The weaving was done after three months and three days;
The linen cloth was long, ninety-nine arm spans.

这多的麻布两老咋个用得完？
卷成一筒放在枕头边。
这多麻布到底谁来穿？
阿奈心中有个大疑团！

Too much cloth, how could the two old folks use it up?
Rolling it up, beside the pillow they put it, the cloth crisp.
Too much linen cloth, who on earth would dress in it?
In her heart, Mom had a grave doubt!

---

① 拏：读如pái，方言，量词，两手向左右伸开的长度。

三 III

星星分外明，	Stars were exceptionally bright;
月亮挂山顶。	Up hung the moon on the mountain summit.
阿奈躺在床上做了个梦——	Mom, on her bed, had a dream–
梦见到河边洗褶裙。	She was washing a pleated skirt in a stream.
那只凤凰又飞来，	The phoenix flew back,
口衔葡萄亮晶晶；	A gleaming grape in its beak.
葡萄放在阿奈手，	Dropping the grape in Mom's hand,
叽叽叫几声：	The phoenix chirped several times and said:
“你将葡萄吃下去，	“Chew the grape and swallow it down;
就会越活越年轻。	Younger you'll feel when you live on.
好花自有好雨淋，	Beautiful flowers will have timely rain;
好人自有好福分……”	Kind people will meet good fortune…”
阿奈手捧葡萄暗思忖：	The grape in her hand, Mom was thinking:
“想来凤凰是好心。”	“Perhaps, good intentions the phoenix's having.”
她将葡萄吃下去，	Chewing the grape, down she swallowed it;
果然满嘴甜津津。	Sure enough, her whole mouth became sweet.

就在同天同一晚，
阿支也遇好梦境——
他到深山去打猎，
蜜蜂嗡嗡眼前飞：
“山再高也有路穿林，
命再苦也会交好运，
祝你喜事就临门！”

On the same day and the same night,
Pop also had a dream so sweet–
In the remote mountains he was hunting;
In front of his eyes a bee was buzzing:
“High as the mountain is, through a forest there's still a track;
Bitter as life is, it'll yet bring one good luck.
May a happy event come to your door in steps quick!”

阿支好纳闷：
“枯树上开不出花朵，
我年过半百能交什么好运？
莫拿假话来骗人！”

Pop felt extremely puzzled:
“Flowers will never be produced by a tree withered;
Being over fifty, how can I have any luck?
Don't fool me with such a joke!”

蜜蜂说：
“给好马配鞍要配新的，
跟好人说话要说真的，
我说的话不会假，
不久你家就会有贵子生。”

The bee did continue:
“When saddling a steed up, you use something new;
When talking to a good man, you say something true.
What I said will never be phony;
Your family will soon have a baby.”

四

天空说晴就放晴，
地上有水庄稼就返青；
自从吃了红葡萄，
阿奈果然变年轻。
脸上皱纹天天少，
不久怀中有了孕，
十个月后坐月子，
一个咪朵坠地生！

咪朵眼睛亮闪闪，
配着一对弯弯眉。
别人生下地来嘛，
第一声是哇哇哭，
这咪朵生下地来呀，
咯咯笑出第一声。

阿支最称心，
望着小宝宝，
就是不吃饭，
肚子也饱了。

IV

Speak of fine weather and the sky will clear up;
With water in the field, green turns the winter crop.
After the eating of the grape red,
Mom became younger as the phoenix said.
Fewer were the wrinkles on her face day by day;
Before long, she was in the family way.
Ten months later, Mom was giving birth;
A baby boy was born, taking his first breath!

Sparkling were the baby boy's eyes;
Curved were his two eyebrows.
When other babies came into the world,
Crying was the first sound they made.
When this baby boy came into the world,
Gurgling was the first sound he made.

Pop was most happy;
Admiring the little baby,
Even if Pop didn't have his meal,
He felt his stomach was full.

阿奈最如意，	Mom was most contented;
抱起小宝宝，	In her arms the little baby she held.
就是不吃蜜，	Even if she ate no honey,
嘴里也甜了。	She felt sweet and sunny.
咪朵的笑声，	Gurgles of laughter the baby boy gave
传遍几十里。	Spread to miles around like many a wave.
凤凰听到了，	The phoenix heard the gurgles,
翩翩飞来祝贺；	And flew to offer its congratulations;
蜜蜂听到了，	The bee heard the gurgles,
嗡嗡赶来道喜。	And came buzzing to give its congratulations.
吊脚楼上好热闹，	Inside the stilted building it was lively;
阿支阿奈真欢喜。	Pop and Mom were really happy.
阿支要给咪朵取名字，	Pop wanted to name the baby boy,
想了五天没想出；	But five days' thinking brought him no joy;
阿奈要给咪朵取名字，	Mom was eager to choose the baby boy's name,
想了七夜没想起。	But after seven nights' consideration, nothing came.
凤凰蜜蜂一齐出主意，	The phoenix and the bee offered their ideas;
你一言来我一语。	One came up with its idea, the other more names.

最后取名扎董丕冉[①]，	Finally, Zhadong Piran[①] was the name they decided on;
这名字响亮又好听，	The name was resonant and had a pleasant sound.
夫妻两个都满意。	The couple was satisfied.
阿支对蜜蜂说：	Pop said to the bee:
“你说把刀打大点，	“To forge the machete larger you asked me;
原来其中有道理。	Actually, there were reasons why you said that.
如今这刀有人使，	Now, there has come the one to use it;
我要感谢你！”	I would like to thank you a lot!”
阿奈对凤凰说：	To the phoenix Mom said:
“你说把布织长点，	“A longer piece of cloth was what you recommended;
现在解了这个谜。	Now, the answer to the riddle has been made known.
如今这布有人穿，	The cloth will be sewn and put on;
我要报答你！”	I'll give you something in return!”
吊脚楼边的桃树，	Near the stilted building, peach trees
开花十五次；	Had blossomed fifteen times;
山坡地里的小米，	On the sloped field of the mountain,
播种十五回；	Fifteen times had millet seeds been sown.
扎董丕冉渐渐长大了，	Zhadong Piran grew up gradually,
满了十五岁；	And was fifteen years old fully;

① 扎董丕冉：意为苗家最漂亮的小儿子。

① Zhadong Piran: (Hmong language) the most handsome boy of Hmong people.

扎董丕冉慢慢长高了，
比青松还俊美。

Zhadong Piran grew tall slowly,
And became more impressive than a pine tree.

树上桃子千万个，
他是最甜的那一个；
夜空星星千万颗，
他是最亮的那一颗。

Thousands of fruits were there on peach trees tall;
He was the sweetest of all.
Millions of stars were there in the night sky;
He was the brightest one hanging high.

苗山上的咪朵，
个个长得很结实，
但是没有一个哟，
像他那样健壮；
苗寨里的咪朵，
人人生得很好看，
可是没有一个哟，
像他那么漂亮。
即使有他那样的身材，
也没有他标致；
即使有他那样的容貌，
也没有他端庄；
即使有他那样的性格，
也没有他诚恳；
即使有他那样的品德，
也没有他高尚。

The boys of the Hmong people's mountains
Were all as strong as stones;
But not one of them
Was as robust as him.
The boys of the Hmong stockade villages
All had good-looking appearances;
But not one of them
Was as handsome as him.
Even if they all, like him, had good statures,
They were not his peers in features;
Even if they shared his appearance,
They were not as dignified as him in countenance;
Even if they shared his personality,
Compared with them, he was a boy of absolute honesty;
Even if they shared his moral character,
Compared with them, he was nobler

扎董丕冉呀，	O Zhadong Piran! You see,
像蜜蜂一样勤劳；	He was as industrious as a bee;
百里苗山呀，	O Hmong mountains, hundreds of miles in circumference!
就数他灵巧。	Of all the lads, he was the most dexterous.
他像阿支一样能干，	As capable as Pop,
会犁会耙会砍柴；	He could plough, harrow and chop;
他像阿奈一样利索，	As agile as Mom,
会洗会煮会撒荞。	He could wash, cook and sow at the farm.
他像阿支一样风趣，	As witty as Pop,
芦笙吹得最好听；	He played the most pleasantly the lusheng;
他像阿奈一样开朗，	As cheerful as Mom,
调子唱得最动人。	He could sing the most beautifully and hum.
他是小咪朵呀，	O! He was a lad,
又是小咪彩，	And also a lass.
他是阿支的希望哟，	He was Pop's hope and expectation;
他是阿奈的依靠。	He was the one Mom could depend on.

第二章 赠笛

Canto 2 Presenting the Gold Flute

五

V

清早太阳升起来，	In the early morning rose the sun.
扎董丕冉上山去砍柴，	To chop firewood, Zhadong Piran went to the mountain;
身背大刀走到泉水边。	The machete on his back, he came to a fountain.
捧口泉水喝下肚，	Holding water up with both hands, he drank it;
坐在石上歇口气。	Sitting on a stone, he took a rest.
一阵微风送来荞花香，	A breeze brought him the fragrance of buckwheat flowers;
一只蝴蝶飞到眼前。	A butterfly came flying before his eyes.
蝴蝶生得很美丽，	The butterfly was very beautiful;
两只翅膀现五彩。	Its two wings were really colorful.
飞来又绕去，	Here, there and everywhere, it flew before his eyes;
活像两根花飘带，	Its wings fluttered like two colorful ribbons.
扎董丕冉看得发了呆。	Admiring it, Zhadong Piran was in a trance.
忽然蝴蝶一闪身，	Suddenly, the butterfly flashed aside from its course;
眨眼飞出三丈外。	In a blink, ten meters away it was.
飞到花丛间，	It flew into flowering shrubs;
飞入金竹林，	It flew into golden bamboo trees;
飞进一片树林里，	It flew into deep forests,
再也没有飞出来。	And never came out of the plants.

扎董丕冉东边寻，	Zhadong Piran looked for it in the east;
扎董丕冉西边找，	Zhadong Piran sought for it in the west;
四处寻找都不见。	All over the place, he failed to find it.
忽然一道金光闪，	Suddenly, flashed a ray of golden light;
一只凤凰站眼前。	Standing before his eyes, a phoenix was in sight.
凤凰披着金羽毛，	With its golden feathers, the phoenix
抖动翅膀舞起来；	Fluttered its wings and began to dance.
凤凰跳舞真迷人，	The phoenix's dancing was really charming;
扎董丕冉乐得心花开。	Zhadong Piran was happy, like a flower blooming.
扎董丕冉呀，	O Zhadong Piran, the lad,
心中暗思量：	Was turning it over in his mind:
"莫非那只蝴蝶有情意，	"Can it be that the butterfly treated me with kindness,
故意引我见凤凰？"	And made me meet the phoenix on purpose?"
扎董丕冉呀，	O Zhadong Piran, the lad,
自言自语讲：	In a murmur, to himself said:
"可爱的金凤凰呀，	"O golden phoenix, so lovely!
看你长得多漂亮。	Look! You are such a great beauty.
红头黄尾金羽毛，	Red-headed, yellow-tailed and golden-feathered,
真不愧是个百鸟王！	The king of birds, you deserve to be called!
如果你愿跟我做伴，	If you are willing to keep me company,

我要找个金笼来喂养……”

扎董丕冉正在想心事，
一只老虎猛然下山冈。
它张牙舞爪一声吼，
扑向那只金凤凰。
这是一只魔虎呀，
凤凰一见就惊慌。
想跑，难抬起双脚，
想飞，难张开翅膀。
即使抬起双脚，
也跑不了几丈；
即使张开翅膀，
也飞不过山梁。
凤凰拼出力气，
一飞一落，
东躲西藏。
老虎施展魔法，
一跳一跃，
紧追不放。
凤凰筋疲力尽，
跌跌撞撞；
魔虎怒吼狂嚎，
天摇地晃。

I'll find you a gold cage and make it homey…”

Zhadong Piran was still daydreaming;
Abruptly, down the hillock a tiger was coming.
Baring its fangs and brandishing its claws, it roared
loudly;
On the golden phoenix it sprang ferociously.
O, it was a monster tiger!
Seeing it, the phoenix felt numb with horror.
It wanted to run, but couldn't raise its feet;
It wanted to fly, but couldn't spread its wings to retreat.
Even if its feet the phoenix did raise,
It could run but a few meters;
Even if the phoenix did spread its wings,
It couldn't fly over mountain ridges.
The phoenix exerted all its strength
To fly up and fall down, though out of breath;
It tried hard to hide here and there.
The monster tiger gave play to its magic power;
It jumped and leapt, following the phoenix's route,
To chase the bird in hot pursuit.
The phoenix was completely exhausted;
Through trees and bushes, it staggered.
The monster tiger roared and howled wildly;

The sky and the earth shook violently.

眼看疯狂的魔虎，
就要抓着金凤凰，
扎董丕冉呀，
愤怒生力量。
他举着大刀追过去，
要跟魔虎斗一场。
他左砍右杀，
势不可挡；
魔虎前闪后避，
只能退让。
直斗得满山树发抖，
直杀得遍地土飞扬。
扎董丕冉越杀越猛，
大魔虎却防不及防。

Seeing that the wild monster tiger
Was about to catch the golden phoenix's feather,
Zhadong Piran, O the young man,
Boiled with rage, built up his force then.
Holding the machete up, he ran toward the tiger;
He was determined to fight the magic monster.
He took swings at the tiger successively,
And he was fighting irresistibly.
The monster tiger dodged his blows aside,
And had no choice but to escape and hide.
All over the mountains, the fighting made trees tremble;
In the sky, clouds of dust flew up as high as possible.
The more he fought, the more vigorous Zhadong Piran was;
The monster tiger found it hard to guard against his blows.

阿支打的大长刀，
这时有了大用场。
魔虎再凶恶，
还是怕刀光。
最后它大吼一声，
夹着尾巴逃进了林莽。

The large machete Pop had forged
Was now turned to good account and used.
Even though the monster tiger was wicked,
It was still afraid of the glints of the machete blade.
It roared fiercely like a peal of thunder, eventually,
And its tail between its legs, fled into the forest quickly.

六

VI

<table>
<tr><td>凤凰终于得救了，
站在石上扇翅膀。
对着扎董丕冉点点头，
伸长脖子开喉唱：</td><td>The phoenix was finally saved;
Standing on a stone, its wings fluttered.
At Zhadong Piran it was nodding;
Its neck poking forward, it began singing:</td></tr>
<tr><td>“就是小蚂蚁，
也知糖最甜；
就是小飞蛾，
也知灯最亮。
我虽是山中一只鸟，
也知道冷暖和炎凉。
是善是恶呀，
我也能分得清清爽爽。
扎董丕冉哟，
你有一副好心肠。
杀退大魔虎，
让我免遭殃。
你的勇敢和机智，
谁也比不上；
你这救命的恩情哟，</td><td>“Small as an ant is,
Sugar is the sweetest thing, it knows;
Small as a moth is,
Light is the brightest thing, it knows.
Though I’m only a bird in the mountains,
I know, too, the hot and the cold of worldly affairs.
Be it a kind act or an evil deed,
The difference between them I clearly understand.
O Zhadong Piran, a youth so smart!
You have a kind heart;
You fought and drove away the monster tiger,
And saved me from great disaster;
Your courage and quick wit,
No one can ever emulate.
Your kindness in saving me from death,</td></tr>
</table>

我永远不能忘！	I can never forget till my last breath.
我要真心感谢你，	I want to express my hearty gratitude;
请你在这儿等一趟。”	Would you please wait a second?”
凤凰唱完歌，	The phoenix finished its singing,
把身子晃一晃，	Its body rocking and swaying.
钻进树林里，	It went into the forest;
树林深处闪金光。	Deep in the forest flashed a golden light.
金光一闪就消失，	The minute the golden light flashed, it disappeared;
凤凰不知飞何方。	The phoenix was nowhere to be found.
扎董丕冉心里想：	Zhadong Piran considered in his mind:
“凤凰怎样谢我呢？	“How will the phoenix show its gratitude?
为何叫我等一趟？	Why did it ask me to wait a second?
给我一坨真金子，	Will it give me a lump of real gold,
还是一件新衣裳？	Or a new coat? O, where is it now?
给我一张栗木弓，	Will it give a wooden chestnut bow,
还是一个花箭囊？……	Or a colorful quiver to me?...
我是正直人，	I’m a man of absolute integrity;
除恶是天良。	I follow the dictates of conscience to remove demons.
遇虎就杀虎，	Meeting tigers, I would kill tigers;
逢狼就打狼。	Facing wolves, I would fight wolves.
要是接礼物，	If I accept the phoenix’s gift,
那就不应当。”	It’s conscience that I will go against.”

东猜西想正入神，
凤凰飞回他身旁。
凤凰嘴里叼金笛，
金笛闪闪现金光。

In random thoughts he was absorbed;
Then, the phoenix flew back to his side.
In its mouth it was holding a gold flute;
The gold flute was glistening with golden light.

凤凰唱：
“扎董丕冉哟，
这支金笛送给你，
请你收下有用场。
愁闷时候吹一吹，
你的心情就舒畅；
高兴时候吹一吹，
你就更加喜洋洋。
它是你最好的伙伴呀，
你要时刻带它在身上。”

The phoenix was heard singing:
“O Zhadong Piran, a young man charming;
I'll give you this gold flute as a gift;
It'll be useful and please keep it.
You can play it when you are gloomy,
And you'll feel free from worry.
When you are happy, you can play it;
With joy you'll feel more radiant.
O! The gold flute is your best partner;
Bring it with you all the time, please remember.”

要是别的礼物呀，
扎董丕冉定然会谢绝；
眼前这件礼物不寻常，
扎董丕冉没有再推让。
凤凰唱完就起飞，
腾云驾雾到远方。

O! If it were some other gift,
Zhadong Piran would definitely decline it.
Too unusual was the gift before him;
Zhadong Piran didn't decline for a second time.
After finishing its song, the phoenix made its way;
Mounting clouds and riding the mist, it went far away.

扎董丕冉拿起金笛吹起来，	Holding the gold flute, Zhadong Piran played it;
学着凤凰的调子越吹越欢快：	Imitating the phoenix's tone, happier and happier he felt:
“布哩布哩布哩噜，	"Boo-lee-boo-lee-boo-lee-lu,
布哩布哩布哩噜……”	Boo-lee-boo-lee-boo-lee-lu..."

吹了一遍又一遍，	Again and again, the gold flute he was playing;
笛声阵阵传天外。	Out of the sky waves of its sound were soaring.
画眉听了不敢再唱歌，	Hearing the music, song thrushes dared not sing songs;
蝴蝶听了不敢恋花来，	Hearing the music, butterflies dared not come for flowers;
金蝉听见着了迷，	Hearing the music, golden cicadas were fascinated;
八哥听到发了呆。	Hearing the music, mynah birds became dumbfounded.
笛声就像珍珠滚银盘，	It sounded as if onto a silver plate pearls were falling,
清脆悦耳响叮当；	Clear, melodious, sweet and resounding;
笛声就像悬崖滴水落千尺，	It sounded as if water dripped down a thousand feet from cliffs,
咚咚哒哒动听又欢畅。	Dong-dong-da-da...the music was pleasant and joyous.

扎董丕冉吹金笛，	Zhadong Piran played the gold flute;
越吹越高兴，	The more he played, the happier he felt.
觉得身子像云彩，	His body was like clouds, he felt,
缥缈又轻盈。	Faintly discernible, graceful and light.
扎董丕冉吹金笛，	Zhadong Piran played the gold flute;
越吹越激动，	The more he played, the more excited he felt.
四肢如同风摆柳，	Like willows in the wind were his four limbs;

如痴又如梦。

He was infatuated as if in beautiful dreams.

七

VII

这支金笛很美观，
世上笛子就数它好看。
笛面又亮又滑，
笛眼又密又圆。
筒子不大不小，
笛身不长不短。
上下镶金嵌银，
头尾画着图案：
这面是——
双龙跃身闹海底；
那面是——
双凤展翅腾云天。
这头是——
鱼眼排对排；
那头是——
鸳鸯面对面。
中间吊着小花穗，
五颜六色多鲜艳。

The gold flute was really pleasing;
Of the world's flutes, it was the best-looking.
Shiny and smooth was the flute's surface;
The holes in the flute were round and close in space;
Neither large nor small was the flute's tube;
Neither long nor short was the flute's tube.
On the surface, gold and silver were embedded;
At its head and end, pictures were painted:
"On this side—
Two Chinese dragons leapt deep into the sea;
On that side—
Two phoenixes fluttered their wings and soared up into
the sky.
At its head—
Two lines of fish's eyes were side by side;
At its end—
Mandarin ducks in twos were face to face.
In the middle of the flute's end hung a tassel;

	It was dazzlingly bright and colorful.
这支金笛最神秘，	Most mysterious was the gold flute;
世上笛子没有它稀奇。	No flute in the world was as curious as it.
只要把它放在嘴边上，	As long as it was put near one's mouth,
就可吹出千歌和万曲；	Thousands of songs and music were heard coming forth;
只要把它放在两唇间，	As long as it was put between one's lips,
还可吹出虫声和鸟语。	Out of it came insects' and birds' chirps.
想吹哪调吹哪调，	With it, you could play any tune you intended;
想唱哪曲唱哪曲。	With it, you could sing any song you wanted.
吹出欢快的调子，	A lively melody that came out of it
可使小河无声息；	Could make a stream silent;
吹出高昂的调子，	An inspiring melody that came out of it
可使飞鹰落下地；	Could make a flying eagle fall;
吹出抑郁的调子，	A gloomy melody that came out of it
可使百兽难呼吸；	Could make all animals' breathing difficult;
吹出幽怨的调子，	A bitter melody that came out of it
可使高山把头低；	Could make a high mountain lower its head;
吹出悲伤的调子，	A sorrowful melody that came out of it
可使万人都哭泣。	Could make ten thousand people weep.
这支金笛最珍贵，	Most precious was the gold flute;
世上笛子没有它值钱。	No flute in the world was as valuable as it.
它是凤凰珍藏的宝贝，	It was a treasure cherished by the phoenix;

它跟凤凰的命运紧相连。
千两黄金呀，
买不下它一根穗子；
万两白银呀，
换不来它一个图案。
虚伪狡诈的歹徒，
永远不能跟它沾边；
只有诚实勇敢的人哟，
才能跟它做伴。
凤凰将它送给扎董丕冉，
这是对他的信任呀，
这是对他的爱恋！

With the phoenix's destiny, it had close links.
O a thousand taels of gold
Could not buy, of the tassel, even a thread;
O ten thousand taels of silver
Could not be exchanged, of the flute, for even a picture.
Those false scoundrels, men of deceit,
Could never have anything to do with it.
O only people of honesty and bravery
Could keep the flute company.
The phoenix presented Zhadong Piran with it;
It showed that in him, the phoenix had great trust,
And expressed its love for him from the heart!

八

VIII

扎董丕冉在家吹金笛，
忘记上山砍柴；
扎董丕冉在外吹金笛，
忘记回到家来。
他对着阿支吹金笛，
阿支也忘了赶街；
他对着阿奈吹金笛，

When Zhadong Piran played the gold flute indoors,
He would forget to go and cut firewood in the mountains;
When Zhadong Piran played the gold flute outdoors,
He would forget to return home and stay on the moors.
When before Pop, he played the gold flute,
Pop would forget to go to the market;
When before Mom, he played the gold flute,

阿奈也忘了洗菜。

To wash vegetables Mom would forget.

阿支笑着说：
“这支金笛真好看，
看见它的样子呀，
我的皱纹就平了！”

Pop said, smiling:
“This gold flute is really good-looking;
O! At the sight of it,
My wrinkles are ironed out!”

阿奈笑着说：
“这支金笛真稀罕，
听到它的声音呀，
我的白发变黑了！”

Mom said, smiling:
“This gold flute is really a rare thing;
O! At the sound of its music,
My white hair turns black!”

这支金笛呀，
扎董丕冉最喜欢。
不管出门和进门，
随时别它在腰间。
它是扎董丕冉的朋友，
它是扎董丕冉的伙伴。

O this gold flute
Was Zhadong Piran’s favorite.
No matter if he was in or out,
He would stick it in his belt.
It was Zhadong Piran’s buddy;
It was Zhadong Piran’s companion.

他放牛时候吹金笛，
爱打架的黄牛不打架；
他挑水时候吹金笛，
爱点水的蜻蜓不点水；
他打猎时候吹金笛，

He played the gold flute when herding cattle,
And aggressive yellow cattle would not scuffle;
He played the gold flute when carrying water on the shoulder,
And water-skimming dragonflies would not skim water;

爱爬树的猴子不爬树；	He played the gold flute when going hunting,
他踩花山时候吹金笛，	And tree-climbing monkeys would stop climbing;
姑娘小伙围着他打转。	He played the gold flute at the Flower Hill Festival,
	And lasses and lads would move around him in a circle.

这支金笛呀，	O! This gold flute
最懂得扎董丕冉的心愿。	Knew Zhadong Piran's wishes best.
春天来了，	When spring came,
扎董丕冉爱看鲜花，	Zhadong Piran loved to see flowers bloom.
他把金笛吹起来，	As he started to play the gold flute,
满山百花越开越鲜艳。	All the flowers over the mountains looked increasingly bright.
夏天来了，	When summer came to the forests,
扎董丕冉爱吃山果，	Zhadong Piran loved to eat wild fruits.
他把金笛吹起来，	As he started to play the gold flute,
遍岭百果越结越香甜。	All the fruits over the mountains became increasingly sweet.
秋天来了，	When autumn came within sight,
扎董丕冉要收小米，	Zhadong Piran was going to harvest the millet.
他把金笛吹起来，	As he started to play the gold flute,
坡上小米长得更饱满。	On the mountain slopes, increasingly plump was the millet.
冬天来了，	When winter came for a year's last run,
扎董丕冉想晒太阳，	Zhadong Piran wanted to bask in the sun.
他把金笛吹起来，	As he started to play the gold flute,
天上阳光变得更温暖。	

The sunshine in the sky turned increasingly pleasant.

一年四季呀，	O! During the four seasons of a year,
金笛与扎董丕冉形影相伴，	The gold flute and Zhadong Piran were always together.
它能使他得到欢乐，	It enabled him to find happiness;
它能帮他消除痛苦。	It helped rid him of sadness.
有了这支金笛呀，	O! With the gold flute's company,
他就觉得不孤独；	He would no longer feel lonely;
有了这支金笛呀，	O! With the presence of the gold flute,
他就感到更幸福！	He was happier than ever, he felt!

第三章　相恋

Canto 3　In Love

九　　IX

当阳的荞菜长得快，
叫你越看越新鲜。
扎董丕冉满了十八岁，
长得比牛犊还矫健。
四肢就像大碓杆，
粗壮又结实；
身躯就像嫩冬瓜，
丰满又浑圆。
他的人品嘛，
没人和他比；
他的容貌呀，
盖过苗家山。

The buckwheat bathed in the sunshine grows fast;
The more you look at it, the fresher you find it.
The age of eighteen Zhadong Piran reached;
Compared with a calf, he was more robust.
Like large pestle poles were his four limbs;
Strong were his legs, brawny his arms.
His body was like a tender white gourd,
Full, well-developed and perfectly round.
O! His character was so great
That no one could ever emulate it.
O! His appearance was so attractive and youthful
That no one in the Hmong mountains could be his rival.

可是树不开花不结果，
天不下雨地就旱。
扎董丕冉不开口，
姑娘跟他也就难交谈。

Yet, without flowers, a tree can never bear any fruit,
And without rain, the land will suffer a drought.
Zhadong Piran would not open his mouth to speak,
So, with him, lasses found it hard to talk.

不是姑娘不爱他，

It's not that the lasses were not fond of the lad;

爱他的姑娘数不完。
眼前的姑娘虽然好，
扎董丕冉就是不喜欢。

Lasses who loved him were too many to be counted.
Though the lasses before his eyes were beautiful and nice,
Zhadong Piran just didn't love any lass.

清早起来时，
扎董丕冉坐在竹楼上，
抬眼朝着树林看。
姑娘轻声唱起歌，
故意逗他下来玩。
可是他假装搓索子，
看也不看她一眼。

Getting out of bed in the early morning,
Zhadong Piran sat upstairs in their bamboo dwelling;
Looking up, he was gazing at the forest.
Lasses started to sing in voices soft,
Alluring him to go downstairs to date.
He pretended to be rubbing and making a rope, yet,
And wouldn't look at them for a single minute.

吃过晚饭时，
扎董丕冉去挑水，
走到寨头清泉边。
姑娘等在半路上，
有意帮他换换肩。
可是他假装没看见，
匆匆走过她面前。

In the evening, having finished dinner,
With a shoulder pole and buckets, Zhadong Piran went
to fetch water;
To the spring at the stockade village's entrance he came.
Lasses were waiting halfway for him,
Attempting to shift the pole onto their shoulders.
Yet, he pretended he hadn't seen those beauties,
And hurriedly walked past the lasses.

踩花山时，
扎董丕冉吹金笛，
跑着要去爬花杆。

When to the Flower Hill Festival he went,
Zhadong Piran played the gold flute,
And ran towards the flower pole to climb.

姑娘打开花撑子[1]，	Lasses opened their oil-paper umbrellas for him,
要想罩住他的脸。	And felt like shading his head.
可是他钻进人群里，	He, however, disappeared in the crowd;
过了半天不露面。	Half a day passing, he still couldn't be found.
跳芦笙时，	When dancing to the lusheng instrument,
姑娘向他抛花带，	Each lass threw to him her flower belt,
故意逗他心喜欢。	Wanting eagerly to make him happy.
可是任凭花带缠满身，	Yet, though flower belts were twined completely around his body,
他却不理也不看。	He paid no attention and looked indifferent,
只顾吹着芦笙调，	Completely absorbed in playing the instrument;
在地上滚滚又翻翻。	On the ground, he rolled, tumbled and danced.
就是这样呀，	O, such was the case of the young heart!
年满十八没情人，	At the age of eighteen, he didn't have a sweetheart;
还是一个单身汉。	He was still a bachelor and had no lass.
不是他无情又无意，	It was not that he knew no love or romance,
只因他要挑又要拣。	But that he was choosy and fastidious.
蝶恋鲜花鸟恋林呀，	O! Birds love forests, butterflies flowers;
鹰爱蓝天鱼爱潭。	Eagles love blue skies, fish pools.

① 花撑子：方言，用竹、木、油纸做的花伞。

扎董不冉爱的是哪个？
太阳在打听，
月亮在偷看……

Who was the one Zhadong Piran loved?
The sun was inquiring around;
The moon was peeking from behind the cloud…

这年春天桃花开，
蜜蜂忙着来采蜜。
苗家山上很热闹，
家家忙着种小米。
偏偏就在这时候，
家中忽然出岔子。
为了儿子的婚事，
阿支心烦闷，
阿奈也焦急。
双双愁出一身病，
躺在床上爬不起。
你看阿支呀，
不吃不喝只呻吟；
你瞧阿奈呀，
不说不笑光叹气。
眼看节令快晃过，
还没打算去犁地。
今年小米种不下，
明年怎样过日子？
想起这件事情呀，

Right that year, spring coming, the peach trees blossomed as ever;
In happy, humming voices, bees were busy gathering nectar.
The Hmong mountains were bustling with excitement;
Each family hurried to sow seeds of millet.
Against all expectations, right at that time,
Some troubles came to Zhadong Piran's home.
Due to their worries about their son's marriage,
Pop was unhappy and had a gloomy visage;
Mom was also full of worry.
Both of them fell ill because of anxiety;
Lying in bed, they couldn't get up.
O, look at his beloved Pop!
He neither ate nor drank, but moaned.
O, look at Mom, his beloved!
She neither talked nor smiled, but sighed with disappointment.
Very soon, the farming season would flash past;
The family hadn't planned to plough the field.

别说扎董丕冉犯了愁，
就是那头牯牛也怄气！

The millet seeds of that year couldn't be sowed;
How could the family get by the year after?
O! The very thought of the whole matter
Would fill Zhadong Piran with great worry,
And even their bull felt annoyed and sulky.

凡是耕田种地人，
节令就是命根子。
要是节令错过了，
来年就得啃树皮。
普天之下都晓得，
这是一个大道理。
一定不能再等了，
得要赶快拿主意！
扎董丕冉清早就起身，
扛上那张黄木犁。
包起冷饭做晌午[1]，
吆牛上山种小米。
孤孤零零一个人，
又撒种子又犁地；
犁完一沟撒一沟，
撒完一沟又来犁，
来来往往忙半天，

To all that plough and till the field,
The farming season is their lifeblood.
If the farming season has been missed,
The next year, tree bark they have to nibble at.
Everywhere under the sun people know that,
For it's a great truth and a hard fact.
He mustn't wait any longer,
And had to think up an idea!
In the early morning, Zhadong Piran got up from bed,
Carried on his shoulder the plough of rosewood,
Wrapped some cold cooked rice to eat at noon,
And drove the bull to sow millet seeds in the mountain.
Alone, he was all by himself, nobody around,
Sowing seeds and plowing the mountainous field;
After finishing one furrow, he sowed,
And finishing the sowing, he, again, plowed.
Back and forth, he had worked half a day in the field,

① 晌午：在这里是午饭的意思。

才种完一块小坡地。
累得浑身大汗如雨淌，
腰酸眼花腿无力。

But finished plowing only a patch of the sloped land.
He felt tired and was wet all over from sweat,
Dizzy in his eyes, weak in his legs and sore in his waist.

十

X

四山八岭传笑声，
扎董丕冉乱了心。
他抬眼向着远处看，
越看越烦闷。

Laughter was heard in the mountains and ridges around;
Zhadong Piran felt confused and distracted.
Raising his eyes, he looked afar to the distance;
The more he looked, the more anguished he felt.

别家做活都有伴，
人多手快热腾腾，
男的吆牛打犁沟，
女的撒种在后跟，
男耕女播多火热呀，
有说有笑有歌声。
调子出口传得远，
种子落地就生根。
累了双双到地头，
大树底下好躲荫。
打开饭包吃晌午，

Other families went out farming together;
Many heads and quick hands made work easier.
The man drove the buffalo and plowed the furrow;
The woman sowed seeds behind and tried to follow.
What a fervent scene, the man plowing, the woman
sowing!
They were talking, laughing and singing.
Tunes, when sung, spread to the faraway place;
Seeds, when falling to the field, took root at once.
Tired, they went in pairs to the edge of the field;
Under a big tree, they enjoyed the cool in the shade.

吃在嘴里甜在心。
男的递给女的吃，
女的接过抿嘴笑；
女的递给男的吃，
男的接过挤眼睛。
恩恩爱爱甜如蜜呀，
亲亲热热情意深。

They opened the rice wrapper to have the midday meal;
Food in their mouths, so sweet did they feel.
The man passed the woman something to eat;
The woman smiled with closed lips and took it.
The woman passed the man something to eat;
The man winked his eyes and took it.
Deep in love, they felt as sweet as honey;
Intimately, they had, between them, a deep affinity.

扎董丕冉越看越懊恼，
犁地撒种没精神。
别人成双又成对，
只有自己孤零零；
别人有说又有笑，
只有自己闷沉沉。
他跑到树下吹金笛，
金笛声声诉苦情：

The more he looked, the more upset Zhadong Piran felt;
In low spirits, to plow and to sow, he made no attempt.
Others were working in pairs and in company;
He was the only one to work alone and feel lonely.
Others were talking and laughing in the field;
He was the only one to feel gloomy and bored.
Running to stand under a tree, he played the gold flute;
Tune after tune, the gold flute poured his woes out:

“布哩布哩布哩噜，
太阳偏西过晌午。
我又犁泥沟又撒种，
满身汗水湿衣襟。
忙酸了四肢，
累散了筋骨，

“Boo-lee-boo-lee-boo-lee-lu,
Passing noon, the sun is to the west and setting low.
I plow the furrow, sow the seeds and do my best;
I'm soaked with sweat, my clothes all wet.
I'm busy working, my four limbs aching;
I'm worn out; apart my bones and muscles are falling.

可怜我扎董丕冉呀，	O how pitiful I am, Zhadong Piran, a young man!
为何这般受苦楚？	Why should I suffer from such misery and pain?
可怜我扎董丕冉呀，	O how pitiful I am, Zhadong Piran, a lad!
何时才会有人来帮助？”	When will someone come to my aid?”
笛声阵阵多惆怅，	The waves of flute melody sounded melancholy and sad,
幽怨婉转绕山冈。	Lingering over hillocks, faintly bitter and mild.
一直传到九霄云，	The music soared skywards and out of the world,
惊得太阳也无光。	Shocking and outshining the sun, making it dazzled.
只见天上起火闪，	In the sky, lightning was seen to flash past,
照得四周明晃晃。	Lighting up the mountains and making them bright.
就在这时候，	Right at that time,
怪事出一桩。	Something strange happened as if he was in a dream.
空中忽然传来木叶声，	Suddenly, in the sky, leaf music was heard;
一声一声多响亮：	Tune by tune, the music was clear and loud:
“布哩布哩布噜哩，	“Boo-lee-boo-lee-boo-lu-lee,
扎董丕冉别心急。	O Zhadong Piran, don’t be as impatient as a bee.
只要你不嫌我手脚笨，	As long as you don’t regard me as clumsy,
我一定会来帮助你！	I’ll come to give you a hand definitely!
人到难时有人怜呀，	People feel sympathetic when one has difficulties;
鸟到山边有林栖。”	There are trees to perch on when birds are near mountains.”
木叶声从哪里来？	From where had the leaf music come?

来自天上云彩里。	It had come from the clouds up in the dome.
扎董丕冉听到木叶声，	Having heard the leaf music sound,
呆呆站着出了神。	Frozen, Zhadong Piran was spellbound.
这声音很像凤凰叫，	The sound was like the voice of a phoenix,
清脆响亮最好听。	Crisp, resounding and nice.
扎董丕冉越听越畅快，	The more he listened, the happier Zhadong Piran felt;
像喝口泉水甜透心。	As if drinking spring water, he felt sweet in his heart.
他抬头朝着天上看，	Raising his head, he looked up at the sky,
只是听见声音不见人。	But he heard only the sound, nobody coming to his eye.
这木叶是谁吹的呢？	Who had played the leaf music?
吹得真迷人！	It was so charming and magical!
扎董丕冉吹金笛，	When Zhadong Piran played the gold flute,
调调吹出心里话；	Every tune came straight from his heart;
这人吹的木叶呀，	The leaf music the person was playing
曲曲吹的是真情。	Revealed in each melody her true feeling.
扎董丕冉已明白：	Zhadong Piran had come to understand:
他已找到好知音；	A good and understanding friend he had found;
扎董丕冉已知道：	Zhadong Piran had begun to realize:
他到难处有人怜。	When he had difficulties, someone would sympathize.
他的知音是哪个？	Who was his true and understanding friend?
就是这个吹叶人！	It was the one who played the leaf music!
可怜他的是哪个？	Who was the one that felt sympathetic?
也是这个吹叶人！	It was also this person who played the leaf music!

这人究竟是谁呢？	Who was, actually, this person?
扎董丕冉在判定：	Zhadong Piran wondered and felt uncertain:
寨子里的姑娘呀，	O the lasses in the stockade village, true,
木叶也还吹得成，	Could play the leaf music, too,
可是她们嘴不灵，	But their mouths weren't nimble,
没有这个好本领。	And of playing so well they were incapable.
她们吹起木叶来，	When they played the leaf music,
好瞧不好听；	It was unpleasant to hear, though they looked fantastic;
她们吹出调子来，	When they played their tunes,
入耳不入心。	They touched no hearts, though pleasing to ears.
如今这个吹叶人，	Now, this very leaf music player,
来历怕是有原因。	Maybe, had come here for one reason or another.
绝不是寨里的小姑娘，	She couldn't be a lass in the village, anyway;
定是远方来的好客人！	She must be a good guest from a place far away!
扎董丕冉正猜想，	Zhadong Piran was still guessing;
忽然眼前闪金光。	Suddenly, before his eyes, golden rays were flashing.
一个姑娘微微笑，	A lass, who was smiling faintly,
已经站在他身旁。	Had stood by his side already.
花衣彩裙随风舞，	In the wind, her colorful coat and skirt were dancing;
项圈手镯响叮当。	A necklace and bracelets were resounding.
头顶有颗夜明珠，	Her hair was decorated with a night-luminescent pearl;
就像星星在眨眼；	Like a sparkling star was the jewel.

鞋尖有对红玛瑙，	On each shoe toe there was a red agate,
晶莹璀璨在发光。	Which was crystal-clear and dazzling with light.
浑身上下亮闪闪，	From head to foot, sparkling was the lass,
活像一只金凤凰。	Who looked exactly like a golden phoenix.
扎董丕冉前边瞧，	Zhadong Piran looked up at her ahead;
扎董丕冉后边看，	Zhadong Piran sized her from behind;
扎董丕冉左边瞅，	Zhadong Piran glanced at her from the left;
扎董丕冉右边望。	Zhadong Piran gazed at her from the right.
最后站在对面不动了，	Facing her, he stood still, finally;
就像一棵木桩桩。	Like a wood stake, he was motionless, perfectly.
他见的姑娘千万个，	The lasses he had met were multitudes;
可是面前这个呀，	However, the one, now, before his eyes,
谁也比不上！	Surpassed all the others!
她的眉毛像月牙，	Like crescent moons were her eyebrows,
又细又弯真好看；	Good-looking, thin and arched;
她的眼睛像湖水，	Like lake water her eyes looked,
又明又亮清汪汪；	Bright, clear and crystal;
她的脸庞像桃花，	Peach flowers did her face resemble,
又红又润粉泱泱；	Red, smooth and fair.
她的头发像青丝，	Like black silk was her hair,
又长又软拖到地面上。	Long, soft and falling down to the ground.
蝴蝶围着她跳舞，	Joyously, butterflies danced around;

蜜蜂绕着她歌唱。	All around her, bees sang happily aloud.
扎董丕冉笑眯了眼睛呀，	Zhadong Piran was all smiles, eyes narrowed;
姑娘羞红了面庞。	The lass blushed, feeling awkward.
扎董丕冉望着姑娘不眨眼，	Zhadong Piran gazed at the lass, eyes frozen;
金笛落地他也顾不上，	The gold flute falling to the ground, he cared not.
不知过了几多时，	Not knowing how much time had passed,
他才如梦初醒眼发亮，	As if awakening from a dream, eyes bright,
赶忙爬上一棵老桃树，	He hurriedly climbed up an old peach tree,
摘下一朵红桃花，	Plucked a red peach flower in high glee,
轻轻插在姑娘的鬓角上。	And placed it in her hair on the temple gently.
扎董丕冉低声问，	In a low voice, Zhadong Piran asked,
心中却是有点慌：	And yet felt a bit embarrassed in his heart:
“你是天上的仙女，	“Are you a fairy maiden in the heavens,
还是林中的凤凰？	Or a phoenix in the woods?”
你怎么生得这样美？	Why were you born so beautiful?
高山因你增颜色，	With you, the mountains become more colorful;
河水因你泛银光！”	With you, in the rivers, silvery lights twinkle!”
姑娘脸上飞红云，	Swiftly, the lass' face blushed scarlet;
启动双唇轻开腔：	Lips parting, she spoke in a voice so soft:
“我是一只金凤凰，	“I'm a golden phoenix,
住在遥远的地方……”	And live in a distant place…”

她顿觉自己已失口，
赶忙改了腔：
“不，不……
我不是凤凰，
我是蒙诗彩奏[①]，
我的家就在山顶上。
看见你一个人种小米，
我特地来帮忙。”
蒙诗彩奏笑盈盈，
欠欠身子显得很端庄。
弯下腰去拾起那金笛，
亲手别在他的腰带上。

She knew she'd made a slip of the tongue immediately,
And changed her speech hurriedly:
"No, no…
I'm not a phoenix, and it is so;
Mengshi Caizou[①] is my name,
And high up on the mountain top is my home;
Seeing you sow alone the millet seed,
I came especially to give you my aid."
Mengshi Caizou was smiling winsomely;
She looked so dignified, bowing slightly.
Stooping to pick up the gold flute,
With her own hands, she stuck it in his belt.

十一

XI

蒙诗彩奏抬起脚，
迈步走进小米地。
扎董丕冉想阻止，
可是没有来得及。
她右手扶犁把，

Mengshi Caizou raised her feet,
And walked onto the field for millet.
Zhadong Piran wanted to stop her,
But he was much slower.
The plough handle her right hand holding,

① 蒙诗彩奏：苗语，意为花苗的小女儿。

① (Hmong language) The youngest daughter of the Flower Hmong people.

左手拉牛鼻索，
口里不住吆着牛，
一铧一铧犁过去。

A tether her left hand pulling,
Tenderly and continuously, she urged on the bull;
One plough after another, away did she toil.

姑娘也会犁地呀！
扎董丕冉觉得很稀奇。
看着她那苗条的身影，
心中又有些不过意：
“还是让我来犁吧，
莫弄脏了你的彩裙和花衣！”

O, a lass could also plough the field!
Zhadong Piran felt it strange and was surprised.
Looking at her slender figure,
He felt somewhat apologetic for his manners:
“Let me still plough the field, please.
Do not make dirty your colorful skirt and clothes!”

“游鱼离不开池塘，
蒙诗彩奏离不开土地，
怕脏怕累就不是苗家女！”
扎董丕冉赶紧拿起一个大粪箕，
撮了一些小米种，
沿沟撒种赶上去。

“A fish can’t live out of a pond;
Mengshi Caizou can’t be separated from the land;
One that fears dirty or heavy work can’t be a Hmong daughter!”
Zhadong Piran picked up a big manure basket in a quick manner,
Scooped up some millet seeds, and
Sowed them along the furrow in the field.

扎董丕冉撒着种，
就像喝醉酒一样。
一步一摇跟她走，
两眼不住朝她望。

Zhadong Piran sowed the seeds,
And just like a drunkard,
He walked unsteadily, one step after another,
And couldn’t take his eyes off her.

一粒一粒小米种啊，
全都撒在沟帮上。

O! One grain after another, the millet seeds
Were all sowed on the furrow's sides.

蒙诗彩奏心里暗发笑，
脸也觉得有点烫，
开口轻轻唱起歌，
教他不该分心肠：

Mengshi Caizou was inwardly smiling,
But also felt her face burning.
She opened her mouth to sing tenderly,
And reminded him to sow carefully:

“种子撒在石头上，
不会生根不会长；
种子撒在沟帮上，
会被鸟雀全吃光；
种子埋得太深了，
就会沤烂在泥塘；
种子盖得太浅了，
将来苗棵长不壮。
我的阿哥哟，
乱撒种子的人，
他的收成无指望！”

“When seeds are sowed on stones,
They can neither take root nor have blooms;
When seeds are sowed on furrow sides,
They will be eaten completely by birds;
When seeds are covered with too much dirt,
They will become mildewed and rot;
When seeds are shallowly covered with earth,
They will never have strong sprouts of growth.
O my beloved big brother!
People who sow carelessly, please remember,
Will harvest nothing, if ever!”

这歌像股清泉水，
潺潺流进他心房，
他边撒种子边唱歌，
也用歌来答姑娘：

Like a crystal stream of spring water was her singing
That flowed into his heart, murmuring and murmuring.
He was singing while sowing,
And with a song he was replying:

“不是我将种子随意撒，	“It's not that I sow the seeds randomly,
是你天仙般的美貌呀，	But that your goddess-like beauty
使我神乱心发慌。	Has made me lose my wits and be nervous.
我的阿妹呀，	O my beloved younger sister! O lass!
我一定专心撒好种，	I promise to focus on sowing,
等到秋天收割时，	And when autumn brings us the season of harvesting,
定让小米装满仓！”	With millet the granary will definitely be bursting!"
歌没唱完小米已撒完，	Still singing, he had finished sowing the seeds;
整整撒了三块大坡地。	Totally, they had sown three sloped fields.
两人你看我来我看你，	Eyes meeting, glances they were exchanging;
还有多少话儿埋心底。	Deep in their hearts, left unsaid was their longing.
可是这时日落天将晚，	Just then, the sun setting, there came the night;
只好依依不舍相别离。	Unwillingly, they had no choice but to part.
扎董丕冉看着她，	Eyes following, Zhadong Piran saw her,
慢慢走进树林里。	Slowly, walk deep into the forest, and even deeper.

十二

夏天地里杂草长，
长得跟小米一样齐。
扎董丕冉铲杂草，
铲一阵呀，吹一回笛：

“布哩布哩布哩噜，
太阳当顶正晌午。
红火辣日头，
铲草最辛苦……”

只听一阵木叶响，
声声传到他耳里：
“布哩布哩布噜哩，
铲草阿哥莫心急。
天热太阳辣，
我来帮帮你……”

木叶声刚停，
蒙诗彩奏又来到地里。
两人一边铲草一边唱，

XII

In summer time, with weeds were the fields growing;
Each grew as high as a millet seedling.
With a hoe, Zhadong Piran was weeding;
Hoeing for a while, the gold flute he was heard playing:

“Boo-lee-boo-lee-boo-lee-lu,
‘It’s noon, and the sun’s right above in the sky blue.
The sun’s shining and scorching;
So hard is hoeing…”

Just then, he heard leaf music sounds;
Tune after tune, they came into his ears:
“Boo-lee-boo-lee-boo-lu-lee,
O my hoeing brother, don’t behave impatiently!
The weather’s hot, the sun scorching,
And to help you I’m coming…”

The leaf music just came to an end;
Mengshi Caizou was already in the field.
They two were singing while hoeing;

太阳不再辣，	The sun was no more scorching;
热风也像有凉意。	The hot air seemed to begin cooling.
你一铲，	One weeded with a hoe;
我一铲，	The other was quick to follow;
一直铲到日偏西；	They weeded till the sun set low.
你一调，	One finished singing a song;
我一调，	The other was quick to sing along;
一直唱到月升起。	They sang songs till the moon hung long.
铲完三块大坡地，	They finished hoeing the three sloped fields finally,
两人恋恋不舍又分离。	And had to part with each other, but unwillingly.
扎董丕冉看着她，	Zhadong Piran looked at her with sadness,
见她姗姗隐进夜幕里。	And saw her disappear slowly into the gathering darkness.
秋天小米一片黄，	The millet fields were yellow when autumn came along;
穗子粗又长。	The millet ears were thick and long.
扎董丕冉割小米，	Zhadong Piran was reaping the millet crop alone,
孤单一人心惆怅。	And felt in his heart fairly melancholy.
他想起心上人，	He was thinking of his beloved,
又把金笛来吹响：	And played the gold flute aloud:
“布哩布哩布哩噜，	“Boo-lee-boo-lee-boo-lee-lu,
小米丰收人幸福。	One feels happy with a good harvest, as is true.

可是人少地多收不完，
怕要收到日落月亮出。
叫声蒙诗彩奏呀，
请你快快来帮助！”

But, with few people and large fields, I can't finish reaping;
I may reap them till the sun's setting and the moon's rising.
O, I'll call the name "Mengshi Caizou" out;
How I wish you can come quickly to assist!"

远处又是一阵木叶响：
“布哩布哩布噜哩，
小米丰收人欢喜。
人少地多不要紧，
妹妹来帮你！”

From a distant place, leaf music was heard again distinctly:
"Boo-lee-boo-lee-boo-lu-lee,
With a bumper harvest one's delighted.
About few hands and large fields you needn't be worried;
I, your sister, will come to your aid."

随着悠扬的木叶声，
蒙诗彩奏又来到地里。
两人心相印，
一齐收小米。
他割得快，
她掼得勤。
又割又掼不歇气，
很快收完三块大坡地。
小米堆得像金山，
两人相对笑嘻嘻。

The melodious leaf music was still in the air;
Mengshi Caizou came again to the field then and there.
The two hearts had mutual affinity,
And were cutting the millet crop in company.
He reaped quickly;
She threshed diligently.
They reaped and threshed without a break;
Before long, the three large sloped fields they finished.
Like a gold mountain, the millet piled up brightly;
They stood face to face and smiled broadly.

十三 XIII

春天犁地种小米，	In spring, they ploughed the field to sow millet seeds;
夏天铲草薅小米，	In summer, they hoed weeds in the fields;
秋天拿刀割小米，	In autumn, they reaped millet crop with sickles;
他俩都是在一起。	They were always together all those times.
金笛诉衷肠，	The gold flute spoke words right from his heart;
木叶传情意。	The leaf music expressed the affection of a sweetheart.
小米黄澄澄，	The millet was yellow and glistening;
心中甜蜜蜜。	The two young hearts shared a sweet feeling.
种小米的时候，	When the sowing time for millet came,
他俩播下种子，	They sowed the seeds, and at the same time,
也播下爱情；	They also sowed the seeds of love.
薅小米的时候，	Came the weeding time, and weeds they tried to remove;
小米长得旺盛，	The millet crop was growing luxuriantly,
爱情也生了根；	And their love was taking root deeply.
小米收割了，	The millet crop had already been reaped;
何时才能收割爱情？	When could they reap love's fruit?
扎董丕冉有点纳闷。	Zhadong Piran felt a bit puzzled.
小米收完了，	The harvest season was coming to an end;

蒙诗彩奏又要别离，
扎董丕冉更加伤心：
“我的阿妹呀，
今天分别了，
何时才相见？
是三年五载，
是几个秋夏几个冬春？”
蒙诗彩奏微微笑：
“我的阿哥呀，
不要三年五载，
也不要几个秋夏冬春，
正月初三踩花山，
我们来相逢，
我俩来对歌，
那时我俩把亲定，
阿哥你莫错过好时辰！”

Mengshi Caizou was again departing.
Zhadong Piran felt it more heart-breaking:
“O my beloved sister!
Here comes the time for departure;
When can we again meet each other?
Is it three or five years later?
How many springs should go before we meet finally?”
Mengshi Caizou was smiling faintly:
“O my beloved big brother!
It’s neither three nor five years later,
And we don’t have to wait years for the day’s arrival!
The third day of the first lunar month is the Flower Hill Festival;
The Flower Hill is the place for our meeting,
And there, we can have antiphonal singing.
Then and there, we’re going to get betrothed;
O brother! You should not miss the day predestined!”

第四章　拦路

Canto 4　Blocking the Way

十四 XIV

八月过了到九月，
九月过了到十月，
十月过了到冬月，
冬月过了到腊月，
时间就像撵兔子，
紧跑快追不停歇。

After the eighth lunar month came the ninth month;
After the ninth lunar month came the tenth month;
After the tenth lunar month came the eleventh month;
After the eleventh lunar month came the twelfth month;
Time is like chasing a rabbit,
And you dash without taking a rest.

正月初三来到了，
欢欢喜喜度佳节。
正月初三踩花山，
高山顶上立花杆。
红绸挂在花杆上，
飘飘扬扬真耀眼。
群群姑娘和小伙，
说说笑笑上花山。

Of the first lunar month, the third day was coming;
Happily and joyously, the Festival people were celebrating.
On the very day, the Flower Hill Festival people were attending;
High on the mountain top, a flower pole they were erecting.
From the flower pole hung a piece of red silk fabric;
Fluttering in the wind, dazzling it did look.
Crowds of lasses and lads were talking and laughing;
Towards the Flower Hill they were climbing.

扎董丕冉穿新衣，
拿起金笛跨出门。
顺着弯弯小路走，

Zhadong Piran put on his new clothes,
Picked up the gold flute and left his house.
Along the zigzagging path, he walked;

越走越精神。	The more he walked, the more energetic he felt.
因为他到花山上，	For when he was on the Flower Hill,
就要会情人。	He was sure to meet his dream girl.
一边赶路一边吹金笛，	While busy making his way, the gold flute he was playing;
笛声传遍山和岭。	From valleys to ridges, the flute music was spreading.
蒙诗彩奏等在大树脚，	Mengshi Caizou was waiting under a big tree,
隐隐听到金笛声。	And heard the flute music, though faintly.
凭着笛声来判断，	Judging from the flute music, she knew
知道扎董丕冉已来临。	Zhadong Piran was soon coming into view.
她站在地上摇摇身，	Standing there, she swayed from left to right,
摆动一下长褶裙，	And swung her long pleated skirt.
使个法术隐真形，	Practicing magic art, she made invisible her true self,
变成另外一个人。	And changed into another lass to cover up herself.
变成糯珠彩奏①呀，	O! Into Nuozhu Caizou① she changed,
她要试探他的心。	And to put his heart to the test she wanted.
扎董丕冉来到泉水旁，	Zhadong Piran came to the spring side,
一颗心儿在跳荡。	And with excitement his heart throbbed.
马上就要见到情人面，	Very soon, he was to see his sweetheart;
止不住阵阵脸发烫。	Uncontrollably, his face was burning with heat.

① 糯珠彩奏：苗语，意为官家的小女儿。

① (Hmong language) The youngest daughter of an official family.

他在泉边停住脚，
俯下身子望一望。
身影映在水里头，
随着水波在荡澜。
一边望来一边理头发，
又伸出手来扯衣裳。
泉水清清多明净，
自己的身影更漂亮。
看着影子微微笑，
自言自语诉衷肠：

He stopped by the spring side;
Bending down, into the water he gazed.
His reflection in the water
Was waving as ripples spread farther.
While gazing, he was combing his hair with his fingers
And hurried then to straighten out his clothes.
So clear and bright was the spring water
That it made his reflection much smarter.
Looking at the reflection, he smiled,
And to himself he murmured:

“蒙诗彩奏呀，
正月初三来相会，
我俩定下好时光。
收拾打扮来会你，
见面就在花山上。
请你耐心等着我，
照照影子我就上山梁。”

“O Mengshi Caizou, my sweetheart!
The third day of the first lunar month is the time for
our date;
It’s a good time we’ve decided.
Dressing up, I come to meet you as promised;
It’s on the Flower Hill that we’re to meet.
Please, wait for me and be patient;
Taking a look at the reflection, I’m coming for our date.”

忽然水面影子闪，
水里现出一个小姑娘。
姑娘生得很漂亮，
紧紧挨在他身旁。

Onto the water, an image flashed all of a sudden;
Right there in the spring appeared a maiden.
The lass was truly beautiful and lovely;
She stood beside him so closely.

她扭着身子眯眯笑，	Turning towards him and narrowing her eyes, she smiled;
脉脉含情把话讲：	Her soft eyes exuding tenderness and love, she said:
“扎董丕冉呀，	“Zhadong Piran, O!
我是糯珠彩奏，	I'm Nuozhu Caizou.
只因你生得像只金鹿，	Just because you look like a golden deer,
我早就偷偷把你爱上。	I've fallen in love with you secretly, my dear.
你有一支神奇的金笛，	You have a magical gold flute;
能吹出欢乐和忧伤。	Happiness and melancholy can be played from it.
我特地在这里等着你，	I'm right here waiting for you on purpose,
把贴心的话语跟你讲。	And want to tell you my inner feelings in confidence.
望你不要嫌弃我，	Hope that you don't turn a cold shoulder to me,
定要将我贴心上。	And keep me dear to your heart and be friendly.
今天踩花山，	Today is the Flower Hill Festival,
我俩正好配成双。”	And it's the best time for us to become a couple.”

扎董丕冉看着她，	Zhadong Piran looked at her, and immediately,
一下被她迷住了。	He was charmed by her beauty.
她的腰身像柳枝，	Her waist was like a willow twig, and
匀称又苗条。	She was of slim and proportional build.
她的脸盘像葵花，	Like a sunflower was her face;
眼睛像葡萄。	Her eyes were likened to grapes.
她比蒙诗彩奏还好看，	Compared with Mengshi Caizou, she was better-looking;
一颗心止不住咚咚跳。	Zhadong Piran's heart couldn't help throbbing.

又仔细瞄了她一眼，	He shot again a glance at her, so attentively,
频频向着她微笑。	And smiled at her repeatedly.
接着吹起金笛来，	After that, the gold flute he began playing;
笛声在她耳边绕：	Around her ears the flute music was circling:
“布哩布哩布哩噜，	“Boo-lee-boo-lee-boo-lee-lu,
我把心事向你来倾吐。	I'm pouring my inner feelings out to you.
你的美貌已使我动心，	Your beauty has made my heart sway, honestly;
你的好心又使我佩服。	Your good intentions I admire, really.
但我不能爱你呀，	Still and all, I can't fall in love with you,
我的心早已有归宿。	Because my heart has found the one it belongs to.
我已爱上蒙诗彩奏，	I've already fallen in love with Mengshi Caizou;
她会给我人生的幸福。	She'll bring me life's happiness, and that is so.
要是我再爱你呀，	Suppose I fall in love with you,
那我就连禽兽也不如！	I'll then be inferior to birds and beasts, ooh!
一双麂子歇个窝，	A couple of muntjacs would sleep in one lair;
一对锦鸡栖一树；	A tree a pair of golden pheasants would share.
我跟蒙诗彩奏已相爱，	Mengshi Caizou and I are in love with each other;
永远只能将她牢记住。	I should keep her in my heart forever.
她在花山上面等着我，	She's now waiting for me on the Flower Hill;
从早等到正晌午。	From morning to noon, she's been waiting still.
为了趁早去会她，	In order, as early as possible, to meet her,
我正忙赶路。”	I'm now in a hurry and have to scutter.”

糯珠彩奏不听他的话，	Nuozhu Caizou wouldn't listen to what he was saying;
左拉右扯缠住他。	She pestered him to stop, pulling and dragging.
不想吃果子，	If one doesn't want to eat peaches,
就不上树丫；	He won't climb up tree crotches;
不愿交朋友，	If one doesn't want to make friends,
就很难说话；	He won't try to exchange words.
扎董丕冉铁了心，	Zhadong Piran was unshakable in his determination;
一心不理她。	He made up his mind to pay her no attention.
糯珠彩奏不死心，	Nuozhu Caizou was unwilling to give up easily;
紧紧跟住他。	She followed him closely.
扎董丕冉上高山，	When Zhadong Piran was on top of a mountain,
她也追到高山上；	She would follow him without a moment's hesitation;
扎董丕冉走进石旮旯，	When Zhadong Piran got into a stone corner,
她也撵到石旮旯。	She would follow him in his steps right after.
追了一山又一山，	One mountain after another, she followed the lad;
撵了一程又一程。	One league after another, to chase him she tried hard.
糯珠彩奏追不着，	Nuozhu Caizou was unable to catch up with him; yet,
可是心中很高兴。	She was quite happy in her heart.
她想扎董丕冉没变心，	Zhadong Piran didn't cease to be faithful, she thought,
正是她的意中人！	And he was just the man of her heart!
可是她又打主意，	However, she thought up another idea suddenly,
钻进一片大树林。	And went into a big stretch of trees promptly.

摇身变成花太彩奏①，	Within seconds, into Huatai Caizou① she changed;
花枝招展真迷人。	Gorgeously dressed, very charming she was indeed.
要论她的容貌呀，	As far as her appearance was concerned, O,
比糯珠彩奏美十分。	She was much more beautiful than Nuozhu Caizou.
穿戴齐整又华丽，	She was neatly and gorgeously dressed and richly adorned,
石头见了也动心。	And even a stone would be magnetically attracted.
她坐在河边弹口弦，	Sitting by the riverside, the mouth harp she was playing;
弹出曲曲好歌音。	Out of it, each tune was sweet and pleasing.
故意等着扎董丕冉来，	She was waiting for Zhadong Piran purposefully;
二次试探他的心。	For a second time, she wanted to sound him out, so eagerly.
一会扎董丕冉走过来，	After a while, Zhadong Piran came to her side;
她闪动一双大眼睛。	Her big eyes beautifully twinkled.
立刻伸出一只手，	Right away, a hand she stretched out,
紧紧拖住他的大衣襟。	And dragged tightly the edge of his coat's front.
又将口弦举起来，	With the other hand, the mouth harp she raised;
嘴里唱得更迷人：	The song was far more enchanting and it said:
“我是花太彩奏，	"I'm Huatai Caizou, a princess;
家住金碧辉煌的宫殿里。	I live in a resplendent and magnificent palace.
虽说山高路又远，	Though beyond high mountains and far away I live,
早已听见你的好名声。	I've heard about your good repute and feel appreciative.
你是苗家最出众的男子，	You're the most outstanding Hmong man,

① 花太彩奏：苗语，意为皇帝的小女儿。

① (Hmong language) The youngest daughter of the emperor.

早就使我动了心。	And have long drawn my attention.
收下我的口弦吧，	Take my mouth harp as a gift;
请你莫嫌礼物轻。	Please, don't think it trifling and belittle it.
它是我的好伙伴，	It's my best friend;
它是我的命根根。	It's my dear lifeblood.
你若把它收下了，	If you accept it,
我俩就算定了情。	Our pledge of love will be self-evident.
我俩在一起，	When we two are together as a family,
就像一对小蜜蜂。	We're like a pair of bees, humming happily.
你会犁地种小米，	You can plow fields and grow millet;
我会织布裁衣裙。	I can weave cloth and make a skirt.
我俩勤勤恳恳过日子，	Let's live diligently and conscientiously;
同甘共苦心贴心。	Let's share comforts and hardships understandingly.
我俩在一起，	When we two are together as a family,
就像一对小百灵。	We're like a pair of skylarks, singing happily.
你吹金笛很好听，	You play the gold flute, so pleasant;
我弹口弦也动人。	I play the mouth harp, so sweet.
你一吹，	The moment you play, O;
我就应。	I will echo.
我俩永远在一起，	Let's live all our lives together;
欢欢乐乐过一生。”	Let's spend our time happily forever."
扎董丕冉一见她，	The minute Zhadong Piran saw her,
不禁赞叹她的好人品。	He couldn't help praising her excellent character.

她的脸蛋呀，	O, her cheeks
像刚剥的竹笋一样白嫩；	Were as white and delicate as newly pealed bamboo shoots;
她的眼睛呀，	O, her eyes
像荷叶上的水珠一样透明。	Were as crystal and transparent as dew on lotus leaves.
绣花的锦缎上衣，	She was in an embroidered brocade jacket
配着美丽的长裙，	And a beautiful long pleated skirt;
手镯是拿金子铸造，	Her bracelets were made of gold,
项圈是用珍珠串成。	And with a pearl necklace her neck was adorned.
如果跟她相爱，	If he fell in love with her,
定是美满婚姻……	They would lead a happy married life forever…

扎董丕冉越想越甜蜜，	The more Zhadong Piran thought, the happier he was;
昏昏沉沉像是入梦境。	As if having a dream, he was in a daze.
可是耳边好像有人在说话，	Yet in his ears, someone seemed to be talking;
那是蒙诗彩奏的声音：	It was Mengshi Caizou who was speaking:
“正月初三踩花山，	“The third day of the first lunar month is the Flower Hill Festival,
我们来相逢……”	And we're to meet on that day so special…”
扎董丕冉心一惊，	Zhadong Piran's heart was alerted,
立刻就猛醒！	And in a flash he became clear-headed!

他又拿起金笛吹，	Picking up the gold flute, he began to play;
金笛声声传真情：	Tune after tune, true feelings he tried to display:
“布哩布哩布哩噜，	“Boo-lee-boo-lee-boo-lee-lu,

你是皇家贵公主。	You're a princess from the imperial family, ooh!
我是一个穷小子呀，	O, I'm a poor lad,
跟你配不住。	And don't deserve you, a princess so good.
你再生得美，	Even if you were more beautiful,
我不能把心转向你；	I wouldn't turn my heart to you, though thankful;
你再长得好，	Even if you were better-looking,
我不能把情移给你；	I wouldn't shift my affections to you, though adoring;
你再说得甜，	Even if your words were more pleasing,
我不能把爱向你倾吐。	I wouldn't pour out my love to you, though heart-aching.
你的口弦我不能接，	Your mouth harp I can't accept;
你的心意我只能婉谢，	Your kind feelings I can only decline and be polite.
我已爱上蒙诗彩奏，	I'm already in love with Mengshi Caizou, the girl;
她是我心中的一颗明珠。	In my heart, she is a bright pearl.
衣裳可以穿两件，	In two garments a man can be dressed;
烂了可以再缝补；	You can mend them when they're worn-out.
情人只能有一个，	But a man can have but one sweetheart,
纯洁的感情容不得亵渎。	And pure love should never be hurt.
她在花山上面等着我，	She's waiting for me on the Flower Hill;
从早等到正晌午。	From morning to noon, she's been waiting still.
为了趁早去会她，	In order to meet her sooner,
我得立刻就赶路。”	I have to hurry right now to scutter."

花太彩奏脸发红，	Huatai Caizou's face flushing,
故意嘟着嘴巴唱一曲：	She pouted on purpose and began singing:

“蒙诗彩奏不爱你，
她是财主家的小幺女。
你是一个穷小子，
她怎把你放眼里？
我见她打着花伞上花山，
跟着一个小伙唱调子，
唱完调子就说话，
亲亲密密坐一起。
她已爱上别个人，
早就忘了你！
劝你不要再想她，
再想也无益。
虽说我是皇家大公主，
却是真心爱着你！”

“Mengshi Caizou isn’t in love with you surely;
She’s the youngest daughter of a rich man’s family.
You’re just a poor lad;
How could she care about you, indeed?
I saw her holding a colorful umbrella and climbing the flower hill;
She was singing tunes together with a young man.
Finishing their tunes, they talked happily,
And sat side by side intimately.
She’s already in love with another man,
And long ago, you’ve been forgotten!
You’d better stop missing her,
And it’s useless to go any further.
Though I’m a princess of the imperial family,
I’m in love with you sincerely!”

扎董丕冉哈哈笑，
吹起金笛又回答：
“布哩布哩布哩噜，
请你不要再啰嗦。
顽石堵不住山泉的水，
臭藤缠不死爱情的花。
我跟蒙诗彩奏早交心，
死死活活都要成一家。

Zhadong Piran burst into laughter;
Playing the gold flute, he tried to answer:
“Boo-lee-boo-lee-boo-lee-lu,
Please, stop meddling! So long-winded are you!
A rock can’t stop the mountain spring from streaming down;
The flower of love can never be stifled by rotten rattan.
Mengshi Caizou and I have opened our hearts to each other;

她贴肝贴肺爱着我，	We, dead and alive, are destined to be a couple forever.
我直心直肠想着她。	She loves me soul and heart;
要是她去爱别人，	I miss her day and night.
除非石头会开花！	She'll love another,
请你不要纠缠我，	Only if the stone can flower.
让我早点去会她！”	Please, pester me no longer,
	And let me meet her sooner!"

花太彩奏一点不放松，	Huatai Caizou wouldn't let him go as he would,
仍然把他拦在大路边。	And still stopped him by the roadside.
又弹口弦又是唱，	She was playing the mouth harp and singing;
在他身边团团转。	Around him she was revolving.
他被缠得无路走，	He was pestered and couldn't make his way,
只好假意答应她：	And had to pretend to consent and say:
“请你别再把路拦，	"Please, don't stand in my way and stop me;
我愿跟你结伙伴。	I'm willing to keep you company.
我们二人一路走，	Let both of us walk together uphill,
双双同去踩花山。”	And as a pair, go to the Flower Hill."

花太彩奏心里想：	In her mind, Huatai Caizou thought:
莫非他已变了心？	Can it be that he's changed his heart?
等我同他一路走，	I'll go with him for the rest of the journey,
看他可会跟我来谈情？	And see whether he's going to court me!
他若跟我谈情，	If he courts me,

就是变了心； It means that he's ceased to be faithful absolutely.
要是不跟我谈情， If he doesn't court me,
也就没变心。 It means that he's been faithful steadily.

花太彩奏让开路， Huatai Caizou stepped aside;
扎董丕冉朝前奔。 Zhadong Piran ran forward.
花太彩奏忙追赶， Huatai Caizou hurried to chase after him;
跨沟翻梁又过岭。 Down the valleys and up the ridges she tried to climb.
扎董丕冉跑得快， Zhadong Piran ran very fast;
一会就不见踪影。 Soon he was nowhere to be found, like a blast.

他越跑得快， The faster he ran,
她就越高兴： The happier she felt with the young man:
"他没跟我同路行， "He didn't keep me company along the way,
没唱曲， Nor sing songs to make me gay,
没谈情， Nor try to court me,
看他确实没变心。 And he didn't change his mind, surely.
不过还得考验他， But I need to put further his love to the test,
三次才会有定准。" And three times of testing can certainly prove best."

花太彩奏又使法， Huatai Caizou practiced again the magic art,
忙将身子扭几扭。 And hurried to wiggle her waist.
只听一阵风吹过， A gust of wind was heard to blow,

她就变成竺妞彩奏①。	And she turned into Zhuniu Caizou①.
竺妞彩奏驾云雾，	Zhuniu Caizou rode the cloud,
悄悄绕到他前头。	And noiselessly she landed ahead.
一直跑到花杆下，	Up to the flower pole she ran straight,
静静地等候。	And stood quietly under it to wait.
她打着一把花撑子，	A colorful umbrella she was holding;
坐在那里等得久。	For quite a long time she'd been waiting.
扎董丕冉一到来，	The minute Zhadong Piran arrived,
就拿撑子罩住他的头。②	She used the umbrella to cover his head②.
扎董丕冉被罩住，	Under the umbrella Zhadong Piran was shaded
觉得很害羞。	And he felt very shy and awkward.
以为蒙诗彩奏在眼前，	"Mengshi Caizou is right here!" thought the boy;
不禁喜上眉梢头。	He couldn't help becoming radiant with joy.
他抬眼瞅见姑娘很美丽，	Raising his eyes, he saw a beauty standing before him;
不禁吃一惊，	He couldn't refrain from being struck dumb.
再把姑娘细端详，	He looked the lass up and down again,
认出她不是蒙诗彩奏，	And realized she wasn't Mengshi Caizou there and then.
不禁浑身发起抖。	He couldn't help shaking all over,
他不愿再打听，	And was unwilling to ask further.

①竺妞彩奏：苗语，意为上帝的小女儿。
②拿撑子罩住对方的头，是苗族男女表达爱情的一种方式。

① (Hmong language) The youngest daughter of God.
② In Hmong culture, this is a way to show one's romantic love towards a certain person

也不敢再停留。
一把掀开花撑子，
立刻就逃走。

He didn't dare to stay any longer,
And pushed aside the colorful umbrella;
Immediately, he ran away from her.

扎董丕冉跑得快，
一下跑到斗牛场；
竺妞彩奏追得紧，
跟着追到斗牛场。

Zhadong Piran ran very quickly,
And came to the bullfighting site promptly;
Zhuniu Caizou followed him closely,
And was in the bullfighting site presently.

扎董丕冉跑得急，
忽然钻进人群里；
竺妞彩奏撵得狠，
跟着撵到人群里。

Zhadong Piran ran at high speed,
And suddenly he got into the crowd;
Zhuniu Caizou chased him hard,
And she was soon seen in the crowd.

扎董丕冉没有地方躲，
重新跑回花杆下。
这时爬杆比赛才开始，
花杆底下的人多如麻。

Zhadong Piran had no place to hide,
And to the flower pole he returned.
Just then, the pole-climbing contest began;
Under the flower pole there was many a man.

小伙子们显身手，
一个跟着一个爬。
没有一个人，
能够爬到花杆顶，
爬了一半就滑下。

Each young man wanted to display his talent eagerly;
In turn, they tried hard to climb the pole voluntarily.
But not any chap
Could climb to the flower pole top;
Only reaching half the pole, they slid down to the ground.

个个累得汗水淌，	Sweat dripping down, each was utterly exhausted;
人人急得眼发花。	All anxious, their eyes blurred.
扎董丕冉跳过去，	Towards the flower pole Zhadong Piran jumped,
抱起花杆往上爬。	And began to climb up it.
倏倏倏！	Shu shu shu!
刷刷刷！	Shua shua shua!
一下爬到花杆顶，	In a minute, he was up to the top;
引得全场笑哈哈。	The crowd burst out laughing and couldn't stop.
小伙齐欢呼，	The lads all greeted him with acclaim,
向他抛彩带；	And with colorful ribbons they showered him.
姑娘齐拍掌，	The lasses all clapped their hands,
向他甩鲜花。	And tossed him fresh flowers.
扎董丕冉来这里，	Zhadong Piran didn't come here to compete
不是爬杆比输赢。	To climb the pole and prove himself the best.
只是为脱身，	He climbed it only for making his escape,
才几下爬到花杆顶。	And so, in seconds, he climbed up to the top.
说不巧来也很巧，	Out of destiny or coincidence,
他夺得爬杆第一名。	In the pole-climbing contest, he won first place.
使得全场都轰动，	His excellence caused a stir among the crowd,
发出阵阵喝彩声。	And admiringly, they cheered and cheered.
竺妞彩奏站在花杆下，	Under the flower pole Zhuniu Caizou stood smilingly;

不住向他表深情：	She expressed her deep love to him ceaselessly:
“我是竺妞彩奏，	“Zhuniu Caizou is my name,
我要跟你成亲。	And I want you to be my bridegroom.
多好听的话呀，	Words which are fine and pleasant
我也不会说，	Are beyond my tongue, O, sweetheart.
我只有一颗真心，	I've but a true and sincere heart;
我只有一片痴情；	I've but a passion deeply felt.
多甜蜜的话呀，	Words which are as sweet as honey,
也不要你讲，	I don't want you to speak to me.
只要你点头，	I want you but to nod your head;
只要你答应！”	I want you but to consent to what I said!”
扎董丕冉见她那容貌，	Zhadong Piran looked at her appearance;
又比花太彩奏美十分。	More beautiful than Huatai Caizou's was her face.
只见她——	Look! She was dressed–
身上裹着红霞紫雾；	In red and purple, top and skirt;
又见她——	Look! She was wearing–
头上戴着明月亮星。	On her head pearls sparkling.
好一派仙女风度呀，	O, she looked like an elegant fairy!
怎能不使人迷恋，	How could one help falling in love with her deeply!
怎能不叫人倾心！	How could one help adoring her whole-heartedly!
是拒绝她的求婚呢，	To decline her proposal,
还是答应跟她成亲？	Or to agree to make a couple?

扎董丕冉的心中，
In Zhadong Piran's heart,
就像海浪在翻腾，
Waves of passion were becoming turbulent;
他稍稍定一定神，
He tried to collect himself immediately,
赶忙闭上眼睛：
And closed his eyes hastily:

"不，不能答应！
"No, I can't say yes to her proposal!
一定不能答应！
I must give her a point-blank refusal!
什么仙女下凡，
I care nothing about whether she's a fairy;
我决不能迷恋，
About her I will never be crazy,
决不能动心！"
And never become addicted to her beauty!"

他随手取出金笛来，
Presently, he took out the gold flute,
就在花杆顶上吹出声：
And on top of the flower pole he played it:
"布哩布哩布哩噜，
"Boo-lee-boo-lee-boo-lee-lu,
心中有苦难说出。
Sorrows in my heart, I can't tell you.
我与蒙诗彩奏早约定，
Mengshi Caizou and I have decided on a date,
花山上面来相会，
And on the Flower Hill we're to meet;
好把真情诉。
It's the best place to open our hearts.
好不容易等到踩花山，
Finally came the Festival, after painful days and nights;
我心中感到最幸福。
I felt the happiest inwardly.
赶忙换上新衣裳，
My new clothes I put on hurriedly;
翻山越岭过深谷。
Mountains, ridges and deep valleys I crossed over.
本想趁早来会她，
I wanted right away to meet her,
可是三个姑娘呀，
But on my way, three lasses came

死搅活缠来拦路。	To pester me to marry them.
一个叫糯珠彩奏，	The first one is named Nuozhu Caizou,
一个叫花太彩奏，	The second one Huatai Caizou,
一个叫竺妞彩奏，	And the third one Zhuniu Caizou.
一个更比一个漂亮，	Compared with the former, the latter's more beautiful;
一个更比一个杰出。	Compared with the former, the latter's more remarkable.
她们个个都爱我，	Each lass loved me without doubt,
抢着跟我诉肺腑。”	And rushed to pour out her heart."
“最清亮的泉水呀，	"O, the most crystal springs
是从山箐沟里淌来；	Always flow down from verdant valleys;
最甜蜜的话语呀，	O, words that are the sweetest
就从她们心中流出。	Flowed freely from each lass' heart.
个个说的都入耳，	To the ear, what they said was pleasant,
叫我心里热乎乎。	And they were so heartwarming, I really felt.
不过我也不迷糊，	But I'm not lost or confused,
我心中有数。	And I knew fairly well where I stand.
因为我爱的是蒙诗彩奏，	'Cause Mengshi Caizou is the one I love,
想的是蒙诗彩奏。	And she's the only one I long to have.
我只有找到她，	Only when I find the lass in my heart
才会心满意足。	Can I feel fully fulfilled and content.
找不到蒙诗彩奏呀，	If I can't find Mengshi Caizou,
才是我最大的痛苦！”	It'll be my greatest pain, I know!"

“蒙诗彩奏呀，	“O Mengshi Caizou!
你今在何处？	‘Where are you?’ I want to know.
莫非你病了，	Have you fallen ill? Can it be that?
还是事情有变故？	Or, is there an accident?
请你快来搭救我，	Please, come soon to rescue me,
快将我的痛苦解除！	And help me out of this pain early!
要是你再不来呀，	If you don’t come to me right now,
眼下我也没生路。	To find my way out, I don’t know how.
蒙诗彩奏呀，	O Mengshi Caizou!
如今你究竟在何处？”	Where exactly are you?”

竺妞彩奏说：	Zhuniu Caizou said:
“你想蒙诗彩奏呀，	“O, you miss Mengshi Caizou so much, lad,
想得快要发疯啦。	And you’re going crazy for her.
可是你俩分手后，	But when you two parted from each other,
她已埋进深山洼。	She was buried in a deep valley.
只因害了一场病，	’Cause she fell ill unexpectedly,
灵丹妙药难救她。	And no wonder drug could save her.
如今她的坟旁边，	Now, beside her grave, and right there
常来一群黑老鸦；	Came very often a flock of crows;
如今她的坟头上，	Now, all over her grave mound are vines
野蔓荒藤到处爬。	And rattan, wildly running over the place.
劝你还是死了心，	Better for you to drop the idea at once,
不要再牵挂。	And don’t think about her endlessly.

我真心实意爱着你，	I'm in love with you, truly and whole-heartedly.
我俩快成家！”	Let's get married promptly!"
扎董丕冉听她说，	Having heard her words, Zhadong Piran felt
心痛如刀扎。	As if his heart had been pierced.
气得两眼冒金星，	Annoyed, he was suffering and saw stars;
哽哽咽咽难说话。	Dumbfounded, he groaned in sorrow and tears.
他又拿起金笛吹，	He took out again the gold flute,
泪珠滚滚湿衣褂：	Tears rolling down and soaking his coat:
“布哩布哩布哩噜，	"Boo-lee-boo-lee-boo-lee-lu,
世上男子千万个，	There's many a man under the sky blue,
就数我命苦。	And I'm the one to suffer the bitterest.
只望来到花山会情人，	I came here, hoping to meet my love sweetest,
哪知情人早已进黄土！	Only to find she's been in the loess!
蒙诗彩奏呀，	O Mengshi Caizou, my sweetest lass!
你别抛下我，	Don't leave me behind!
我也要跟你走一路。	I want to be by your side.
我俩共埋一座坟，	Let's be buried in the same tomb,
去到阴间在一处。	So, in the nether world, we can share a room.
要我再爱别人呀，	I won't fall in love again,
除非地陷井干枯！”	Unless the well dries up and the earth caves in!"

十五　　XV

竺妞彩奏听完这支歌，
心中很快乐。
扎董丕冉情意真，
三次引诱心不动，
不愧是个好哥哥。
她越想越高兴，
两颊笑出小酒窝。
走到僻处摇摇身，
一道金光在闪烁。
现出蒙诗彩奏真身子
亭亭玉立像天鹅。
打开那把花撑子，
坐在那里抿嘴角。
拿起一片木叶吹，
美妙歌声出心窝：

“布哩布哩布噜哩，
扎董丕冉莫心急。
我早就来到花山上，

Zhuniu Caizou, having heard the song,
Felt as happy as the day is long.
Zhadong Piran was sincere in his love;
Three times, her lure stirred up not a single wave;
He was really a worthy sweetheart.
The more she thought, the happier she felt;
Dimples appeared on her smiling cheeks.
She walked to a secluded place,
A wave of golden light flickering.
She turned back into Mengshi Caizou, standing
As slim as a white swan, gracefully.
She opened the colorful umbrella gently;
Sitting there, she compressed her lips lightly.
She plucked a tree leaf to play;
From her heart a beautiful song spread away:

“Boo-lee-boo-lee-boo-lu-lee,
Please, Zhadong Piran, take it easy.
I've already been on the Flower Hill,

坐在这里等着你。	Sitting and waiting for you all the while.
竺妞彩奏说我得病已死去，	Zhuniu Caizou said I had died of illness;
你泪流满面吹金笛。	You played the gold flute, tears down your face.
金笛声声好凄惨，	One note after another, the music sounded miserable;
我听着心里也悲戚。	Hearing them, I felt in my heart sorrowful.
你爬花杆摆脱她，	You climbed the flower pole to avoid her,
我就暗暗敬佩你。	And inwardly, I admired you right after.
风刮不倒的红椿树呀，	Red toons that can't be uprooted by strong storms
才能成材做桌椅；	Can grow to full size for tables and chairs;
水泡不烂的好种子呀，	Millet seeds, which, after being steeped, don't rot,
才能生根长小米；	Can root, sprout and produce a harvest;
女色迷不住的男子汉呀，	A man who'll never be seduced by a woman
才算坚贞有出息。	Can be seen as a faithful and promising one.
扎董丕冉呀，	O Zhadong Piran, my sweetheart!
我把真情告诉你：	I'll tell you the true fact:
蒙诗彩奏没死去！	Mengshi Caizou didn't pass away.
快来吧，	O, hurry up, and make your way!
我在这里等着你！	I'm waiting for you right here!
快来呀，	O, hurry up, my dear!
蒙诗彩奏在这里！”	Mengshi Caizou is over here!

扎董丕冉听见木叶声，	Zhadong Piran, hearing the leaf music clearly,
感到亲切又熟悉；	Felt it cordial and familiar inwardly.
声声入耳又入心，	Successively, the notes were pleasant to ears and heart;

觉得温暖又甜蜜。	He felt deep down warm and sweet.
他揩干眼泪往下看，	Drying his eyes, he looked down,
竺妞彩奏早已无踪迹。	And Zhuniu Caizou's trace couldn't be seen.
他从花杆顶上跳下地，	Jumping down from the flower pole top,
三步两步跑过去。	He ran toward the lass without a stop.
跑到蒙诗彩奏的身边，	He stood by Mengshi Caizou's side,
不知是悲还是喜！	Not knowing whether he was happy or sad.
两人并肩罩在撑子下，	Under the umbrella, they stood side by side,
双双钻进人群里。	And made their way as a pair into the crowd.
一个唱长捎①，	A ballad one was singing,
一个吟四句②。	Four-line songs① the other chanting.
金声玉嗓来相合，	Golden and jade-like voices sang in perfect harmony;
声声有情又有意。	Note by note, their singing affectionate and rosy.
扎董丕冉对着她，	Facing her, Zhadong Piran related
诉说路上的遭遇。	All his misfortunes on the road.
蒙诗彩奏听完了，	Hearing his words, Mengshi Caizou laughed heartily,
笑得腰也直不起。	And couldn't straighten her back readily.
她脱下一只金手镯，	She took off a gold bracelet,

① 长捎：苗语，苗族叙事民歌。
② 四句：苗族中的一种即兴式民歌，也叫主意歌或四句歌。

① A form of impromptu singing, usually consisting of four lines, in Hmong folk music.

戴在扎董丕冉手腕上，	And put it around Zhadong Piran's wrist;
轻轻对他说：	She said to him softly:
“见了金手镯，	“The moment the gold bracelet you see,
你就想起我。”	You'll naturally miss me.”
扎董丕冉脱下一副银项圈，	Zhadong Piran took off a silver neckband,
挂在蒙诗彩奏脖颈上，	Put it around Mengshi Caizou's neck, and
低低对她说：	Said to her in a voice so soft:
“项圈在你脖颈上，	“The neckband is around your neck, my sweetheart;
我就挂在你心里。”	I'm now residing in your heart.”

十六 XVI

花山踩了一整天，	On the Flower Hill, they played the whole day,
情话也说了一整天，	And also whispered sweet nothings the whole day.
扎董丕冉沿着羊肠路，	Walking along a meandering footpath smilingly,
又唱又笑回家转。	Zhadong Piran sang and returned home happily.
檐口挂着的小画眉，	The caged song thrush hanging from the eave, chirping,
没有他唱得好；	Was no match for him in singing;
吃饱归家的小牛犊，	A calf, returning to the pen after eating its fill,
没有他跳得欢。	Didn't gambol more happily than him still.

出门时脸上常带笑，
吃饭前还要唱一段。

With a big smile on his face, he often went out;
Before a meal he would sing a part.

阿奈坐在堂屋吃草药，
扎董丕冉端水到面前。
她见儿子没戴银项圈，
又见儿子展笑颜。
心想定是找到了好姑娘，
才会这样喜地欢天。
阿奈越想越高兴，
病也好了一大半。
皱紧眉头故意问：
“你的项圈哪去了？
为何不见挂胸前？
拿去街上卖掉了，
还是丢在大路边？
这是我家的传家宝呀，
一代一代传了几百年。
千两黄金也不卖，
万两白银也不换。
我要留着它，
送给儿媳妇。
我一生一世呀，
就是这心愿！

Mom was in the central room, taking herbal medicine;
A bowl of water Zhadong Piran brought in.
Seeing her son's silver neckband was gone,
And the boy's face a broad smile was on,
She thought he must have found a nice lass,
So his joy seemed to be boundless.
The more Mom thought, the happier she felt;
Her illness had already begun to melt.
Knitting her brows, she asked purposefully:
"Where's your neckband, honey?
Why isn't it there upon your chest?
Did you sell it in the market,
Or lose it on your way?
It's our family heirloom, anyway;
For generations, it's passed on in our family.
One thousand taels of gold can't buy it, honey.
Ten thousand taels of silver can't be exchanged for the neckband.
I'm going to keep it, and
Give it to my son's future wife.
O, my son, all my life,

你要把它找回来，
期限给三天。
三天要是找不回来呀，
你就别进家门槛！”

I have only this wish!
You have to get back the thing I cherish,
And three days is the time limit.
Within three days, if you can't find it,
You should never come back home. Don't forget!"

扎董丕冉抿嘴笑，
不禁红了脸。
他取出金笛吹起来，
欢快的笛声响不断：
“布哩布哩布哩噜，
我劝阿奈别发怒。
项圈没卖也没丢，
我为它找到一个好去处。
将它送给一个小姑娘，
她名叫蒙诗彩奏，
就是你的儿媳妇！”

Zhadong Piran flashed a toothless smile,
And his face couldn't help turning red awhile.
He took out the gold flute to play;
Cheerful music resounded all the day:
"Boo-lee-boo-lee-boo-lee-lu,
I advise you, Mom, not to get angry, will you?
I neither sold the neckband nor lost it, mother;
I've found it a new and good owner.
I've given a lass the neckband;
Mengshi Caizou is her name, and
In marriage I've asked for her hand!

这歌正合阿奈的心意，
她越听越喜欢，
赶忙拿起纺车来，
高高兴兴纺麻线。

The song was to Mom's liking;
She felt happier and happier while listening.
Hurriedly, she sat before the spinning wheel;
Spinning linen thread, so happy did she feel.

阿支躺在床上干咳嗽，

Pop was lying on the bed, coughing;

扎董丕冉给他揉胸口。	His chest Zhadong Piran was rubbing.
他见扎董丕冉哼着歌，	Seeing Zhadong Piran was humming,
又见他戴着金手镯。	And a gold bracelet he was wearing,
心想儿子定是找到了好姑娘，	His son must have found a nice lass, he thought,
才会这样哼不停呀唱不够。	So the lad kept humming and stopped not a moment.

阿支越想越开心，	The more Pop thought, the happier he was;
丝丝笑意挂眉头。	Traces of a smile were creeping up his brows.
顿觉疾病全消了，	All his illness disappeared suddenly;
真想起床去喂牛。	He wanted to get out of bed to feed the cattle eagerly.
收起笑容故意问：	Hiding his smile, he purposefully asked:
“你这手镯哪里来？	“Where did you get the gold bracelet?
到底是抢还是偷？	Did you commit a robbery or a theft?
家穷也要有志气，	Though poverty stricken, we should be upright
要有一架硬骨头。	And be men of integrity.
别人的手镯决不要，	We want no other's bracelet resolutely;
戴在手上也害羞！”	If not, wearing it, we're to feel shameful, really!"

扎董丕冉暗发笑，	Zhadong Piran was inwardly laughing,
忸忸怩怩低下头。	And behaved coyly, his head drooping.
拿出金笛吹起来，	He took out the gold flute to play;
笛声传遍吊脚楼：	The music spread to stilted buildings far away:
“布哩布哩布哩噜，	“Boo-lee-boo-lee-boo-lee-lu,
我劝阿支莫发怒。	I advise you, Pop, not to get angry, will you?

我没去抢也没偷，	I committed neither a robbery nor a theft;
这只手镯有来路，	From a good source came the gold bracelet.
是蒙诗彩奏送给我，	It's Mengshi Caizou who gave it to me;
她就是你的儿媳妇。”	Your son's wife she is going to be."
阿支听罢笑起来，	Hearing that, Pop started to laugh,
几步跑出堂屋外。	And ran out of the central room to fetch chaff.
忙到牛厩去喂牛，	He hurried to the cowshed to feed the cattle.
添草上料心自在。	Adding forage and fodder, he felt comfortable.

第五章　中计

Canto 5　Being Trapped

十七

那次凤凰在山上游玩，
魔虎猛然下山冈。
它将凤凰紧追赶，
眼看很快就追上。
扎董丕冉拿起刀，
跟那魔虎斗一场。
魔虎终于被赶跑，
凤凰才得免祸殃。
躲荫不忘栽树人，
脱险常念救命郎。
为了报答扎董丕冉，
凤凰施法变姑娘。
她就是蒙诗彩奏呀，
美丽又善良。
她跟扎董丕冉结良缘，
二人配成称心的一双。
大魔虎没有得到凤凰，
整天把牙咬得咯咯响。
凤凰变成了蒙诗彩奏，

XVII

That time, the phoenix was playing in the mountain
happily;
A monster tiger rushed down from a hillock abruptly.
It was chasing after the phoenix closely,
And was about to catch the phoenix immediately.
Zhadong Piran took up his machete,
And fought the monster tiger bravely.
The monster tiger was driven away finally,
And the phoenix was rescued from a calamity.
Taking shelter from the sun, one forgets not the tree-
planting man;
Saved out of danger, the phoenix longed to see its savior
again.
To repay Zhadong Piran for his kindness,
The phoenix, performing magic arts, turned into a lass.
O, Mengshi Caizou was the lass,
A lass of beauty and kindness.
She and Zhadong Piran had gotten engaged,
And a perfect couple they had made.

爱上了扎董丕冉， 它更是妒火烧胸膛： “既然凤凰变成了美女， 那就应该抢来做婆娘！” 魔虎打定鬼主意， 只等时机一到又要逞凶狂。	The monster tiger failed to get the phoenix; Every day it clenched its teeth in the sticks. Into Mengshi Caizou the phoenix had changed, And fallen in love with Zhadong Piran, the lad. The monster tiger was burning with jealousy: “Now that the phoenix has turned into a beauty, Why not kidnap her and make her my woman?” The monster tiger had devised an evil plan; Chance coming, it would act violently like a madman.
大魔虎共有十弟兄， 虎兄虎弟同住一个洞。 抬牛抓羊拿手戏， 吃人害人是天性， 只要碰上好机会， 它们就一齐倾巢出动。 大魔虎要抢蒙诗彩奏， 九弟兄自然一致赞同。 它们天天出来游串， 奔西又跑东， 只要哪里有动静， 就去向大哥报信请功。	The monster tiger had nine younger brothers; In a cave lived together the ten tigers. Past masters in hunting cattle and goats, They devoured people and were born cutthroats. Whenever there was a good chance, They turned out in full force. First monster tiger wanted to kidnap Mengshi Caizou, And its nine brothers naturally agreed to do so. Every day they turned out to run about From east to west to check her out. Whatever the news was, They let their big brother know without pause.

十八	XVIII
就在那年春三月，	In March of that year, spring came;
扎董丕冉出家门。	Zhadong Piran left home.
到了远方寨子里，	He went to a faraway stockade village, and
去跟吹师学芦笙。	Learned to play the lusheng from a deft hand.
日子过得飞飞快，	Time flew away without delay;
一去就是一年整。	For a whole year he had been away.
二魔虎得知这消息，	Having heard the news,
笑得浑身抽了筋。	Second monster tiger laughed to tears.
连忙禀告大魔虎，	It reported the news to its big brother hastily.
大魔虎冷冷哼一声：	Humph! First monster tiger said coldly:
“上回追扑凤凰没得手，	“Last time, to catch the phoenix I failed,
只因扎董丕冉当救星。	Just because Zhadong Piran came to her aid.
如今扎董丕冉没归家，	Zhadong Piran hasn't returned home now;
真是老天对我发慈悲，	The gods are really having mercy on me. Wow!
即刻去把蒙诗彩奏抢，	I'm going at once to kidnap Mengshi Caizou;
看有哪个敢救应？”	Who else dares to rescue her? I want to know!”
村头有口大水井，	At the village entrance there was a big well;
蒙诗彩奏常到这儿来挑水，	Mengshi Caizou oft came to carry water with a shoulder

大魔虎抢亲生毒计，	pole.
一个红桃丢井内，	To kidnap the lass, a deadly trap First monster tiger set,
然后吩咐虎兄虎弟躲起来，	And into the well a red peach it cast.
专等蒙诗彩奏来上钩。	Then, it told its younger brothers to hide,
	And wait for Mengshi Caizou on the well side.
这天天气很阴沉，	That very day, the sky was cloudy and gloomy;
蒙诗彩奏心烦闷。	Mengshi Caizou felt unhappy and moody.
她无心唱歌吹木叶，	To play the tree leaf music she was in no mood,
也不想拿针绣衣裙。	Neither would she embroider or eat food.
一年没会情人面，	For a whole year she hadn't seen her sweetheart;
她没有哪天不伤心。	She felt so sad every day deep in her heart.
天天盼着他回转，	She longed for him to come back day after day,
就是不见他的半个影。	But hope of seeing him there was not a single ray.
她挑起水桶走到水井边，	She carried water buckets to the well side,
假装挑水望情人。	Pretending to fetch water and meet him by the wayside.
眼睛朝着东边望，	She looked to the east.
东边有块大乌云；	There was a big black cloud over there.
眼睛朝着西边望，	She looked to the west.
西边是片大森林；	There was a big forest over there.
眼睛朝着南边望，	She looked to the south.
南边有高高山岭；	There were high ridges over there.
眼睛朝着北边望，	She looked to the north.

北边是个老黑箐。
茫然四顾静悄悄，
要会情人呀到哪里寻？
她本想重新变成凤凰鸟，
天涯海角找情人。
可是自从与扎董丕冉订终身，
她就不再露真形。
她想露了真形不打紧，
会惹得风言风语不安宁。
她住在深山茅屋中，
成了凡间一个苗家女，
人人都赞她贤惠，
个个都夸她忠贞。

There was a densely wooded valley over there.
Frustrated, she looked around and it was quiet;
Where could she find her sweetheart?
She wanted to change back into a phoenix,
And look for her sweetheart in the remotest place.
Ever since she and Zhadong Piran got engaged,
Her true shape she had never again revealed.
It didn't matter whether she did or not, she thought,
Afraid that people would talk, which would make her
distraught.
She lived in a thatched cottage in the remote mountain,
And became in the mortal world a Hmong woman.
Everybody praised her for her virtue and decency;
Everybody praised her for her honesty and loyalty.

蒙诗彩奏走到井口上，
看看井水解愁烦。
忽然见个红桃子，
漂在水面溜溜转。
她越看越有趣，
她越瞧越喜欢。
弯下腰肢伸出手，
想捞起桃子玩一玩。
可是井深手短够不着，

Mengshi Caizou walked up to the well;
Looking into it, her vexation she tried to dispel.
Suddenly, she saw a red peach floating
On the surface of the water, spinning and spinning.
The more she looked, the more interesting she felt it;
The more she watched, the more she liked it.
Stooping down, her hand she held out;
She wanted to fish it out and check it out.
So deep was the well that it was beyond her reach;

捞了半天难如愿。	Half a day passing, she failed to get the peach.
她又使劲把腰弯下去，	She tried hard to stoop down further;
离那红桃只差一点点。	Yet it was still an inch away from the Hmong daughter.
忽觉背后被谁推一掌，	Suddenly, she felt someone was pushing her,
扑通一声落到井里面。	And with a splash, she fell into the water.
井水齐腰深，	The water in the well was up to her waist;
井帮滑又软，	The side of the well was slippery and soft.
她左攀右蹬上不来，	She tried hard to climb up the well, but failed;
泡在水里好为难。	Standing in the water, she felt awkward.
最后她急得没办法，	At last, irritated, she still couldn't climb out,
只好对着井口大声喊。	And had to look upward and began to shout.
大魔虎暗地将她推下井，	Stealthily, First monster tiger pushed her down the well,
心想大事已经成一半。	Thinking it was halfway to its goal.
此时听她喊救命，	Now, hearing her shout for help,
跑到井口出狂言：	It ran up to the well and began to yelp:
“我今把你救上来，	“I can save you from the well now,
你要给我许个愿。	But you have to make a vow.
打算怎样报答我，	How you're going to repay me,
这话定要说在先！”	You have to tell me first definitely!”
“你能救得我的命，	“If you can save my life,
保你全家得平安。	I promise to keep your family sound and safe.

女的活到九十九，	Women will be able to live to ninety-nine years old,
男的活到九十三！”	And men to ninety-three years old.”
魔虎听罢哈哈笑，	Hearing her words, First monster tiger burst out laughing.
笑得井水也打战：	Its laughter frightened the well water into shuddering:
“你是这样报答我，	“You want to repay me this way,
我却一点不喜欢。	But I don’t like the idea anyway.
要是你不改主意，	If you don’t change your idea,
要我救你难上难！”	It’ll be extremely hard for me to save you, dear!”
“这个主意怎样改，	“Brother, how should I change my mind?
还请大哥给指点。	Please, give me some advice and be kind.
只要大哥说得好，	If your advice is right,
我就一定照着办。	I’ll act upon it in delight.”
“我今把你救上来，	“If I save you from the well today,
你要跟我结姻缘。	You should marry me without delay.
答应给我做老婆，	You should promise to be my wife,
跟我一起把家还。	And go home with me to start a new life.
如若违背我心愿，	If you go against my wish,
让你小命归西天！”	I’ll kill you. So, don’t be foolish!”
“这事我可不能办，	“O brother, please! I just can’t do that;
大哥不要来为难。	Don’t make things difficult, for my denial’s flat!

我已跟人定了亲，
至今已有整一年。”

I've gotten engaged and made a vow;
It has been a whole year now!"

蒙诗彩奏说到此，
不禁心中一阵酸：
是谁心眼这样狠，
推我落井遭大难？
心想变成凤凰鸟，
展翅飞腾上蓝天，
可是身子泡着水，
再变凤凰难上难。
心中越想越懊恼，
两行泪水挂腮间……

Finishing this, Mengshi Caizou, the Hmong daughter,
Couldn't help feeling sad and bitter:
Who's the one that was so cruel
To push me down the well?
Suffering, I want to turn into a phoenix, and try
To flutter and fly up into the blue sky.
But I'm soaked in the water,
It'll be the most difficult to turn into the bird ever.
The more she thought, the more she felt annoyed;
Down her cheeks two streams of tears rolled…

十九

XIX

人到绝处不由己，
真是心长舌头短。
要想做的做不成，
不愿干的也得干。
如今死活这命运，
操在别人手里边。

In hopeless situations, people have no choice;
Even if the heart longs, the tongue finds no voice.
What the heart desires can't be won;
What the heart despises has to be done.
Now, her destiny—to live or to die
Was already in the hands of some guy

蒙诗彩奏没办法，	How to climb out Mengshi Caizou didn't know,
只得假意许下愿：	And so, she had to pretend to make a vow:
“你若救得我出井，	"If you can save my life,
我就跟你结姻缘。”	I'll marry you and be your wife."
“这话是真还是假？	"Do you really mean it or not, woman?
诺言出口就不能变！”	A vow made should never be broken!"
蒙诗彩奏暗暗想，	Mengshi Caizou thought inwardly;
只要出了井，	As long as she was saved out of the well safely,
事情就好办，	Things would be easy to handle,
又强装笑脸巧周旋：	So she tried to look happy and cheerful:
“这话是真不是假，	"What I said can't be untrue!
你莫多心眼。”	Please, don't be oversensitive, will you?"
魔虎拿根长竹竿，	First monster tiger picked up a bamboo pole,
一头伸到井里面。	And put one end into the well.
蒙诗彩奏抓住竹竿头，	Mengshi Caizou grasped the end immediately,
魔虎将她拖到井外边：	And out of the well the tiger dragged her safely:
“走吧走吧快走吧，	"Let's go! Let's go! Let's go right now!
赶快跟我回家转！”	Let's go back home! Be sure to keep your vow!"
魔虎一边说话一边笑，	While speaking, the monster tiger was laughing;
诡计得逞口流涎。	Its trick working, it was slobbering.

蒙诗彩奏见是一只虎，	Mengshi Caizou saw her savior was a tiger;
吓得心跳腿发软：	Her heart beating fast, her feet did shudder:
“我是人，	“I am a human being,
你是虎，	While you're a tiger roaring;
人虎怎能结姻缘？	How can a human and a tiger make a couple?
我说死说活也不愿！”	I would never do that whatever you babble!”
魔虎听她说“不愿”，	The monster tiger heard her say “would never”,
咆哮如雷气冲天。	And flew into a rage, roaring like thunder.
尾巴一翘三丈高，	Its tail stuck up three feet high;
四脚一纵八丈远。	It leapt forward as if flying in the sky.
又将蒙诗彩奏推下井，	It pushed Mengshi Caizou down the well again,
龇牙咧嘴唾沫溅：	Baring its teeth and drooling there and then:
“叫你吃蜜你不吃，	“When honey was offered, you wouldn't eat it,
偏要去吞苦黄连。	And insisted on swallowing Chinese goldthread root.
我叫你二次再下井，	Now again, down the well,
让你死在井里边！”	You'll die in the cell!”
蒙诗彩奏在井里，	Mengshi Caizou was in the well.
不上不下真为难。	Stuck, she couldn't get out of the living hell.
无可奈何说了话，	Utterly helpless, she opened her mouth unwillingly,
又假意许心愿：	And had to make a vow again, but insincerely:
“谁人拉我出水井，	“Out of the well whoever pulls me,
我就跟他结姻缘；	I'll marry him and keep him company.

谁人救得我的命，	Whoever saves my life,
我就跟他回家转！”	I'll go home with him and be his wife."
魔虎听了笑哈哈，	Hearing that, First monster tiger burst out laughing,
开口忙答话：	And opened his mouth, saying:
“只要你不再骗我，	"Only if you don't cheat me for a second time,
我就再拉你一把；	Out of the well I'll again help you climb;
要是这回再骗我，	If you dare cheat me again,
我就懒得救你啦。	I'll leave you alone, then.
我要死守在井边，	I'll keep staying by the well side;
谁人来救也害怕。	Whoever wants to save you would be horrified.
哪个敢来搭救你，	Anyone who dares to save you
我就一口咬死他。	Will be killed in one bite. O, a sad adieu!
让你泡上一辈子，	All your life I'll keep you soaked in the well
泡成一坨烂泥巴！”	Until you become a lump of mud in the cell!"
蒙诗彩奏心里想，	To herself Mengshi Caizou thought:
事到如今也无法。	"Up till now, no other ways could be sought.
要是淹死在井里，	If in the well, I get drowned,
不是白白受糟蹋？	My life will, in vain, be wasted!
扎董丕冉不见我，	If Zhadong Piran can't find me,
定会气死在山洼。	He'll definitely die of sorrow in the valley.
二人都会遭不幸，	We two are sure to meet with misfortune,
落得树死谢了花。	As trees wither, their flowers go to ruin.

这个结局更悲惨，	Such a result is more miserable,
永世永代难成家。	And forever and ever, we can't make a couple.
还是忍辱先答应，	Better to endure insult and agree temporarily;
出去再想办法对付它。	When getting out, I'll try to deal with it successfully.
于是对着井口说：	So, facing the well's mouth, she said for sure:
“哪有救命不报恩？	'How could the rescued not requite the savior?'
这回说话就算话。	This time, I mean what I said.
一定不会再失约，	I'll certainly honor my promise, instead;
求你快拉我一把。	Out of the well, please, help me climb!
只要拉我出水井，	As long as you save me for a second time,
我就跟你转回家。”	I'll go back with you to your home."
魔虎听罢心里乐。	Hearing her words, the monster tiger felt pleased;
伸下竹竿使劲拖。	Stretching the bamboo pole down and pulling hard,
一下将她拖出井，	All at once, out of the well the monster tiger pulled her.
她浑身不住打哆嗦。	From head to foot, she couldn't help but shiver.
魔虎死死拉住她，	First monster tiger grabbed her tightly
逼她答应做老婆。	And forced her to be its wife eagerly.
蒙诗彩奏没办法，	Mengshi Caizou had no other way,
心想这次难逃脱。	Thinking it was impossible then to run away.
只得跟着老虎走，	She couldn't choose but follow the tiger,
以后慢慢又再说。	Believing she would find a way out later.

那九只魔虎一齐跳出来，
个个得意洋洋笑颜开。
围着蒙诗彩奏打转转，
前呼后拥扯成一大排。
怪声怪气对她叫“大嫂”，
使她又羞又恼红了腮。
大魔虎不住夸赞三魔虎：
“还是三弟办法好，
让我老婆来得快。
是你叫我丢红桃，
诱她落到网中来；
又叫我朝她背后推一掌，
让她成了缸里泡的水酸菜！”
三魔虎一听很得意：
“大哥平时待我恩义重，
我为大哥出力也应该！”

The nine tigers jumped out from their hiding places;
Each felt elated, big smiles on their faces.
Around Mengshi Caizou they revolved,
And in a joyous circle they crowded.
They called her “sister-in-law” in an affected voice;
She felt ashamed and angry, going red in the face.
First monster tiger praised Third monster tiger ceaselessly:
“My third brother, how great your idea was, really!
It helped me soon get a wife, who’s now within my reach.
You asked me to throw into the well the red peach,
And she fell into the trap as you designed;
You asked me also to push her from behind,
And made her newly pickled green vegetables in a jar.”
Hearing that, Third monster tiger felt pleased like a shining
star:
“Big brother, you’re always so kind to me;
It’s a great honor to do something for thee!”

二魔虎听着不服气，
嘿嘿一笑发冷语：
“你们的计策倒是好，
可这是脱掉裤子放臭屁，
白白费憨力。
见她来挑水，

Hearing that, Second monster tiger felt wretched;
It gave a brittle laugh and slightingly added:
“Your plan is good, I must admit from the heart,
Yet it looks as if one takes off his pants to fart,
And it’s a great waste of our efforts.
When she came to carry water with buckets,

一把将她抓住就是了，	We could just catch her, and it was over;
何必设计绕圈子？”	What's the point in troubling us with the matter?"
大魔虎对它摇摇头，	Shaking its head at Second monster tiger, First monster tiger
讲出一番大道理：	Expressed its idea about the matter:
“她来挑水抓住她，	"To catch her when she came to carry water
看来倒是很省力。	Seems to be effort-saving, my brother.
可是她又变成凤凰怎么办？	But what if she turns back into a phoenix?
我哪里还有妻？	How can I have a wife without the tricks?
那回她是个凤凰鸟，	Last time, she was a phoenix bird,
我想抓她填肚子。	And I wanted to catch her for food.
这回她成了个好姑娘，	She's turned into a good lass now,
我要让她跟我拜天地[①]。	And I'll marry her and make her keep her vow.
古时她们的祖先住在大河边，	In ancient times, their ancestors lived by the riverside;
大河涨水淹死多少男和女。	Too many men and women drowned in a flood.
后来逃到深山里居住，	Later, they moved to deep mountains and settled down,
总是害怕洪水再侵袭。	Afraid that there might be a flood again.
将她推进水井里，	I pushed her down the well, and soaked her in water,
就是使她再也不能变把戏。	She was unable to practice her magic power.
这样可以逼她亲口答应我，	So, I could force her to personally consent;
二弟怎懂其中有奥秘。”	My second brother, you're far from knowing the secret.

① 拜天地：成亲时举行的隆重仪式。

二魔虎张口又结舌，	Second monster tiger was tongue-tied, and consequently
只好在一旁生闷气。	Had nothing to say but stand by sulkily.
蒙诗彩奏很难过，	Mengshi Caizou felt so upset and unhappy
急得两眼喷怒火。	That she became anxious, eyes filled with fury.
受到的侮辱真是比天大，	The insult she suffered was bigger than the sky;
暗恨侮辱真是比天大，	She hated inwardly that the insult was bigger than the sky;
暗恨魔虎太凶恶。	She hated inwardly that the monster tigers were ferocious.
水泡过身子再也不能变凤凰，	Having been soaked, she couldn't turn into a phoenix;
气得她嘴唇都咬破。	Being so angry, she bit her lips broken.
半晌她才定住神，	After quite a while, she finally calmed down;
冷冷对着魔虎说：	She said to the monster tigers coldly:
“我在井里泡久了，	“For a long time, in the well I've been soaked pitifully;
现在肚子有点饿。	Now, I'm a bit hungry.
那边有棵羊奶树，	Over there, there is a thorny olive tree,
树上结满羊奶果。	And there are fruits all over it.
我去摘些果子吃，	I'm going there to pick some to eat;
你们好好等着我。”	All of you just wait here for me patiently.”
她想这样哄魔虎，	She wanted to hoodwink the tigers into accepting her plea,
施个巧计好逃脱。	And carry out the good ruse to escape from the danger.
只要魔虎答应她，	As long as the monster tigers said OK to her,
她就可以上山坡。	She could climb up the mountain slope,
上了山坡钻深箐，	

就到自己寨子脚。	And go down into the wooded valley after reaching the top.
大魔虎起初不答应，	At the foot of her stockade village she would then step.
怕她跑掉抓不着。	First monster tiger said no to her firstly,
经她再三说了话，	Afraid that she might escape unexpectedly.
这才准她摘野果：	However, time and again she pled,
“吃饱野果就回来，	And it finally nodded its head:
莫在树上久耽搁。”	“Come back soon when you've eaten your fill.
	Don't stay there for long! There's no time to kill.”

三魔虎冷冷哼一声，	Third monster tiger muttered coldly,
阴阳怪气戳大哥：	And pointed out to its big brother cynically:
“大哥心肠倒是好，	“How kind you are, big brother!
‘麂子’到口还放脱。	You let the 'muntjac' go instead of catching her.
什么野果不野果，	Whatever she's talking about, wild fruits or any fruits,
这是沙蛆在蜕壳。	To slip away by casting off a cloak is what she wants.
我劝大哥莫上当，	Big brother, I advise you not to be fooled by a cheat.
放走‘麂子’吃不着！”	Once you let the 'muntjac' go, you can never eat it!”

二魔虎一下跳起来，	Second monster tiger jumped all at once,
张开嘴巴笑呵呵：	And began to speak, a big smile on its face:
“老三也真太过虑，	“Third brother, really, you worry too much;
何必这样心眼多？	Why should you be alert as such?
谅她长翅飞不了，	I suppose, even with her wings, she can't fly away;
真的飞了还有我。	If she really flies away, I'll be in her way.

就是飞到天边去，	Even if she flies to the horizon,
我也抓来还大哥！”	I'll catch her and return to big brother his woman!"
起先大魔虎夸三魔虎，	When First monster tiger praised its third brother at first,
二魔虎心中就不乐。	Second monster tiger felt really unhappy and upset.
这回它要露一手，	This time, it wanted to take the chance to show off,
显显本事才快活。	And would feel cheerful after doing its stuff.
大魔虎想了好一阵，	First monster tiger thought for a long time, and then
便又开口把话说：	Opened its mouth to speak again:
“你们两个莫争论，	"Please, stop arguing, you two!
这事让我来定夺。	I'll make the final decision as for the issue.
既然她的肚子饿，	Now that she's hungry,
那就让她摘野果。	So, just let her pick wild fruits from the tree.
不过二弟你要陪她去，	But, second brother, you have to keep her company,
也好防备她逃脱。”	And prevent her from escaping, see!"
二魔虎大声叫起来，	Second monster tiger cried out loudly,
好像雷声从天落：	As if thunder had come down from the sky suddenly:
“叫我陪她我不去，	"You want me to be her companion, but I won't go,
别的弟兄也用不着。	Neither do other brothers have to do so.
就是让她一个去，	Just let her go all by herself precisely;
要是她真逃脱了，	If she succeeds in escaping, really and truly,
就砍我这大脑壳！”	Just cut off my big head!"
大魔虎听它这样讲，	First monster tiger heard what he had said,

也就不再说什么。	Added not another word and agreed instead.
蒙诗彩奏跑去摘野果，	Mengshi Caizou ran to pick wild fruits;
野果结成串，	Clustering together, high above grass shoots,
压弯了枝丫，	The wild fruits weighed the branches down.
她心里乐呵呵。	She felt cheerful and gay, her sadness gone.
摘了吃，	Picking and eating,
吃了摘，	Eating and picking,
吃饱肚子上山坡。	Having eaten her fill, she climbed up the mountainside.
不走大路走小路，	She chose the trail instead of the main road;
过深箐，	Going through the deep wooded valley,
直奔自己寨子脚。	She ran towards her stockade village directly.
魔虎们等了大半天，	For quite a long time waited many a monster tiger;
等得心头冒了火。	They waited on until their hearts burned with anger.
总是不见她回来，	After all, there was no trace of her coming back, surely;
大魔虎急得干跺脚。	So, First monster tiger stamped its foot anxiously.
三魔虎对老二说风凉话：	To its second brother sarcastically said Third monster tiger:
“二哥的脑壳呀，	“O, talking of your head, second brother,
到底有几个？	How many do you have really?
还不赶快砍下来，	Why not chop it off presently?
还要等什么？”	What are you still waiting for?”
二魔虎感到很羞愧，	Second monster tiger felt very ashamed, and therefore,
只见它纵身一窜，	It jumped into the air and ran forward;

顺着大路追上大山坡。	Along the main road, a long slope it climbed.

蒙诗彩奏走的是小路，	Mengshi Caizou chose the trail to escape from danger;
二魔虎走的是大路，	Second monster tiger took the main road to chase her.
任凭它跑得如风快，	Even though it ran as fast as the wind,
哪里追得着？	How could it catch up with her as it desired?
追了一阵转回来，	It chased her for quite a while and then came back,
不好意思见大哥。	Feeling embarrassed to meet its big brother due to the setback,
躺在地上就打鼾，	Second monster tiger lay on the ground and snored immediately;
把大魔虎气得直跺脚。	First monster tiger stamped its foot angrily.

三魔虎看看那小路，	Third monster tiger looked carefully at the trail;
小路印着脚迹窝。	On the trail there were definitely footprints of the girl.
它三纵两跳窜出去，	It jumped forward along the trail to chase her,
没跑多远就追着。	And it caught up with her not long after.

“老二差点误了事，	“Second brother, you nearly bungled the matter;
还是老三心计多。”	Fortunately, third brother was much smarter.”
大魔虎又夸三魔虎，	Again, its third brother First monster tiger praised;
三魔虎心中好快活。	Third monster tiger felt cheerful and pleased.

蒙诗彩奏很伤心，	Mengshi Caizou felt heartbroken and upset;
势单力薄受折磨。	Alone and weak, she suffered great torment.

十只魔虎拖住她，
推推搡搡朝前挪。

The ten monster tigers dragged her forward;
Pushing and shoving, they moved at low speed.

走了九山十八洼，
过了十箐百重岭。
不觉来到夺戈底，
蒙诗彩奏更伤情。
那是扎董丕冉家，
触景生情想亲人。
她灵机一动坐地上，
推说走路太多脚杆疼，
要在路边歇一会，
养足力气才好赶路程。
网里的兔子跑不脱，
笼中的斑鸠难飞腾；
魔虎也就没有说什么，
让她歇下养精神。

They climbed nine mountains and crossed eighteen
depressions;
They went through ten valleys and covered hundreds of ridges.
Before they knew it, they reached Duogedi;
Mengshi Caizou felt even more heartbroken inwardly.
It was the place in which Zhadong Piran's family was
located;
Moved by the sight, she missed her beloved lad.
Having a sudden idea, on the ground she sat,
Pretending to say that after such a long walk, her feet hurt,
And she wanted to take a break by the roadside briefly
To refresh herself, so she could push on with the journey.
A rabbit in a net trap can't escape, really;
A turtledove in a cage can't fly upward freely.
The monster tigers said nothing about it,
And let her sit down to take a good rest.

蒙诗彩奏歇一阵，
摘片木叶吹出声，
吹一阵呀望一阵，
试探情人可回村？

Mengshi Caizou had a short rest,
And picked a tree leaf to play it.
She played it for a while and then for a while she gazed;
She was trying to find out whether her honey had

望一阵啊盼一阵，
情人可会来救应？

returned.
She gazed for a while and for a while she longed;
Would her sweetheart come to her aid?

第六章　试刀

Canto 6　Trial Use of the Machete

二十

扎董丕冉学芦笙，
样样调子学得精。
三年期满别吹师，
高高兴兴回家门。

阿支搁下砍柴斧，
欢天喜地笑相迎：
“自从你去学芦笙，
我在家里做活忙不赢。
又打木床又做柜，
又修房顶又做门。
样样家什备办好，
等你回来就成婚。”

阿奈停下小纺车，
连忙将儿唤几声：
“自从你离娘出门去，
娘在家中操持受苦辛。

XX

Zhadong Piran learned to play the lusheng eagerly;
He learned every tune precisely and perfectly.
Three years' learning completed, he bid farewell to the
master,
And returned home happier than ever.

Pop put down his chopping axe, and overjoyed,
He welcomed his son home and said:
"Ever since you went to learn to play the lusheng, son,
I've been busy working at home to get things done.
I've made a wooden bed, chests and wardrobes;
I've repaired the roofs and made new doors.
All the furniture needed has been well prepared;
We're waiting for you to come back and get married."

Mom stopped her work on the spinning wheel, and
Hurriedly called her son several times and said:
"Ever since you left Mom and were away from home,
I've been managing household affairs and having a rough

整日纺麻又织布，
添制被盖和衣裙。
样样穿戴置办好，
等你回来就结亲。”

time.
I weaved linen and cotton cloth every single day;
I made new bedding and clothes when you were away.
I've prepared all the wedding dresses and jewelry needed;
We're waiting for you to come back and get married."

扎董丕冉抬眼望，
眼前一片好光景：
竹篱房间多别致，
木床柜子多齐整；
碗筷瓢盆换了样，
桌椅板凳样样新。

Zhadong Piran looked up, and
Before him, the scene was so grand:
Bamboo strip rooms were uniquely built;
A wooden bed, chests and wardrobes were neat;
Bowls, chopsticks, water ladles and basins had been changed;
Tables, chairs and wooden stools were all newly made.

打开柜子朝里看，
柜中景象更喜人：
新制的被盖绣雀鸟，
才缝的衣裙描花纹。
家中处处有喜气，
扎董丕冉笑盈盈：
“阿支阿奈在家里，
真替孩儿操碎心。
看来万事已齐备，
快请么公定良辰！”
三人正在嘻嘻笑，

He opened a chest and looked inside;
With what was in the chest he felt satisfied:
A new quilt cover was embroidered with birds,
And newly tailored clothes had decorative patterns.
Every place in the house was full of joy;
How happy was Zhadong Piran, now a smiling boy:
"Pop and Mom worked hard at home, and
Have taken a lot of trouble for me, which I understand.
It seems that everything is ready;
Let's ask a shaman soon to choose a lucky day for me!"
The three of them were laughing merrily,

远处传来木叶声。
声声低沉又凄婉，
扎董丕冉仔细听。

“布哩布哩布噜哩，
我把木叶来吹起。
问声扎董丕冉呀，
你可曾回来到家里？
跟你分别整一年，
我天天都在想着你。
你出远门学芦笙，
我俩因此才分离。
我天天走到水井边，
假装挑水来等你。
眼睛望穿不见你回来，
我感到寂寞又孤凄。
今天心里更烦闷，
我又到井边去等你。
为捞一个红桃子，
被虎推落在井里。
魔虎趁机来逼婚，
我已中了它奸计。
如今十只魔虎抓住我，
要将我带到山洞去。

When leaf music was heard coming from afar suddenly.
Tune by tune, the music was low, deep and sadly moving.
So attentively was Zhadong Piran listening.

“Boo-lee-boo-lee-boo-lu-lee,
I'm now playing the leaf music sadly.
O Zhadong Piran, my sweetheart,
Have you returned home yet?
We've been separated for a whole year,
And I miss you every single day, my dear.
To learn to play the lusheng, you went to a faraway place,
So we've been separated ever since.
Every day, I came to the well expectantly,
While pretending to carry water, to wait for you, honey.
I kept gazing, my eyes strained, but you never returned;
I felt lonely, miserable and sad.
Today, I felt more depressed than ever;
To wait for you, I went again to carry water.
In order to fish out a red peach in the well,
I was pushed by a tiger down into the hell.
Taking advantage of the occasion, the tiger forced me to
marry it;
I've fallen into the trap it had set.
Now, ten monster tigers have caught me,

到了山洞就成亲，
我就永远成了魔虎妻。
我若不跟它们去，
定会死在虎口里。
我的扎董丕冉呀，
快来搭救我，
我的扎董丕冉呀，
不要再迟疑！”

And are going to take me to their cave immediately.
Arriving there, First monster tiger will marry me shortly
after,
And I will become a monster tiger's wife forever.
If I don't go with them obediently,
I'll be killed by them definitely.
O Zhadong Piran, my honey,
Please, come soon to rescue me;
O Zhadong Piran, my sweetheart,
Please, hurry up and don't hesitate!"

扎董丕冉在家里，
一字一句听得清。
只觉眼前一片黑，
好像霹雳轰头顶。
蒙诗彩奏遭灾难，
使他气愤又伤心。
生活就像爬山岭，
高高低低路不平。
阿支阿奈也悲痛，
又急又气成泪人。

Zhadong Piran was in the house,
And heard clearly each word and each sentence.
He felt his vision was blurred
As if a thunderbolt struck above his head.
A great disaster Mengshi Caizou suffered;
He felt furious and very sad.
Life was like climbing chains of mountains,
And roads were unsmooth, full of ups and downs.
Pop and Mom were both grieved;
They were all tears, anxious and enraged.

扎董丕冉抹抹泪，
吹起金笛忙答应：

Zhadong Piran wiped away his tears quickly,
And played the gold flute to make a reply:

“布哩布哩布哩噜，	“Boo-lee-boo-lee-boo-lee-lu,
我已知道你受苦。	You are suffering hardships I just knew.
我的心情很难过，	I feel so sad in my heart
就像利箭穿胸脯。	As if arrows are piercing my chest.
只望回到家里来，	I had hoped that when I came back home,
跟你相会诉肺腑。	I could tell you words from my heart’s bottom.
不料祸事从天降，	A disaster descended from heaven unexpectedly,
十只魔虎真狠毒。	And the ten tigers were vicious, really and truly.
趁我不在你身边，	They took advantage of my being away from your side,
什么坏事都干出。	And have done all the evil things they could.
我的蒙诗彩奏呀，	O Mengshi Caizou, my sweetheart,
你不要伤心不要哭。	Don’t cry and don’t feel upset.
等我提起大砍刀，	I’ll take my machete,
为你报仇杀魔虎。”	And kill the monster tigers to avenge thee.”

蒙诗彩奏听到金笛声，	Mengshi Caizou heard the gold flute music,
知道扎董丕冉已回村。	Knowing that Zhadong Piran had come back.
她眼前一亮心激动，	Her eyes brightened and she felt excited in her heart;
紧吹木叶告亲人：	She played the tree leaf unceasingly to tell her sweetheart:
“布哩布哩布噜哩，	“Boo-lee-boo-lee-boo-lu-lee,
你已平安到家里。	You have returned home safely.
我的苦楚你知晓，	My suffering you’ve gotten to know;
你来杀虎要警惕。	To kill the tigers, you should guard against many a foe.
十只魔虎凶恶又狡猾，	The ten monster tigers are crafty and fierce;

你要沉着莫性急。	You should be cool-headed and have more patience.
大刀一定要磨快，	The machete should be made as sharp as a razor;
杀虎才有力。	When used to kill tigers, it'll make you a powerful fighter.
如果有闪失，	If anything should go wrong unfortunately,
我俩都会落进虎口里！”	Both of us will be captured inevitably!"
扎董丕冉怒不歇，	Zhadong Piran couldn't stop his anger,
又吹金笛答木叶：	And played again the gold flute to answer her:
“布哩布哩布哩噜，	"Boo-lee-boo-lee-boo-lee-lu,
你的话语我记住。	I'll remember all the words from you.
魔虎凶恶我不怕，	I'm not afraid of the fierce tigers,
我有心计胆气足。	Because I'm brave enough and have plans.
我就立刻磨大刀，	I'll grind the machete immediately,
将刀磨快好杀虎。”	And making it sharp, I'll kill the tigers easily."
金笛一调接一调，	Tone by tone, Zhadong Piran played the gold flute;
木叶一声连一声。	Mengshi Caizou did the tree leaf note by note.
金笛木叶传情意，	Affections the gold flute and the tree leaf were exchanging;
一个吹来一个应。	One was playing and the other responding.
十只魔虎在旁边，	The ten monster tigers stood nearby,
一调一声也不会听。	And couldn't understand what they tried to imply.
只得坐在石头上，	They had no choice but to sit on stones,
闭起双目养精神。	And to gather their strength, they closed their eyes.

二十一

扎董丕冉不说话，
立刻奔向竹篱笆。
阿支打的大长刀，
正在上面高高挂。
扎董丕冉踮起脚，
伸手忙把刀取下。
又去搬来大磨石，
整天磨个眼不眨。
唰唰唰！
沙沙沙！
磨了三天又三夜，
磨得大刀闪闪放光华。
他拿起大刀晃一晃，
照得竹楼闪闪亮。
到底刀口快不快，
还要试试它。

XXI

Zhadong Piran said nothing and at once,
He ran towards the bamboo fence.
The long machete Pop had forged before
Hung up high on the fence, ready for the coming war.
Zhadong Piran stood on tiptoe without a moment's hesitation,
Stretched out his hand and hurriedly took it down.
Then, to the yard a big grindstone he brought;
Without blinking his eyes, he ground the machete day and night.
Shua-shua-shua!
Sha-sha-sha!
For three days and three nights he ground the machete,
And it glittered in the sunlight brightly.
He took up the machete and shook it;
It shone upon the bamboo house and made it bright.
Was the blade of the machete sharp or not?
He still needed something to test it.

恰巧就在这时候，	Just at that moment, by chance
阿支牵牛到院坝。	Pop led the bull into the yard through the entrance.
扎董丕冉又吹笛，	Again, the gold flute Zhadong Piran played,
对着阿支说起话：	And earnestly, to Pop he said:
“布哩布哩布哩噜，	“Boo-lee-boo-lee-boo-lee-lu,
我正磨刀去杀虎。	To kill the tigers, I'm grinding the machete anew.
不知磨得快不快，	Not knowing whether it is sharp or not,
试它一试才有数。	I'll get to know after I have a test.
要拿什么来试刀？	What can I use to try the machete?
就拿这头大黄牯。”	The best subject the yellow bull would be!”
阿支听罢流眼泪，	Hearing that, Pop shed tears uncontrollably,
歌声随着眼泪出：	And with his tears, a song flew freely:
“儿是爹的心头肉，	“You're my dearly loved son,
牛儿是爹的手中物。	And the bull's my treasured possession.
为了搭救蒙诗彩奏呀，	In order to rescue Mengshi Caizou, your beloved girl,
何惜这头大黄牯！”	I don't feel pitiful about sacrificing the yellow bull!”
阿支献牛试大刀，	Pop sacrificed the bull to try the machete;
深明大义心宽阔。	He was broad-minded and knew its importance clearly.
扎董丕冉奔上前，	Zhadong Piran ran quickly forward without stop,
一刀割断牛鼻索。	And at one stroke, cut off the bull's nose rope.
他又照准牛屁股，	Then, at the bull's rump he aimed,
使劲踢一脚。	And exerted all his strength to kick it hard.

黄牯不防挨了这一踢，	The yellow bull was kicked unexpectedly,
猛跳狂奔窜进山窝窝。	Then, it jumped and ran into a dell wildly.
踏得满山黄尘滚，	Clouds of dust were stirred up all over the mountain,
大树小树打哆嗦。	Big and small trees trembling with each vibration.
扎董丕冉握起刀，	Zhadong Piran held the machete,
纵过石坎跨沟壑。	Jumped over stone steps and strode over ditches bravely.
就像一阵狂风卷过去，	Like a violent gust of wind he swept;
手一举起刀就落。	Raising his hand, he chopped.
一头肥壮的大牯牛呀，	O, a big, stout and strong bull
被劈成两截轱轱辘辘滚下坡。	Was chopped into two parts, rolling down the hill.
滚到坡下才见流出血，	When getting to the foot of the hill, blood appeared,
染红了一片杂草棵。	And dyed a clump of rank grass red.
看来大刀已磨快，	Evidently, the machete had been made sharp;
扎董丕冉不禁喜心怀。	Feeling greatly pleased Zhadong Piran couldn't help,
可是他深思又细想，	But he pondered over the matter deeply and carefully;
杀虎还得再忍耐。	To kill the tigers, he needed to wait patiently.
他又继续磨大刀，	The big machete he kept grinding,
要把大刀磨得飞飞快。	And meant to make it sharp for everything.
磨了三天零三夜，	For three days and three nights, he ground it,
磨得大刀能照出影子来。	And images could be reflected in the blade in daylight.
他拿起大刀晃一晃，	He took up the machete and shook it;
映得山山水水放光彩。	Mountains and streams shone bright before its light.

这回又要试试刀，	Again, he wanted to try the machete,
看看磨得快不快。	And see whether it was sharp already.
要拿什么来试刀？	To try the machete, what could be used?
他半天也想不出主意来。	Half a day passing, he was still confused.
只见阿奈正在织麻布，	Mom was weaving linen cloth, of which he caught sight;
麻布织得细又白。	The linen thread was both thin and white.
扎董丕冉拿金笛，	Zhadong Piran took up his gold flute,
对着阿奈吹起来：	And facing Mom, he played it:
“布哩布哩布哩噜，	“Boo-lee-boo-lee-boo-lee-lu,
我磨大刀去杀虎。	I'm grinding the machete to go to Mengshi Caizou's rescue.
不知磨得快不快，	Not knowing whether it is sharp or not,
试它一试才有数。	I need to have something to try it.
要拿什么来试刀？	What can I use to try the machete?
就拿这匹细麻布。”	This bolt of linen cloth is a good subject surely.”
阿奈听罢很伤心，	Hearing that, Mom felt really sad;
一边唱歌一边哭：	She began to sing, and simultaneously cried:
“儿是妈的心头肉，	“O, you are my dearly loved son;
布是妈的手中物。	The linen cloth is just a possession.
为了搭救蒙诗彩奏呀，	In order to go to Mengshi Caizou's rescue,
何惜这匹细麻布！”	Such a bolt of linen cloth how can I value!”
阿奈献布试大刀，	Mom sacrificed the cloth to try the machete;
通情达理想得全。	She was understanding and considered things thoroughly.

扎董丕冉走上去，
将布一刀就割断。
他将麻布抛上天，
布在天上悠悠转，
布从空中慢慢往下落，
像是降下云一片。
扎董丕冉举刀接住它，
麻布立刻成两段！

Zhadong Piran went up to Mom,
And at a strike, he cut off the cloth on the loom.
He threw the linen cloth up into the sky;
In the air, it rotated lightly, and by and by,
The cloth fluttered down slowly
As if a layer of cloud descended gently.
Holding up the machete, Zhadong Piran met it,
And the linen cloth was cut up in an instant!

大刀磨得飞飞快，
大刀磨得光闪闪。
扎董丕冉摸了又摸，
扎董丕冉看了又看。
轻轻插进刀鞘里，
用根银链挂在腰间。

The machete was ground sharp like a razor;
The machete was ground bright like a mirror.
Zhadong Piran felt it time and time again;
Zhadong Piran looked at it over and over again.
He put the machete into the sheath carefully,
And with a silver chain, attached it to his waist firmly.

扎董丕冉要杀虎，
马上就要离开家。
他用试刀的麻布缝个大口袋，
又用试刀的牯牛烘成香干巴。
他将干巴装进口袋里，
就去告别爹和妈。

Zhadong Piran wanted to kill tigers eagerly,
And was going to leave home immediately.
He used the machete-testing cloth to sew a big sack,
And then the dead bull to dry over the fire for the beef snack.
He put into the sack dried beef fragments,
And went to bid farewell to his parents.

阿支说：	Pop said:
“你要杀虎报大仇，	“Son, kill the tigers and go to Mengshi Caizou's aid;
救出亲人快回家！”	Save your beloved lass and come home quickly with the maid!”
阿奈说：	Mom said:
“你在路上多小心，	“Son, you should be careful on the road;
救出亲人早回家！”	Save your beloved lass and come home early with the maid!”
扎董丕冉抹抹泪，	Zhadong Piran wiped his eyes,
奔出门外去把仇敌杀！	And rushed out to kill the foes!

第七章　追虎

Canto 7　Chasing Tigers

二十二　XXII

穿过苦竹林，	He passed through Bitter Bamboo Forest firstly,
又进冬瓜箐；	And then went into Wax Gourd Wooded Valley;
翻过黄土坡，	He climbed over Yellow Earth Slope at one go,
又跨红石岭；	And then got over Red Stone Ridge for many a foe;
涉过山溪水，	He forded mountain streams,
再钻茅草丛。	And went through thick cogon grass in hot sunbeams.
背淌汗，	His back was wet with sweat,
脚生风。	And the wind blew under his feet.
口里直喘气，	On the way, deeply he breathed;
心中恨难平。	The hatred in his heart couldn't be subdued.
扎董丕冉追魔虎，	Zhadong Piran wanted to catch up with the tigers eagerly;
白昼黑夜赶路程。	So, he hurried on, day and night, with his journey.
他快跑紧追到河谷，	Hurriedly and quickly, he found himself in the river valley,
见个彩伊[①]在啼哭。	And saw a Zhuang lass crying sadly.
扎董丕冉心难过，	Seeing that, Zhadong Piran felt sad,
吹起金笛问缘故：	And played the gold flute to ask why she cried:
“布哩布哩布哩噜，	“Boo-lee-boo-lee-boo-lee-lu,

① 彩伊：苗语，即壮族姑娘。

问声阿妹为何哭？	O sister, what made you cry and feel blue?
有仇我来为你报，	I'll avenge you if you have a foe;
有贼我来为你除。	If there's a robber, I won't let him go.
天大疑难我来解，	However big the trouble is, I'll get it sorted out;
我劝阿妹莫要哭！”	O sister, please stop crying and have no doubt!"
彩伊伸手擦擦泪，	The Zhuang lass wiped away her tears miserably,
凄凄切切放悲声：	And began to speak sadly:
“前天来了十只虎，	"The day before yesterday, there came ten tigers;
张牙舞爪最吓人。	So frightening, they bared fangs and brandished claws.
驮着一个小姑娘，	They carried a lass on the back,
一下冲进我家门。	And dashed into my house without a knock.
吃了我家一头大水牛，	They ate a buffalo of my family,
连毛带骨一口吞；	And swallowed the hide and bones completely;
抬走我家两条大母猪，	They took away my family's two sows,
连儿带崽拖出村。	And dragged away all the piglets in rows.
阿哥呀，	O brother!
看你是个好心好肠人，	You look like a good man with a kindly manner;
请你为我除大害，	Please, rid me of the tigers and get my pigs rescued;
让我慢慢来报恩！”	I'll later on pay you a debt of gratitude!"
扎董丕冉生怒气，	With rage Zhadong Piran was boiling,
拿起金笛吹几句：	And played the gold flute, singing:
“布哩布哩布哩噜，	"Boo-lee-boo-lee-boo-lee lu,

我说阿妹你莫急。	Be patient, sister, and don't feel blue!
魔虎是你的死对头，	The tigers are your mortal enemy, I know,
也是我的大仇敌。	And they are also my deadly foe.
它背上驮着的那姑娘，	The lass carried on the tiger's back
就是我的未婚妻。	Is my fiancée, and the tigers I'm trying to track.
不管山多高呀路多险，	High as the mountain is and the road dangerous,
我定要杀虎来见你！”	I vow to kill the tigers and come to see you, lass!"
扎董丕冉别了那彩伊，	From the Zhuang lass Zhadong Piran parted hurriedly,
赶到一个大箐旁。	And soon he was near a big wooded valley.
看见一个咪尼娇[①]，	There he saw a Yao kid;
一边啼哭一边嚷，	While crying, the boy yelled.
扎董丕冉心发愁，	Zhadong Piran felt worried in his heart;
又吹金笛问端详：	To find out details, he played the gold flute:
“布哩布哩布哩噜，	"Boo-lee-boo-lee-boo-lee-lu,
阿弟哭得好凄楚。	O brother, you cry so bitterly and look so blue.
是你的蓝靛被糟蹋，	Has your indigo blue coat been ruined,
还是死爹或丧母？	Or your dad, or your mom died?
阿弟呀，	O brother!
请你明白告诉我，	Tell me the truth please; it's now or never;
我会对你有帮助！”	I can be of help to you, brother!"

① 咪尼娇：苗语，瑶族小孩。

咪尼娇呀抬起头，	The Yao kid raised his head,
揩干眼泪唱悲歌：	Dried his tears and began singing a melody sad:
“昨天来了十只虎，	“Yesterday, there came ten tigers so savage;
驮着个姑娘进村落。	Carrying a lass, they came to the village.
它们闯进我家里，	They charged into my family’s house;
又吼又叫太凶恶。	Roaring and growling, they were so fierce.
吃了我家枣骝马，	They ate my family’s brown horse,
抓走我家鸡和鹅。	And robbed my family of chickens and geese.
阿哥呀，	O brother!
看你是个有胆有识人，	You look courageous, knowledgeable and clever;
请你为我除大害，	Please help rid me of this great evil,
我的日子才好过！”	So my life can be good and beautiful!”
扎董丕冉怒火起，	Zhaodong Piran flared up, and
吹起金笛劝阿弟：	Played the gold flute to comfort the Yao kid:
“布哩布哩布哩噜，	“Boo-lee-boo-lee-boo-lee-lu,
我劝阿弟莫心急。	O brother, don’t be so anxious and blue!
魔虎是你的死对头，	The tigers are your mortal enemy, I know,
也是我的大仇敌。	And they are also my deadly foe.
它背上驮着的那姑娘，	The lass carried on the tiger’s back
就是我的未婚妻。	Is my fiancée, and the tigers I’m trying to track.
不管河多宽呀水多深，	Wide as the river is and deep the water,
我定要杀虎来见你！”	I vow to kill the tigers and come to see you, brother!”

扎董丕冉别了咪尼娇，	Zhadong Piran parted from the Yao kid in a hurry;
又追到一条山沟里。	He chased and soon found himself in a gully.
见个佑保[1]坐在荞地头，	He saw a Yi elder sitting at the edge of a buckwheat field;
呜呜咽咽在哭泣。	The Yi elder was sobbing in a voice so sad.
扎董丕冉心悲切，	Zhadong Piran felt mournful and grieved,
吹起金笛问情由：	And played the gold flute to ask why he cried:
“布哩布哩布哩噜，	“Boo-lee-boo-lee-boo-lee-lu,
问声阿佑为何哭？	Grandpa, what made you so heartbroken and blue?
是你儿孙不孝顺，	Is it that your children and grandchildren are not kind,
还是媳妇受欺侮？	Or that your daughters-in-law are unrefined?
阿佑呀，	O grandpa!
请你跟我说清楚，	Tell me what really happened, huh?
我会给你解愁苦！”	I can help relieve your sorrow, grandpa!”
佑保开口把话答，	The Yi elder opened his mouth to answer,
满脸挂泪花：	Tears streaming down his cheeks like a river:
“今早来了十只虎，	“This morning, there came ten tigers so fierce;
驮着个姑娘进我家。	Carrying a lass, they rushed into my house.
又是跳呀又是滚，	Jumping, rolling about and shouting,
个个舞爪又张牙。	They brandished claws and bared fangs, so frightening.
咬死我的独儿子，	They bit my only son to death cruelly,
吃光我的一群鸭。	And ate up all my ducks greedily.

① 佑保：苗语，彝族老人。

阿哥呀，
看你是个大智大勇人，
请你为我除大害，
杀死魔虎我死也瞑目啦。”

O young brother!
You look brave, resourceful and clever;
Please, help rid me of those evil creatures;
I'll die content if you kill the tigers."

扎董丕冉怒冲天，
大吼一声震群山。
两眼射出仇和恨，
双手一伸紧握拳。
唰地抽出长刀来，
刀光亮闪闪。
他照准一棵青枫树，
一刀劈下成两段。
他又吹笛劝阿佑，
笛声激昂又威严：

Zhadong Piran's rage shot out of the world;
He roared, and the mountains trembled and swirled.
His eyes shone with hatred and enmity;
Hands stretching out, he clenched his fists tightly.
Swish! He drew his long machete,
And the glint of its blade shone brightly.
He aimed at an oriental white oak,
And cut it into two pieces at a strike.
He played then the flute to comfort the Yi elder reassuringly,
The sound of the flute impassioned and stately:

“布哩布哩布哩噜，
我劝阿佑莫着急。
魔虎是你的死对头，
也是我的大仇敌。
它背上驮着的那姑娘，
就是我的未婚妻。
不管魔虎多凶残，
我定要剥下虎皮来见你！”

"Boo-lee-boo-lee-boo-lee-lu,
Grandpa, don't be so anxious and blue.
The tigers are your mortal enemy, I know,
And they are also my deadly foe.
The lass carried on the tiger's back
Is my fiancée, and the tigers I'm trying to track.
Fierce and cruel as the tigers are,
I vow to flay them and come to see you, grandpa!"

二十三 XXIII

天有风云会下雨，
人有心事就忧愁。
扎董丕冉别了那老人，
来到一个岔路口。
一想起蒙诗彩奏，
他心中就像火上泼了油。

Where there are wind and cloud, it is going to rain;
If something's weighing on one's mind, he'll be under strain.
Zhadong Piran bid farewell to the elder promptly,
And came to a fork in the road hurriedly.
The very thought of Mengshi Caizou, his beloved girl,
Filled his heart with anger, like adding to the flames fuel.

蒙诗彩奏呀，
前天到壮家河边，
昨天到瑶家箐头，
今天到彝家山沟。
此时此刻呀，
不知又到了哪匹梁子，
哪条冲口？

O Mengshi Caizou, sweet and graceful,
The day before yesterday, was by the riverside of the Zhuang people;
Yesterday, she was on the top of the Yao people's wooded valley;
Today, she was in the Yi people's gully.
O, at this very moment,
"Which ridge are you on?" He was filled with puzzlement,
"At which road fork are you standing at present?"

蒙诗彩奏呀，

O Mengshi Caizou,

我的蒙诗彩奏！
魔虎驮着你，
在路上行走，
一定是快如疾风，
绝不是慢如老牛。
你在魔虎背上，
要抱紧它的脖子，
不要碰破了头，
不要跌断了手。
饿了，
叫它给你吃个饱；
渴了，
喊它给你喝个够；
手酸了，
你叫它慢慢走；
头晕了，
你喊它且停留。
魔虎的牙齿很尖利，
魔虎的嘴巴脏又臭。
你不要碰着它的牙，
你不要挨近它的口。
它急了，
你不要去惹；
它怒了，

My Mengshi Caizou!
On the back, the monster tigers carried you, my love,
And made their way towards their cave.
They must run as fast as the strong wind,
And are surely not as slow as a bull old.
When you are on the tiger's back,
Make sure to hold fast to its neck,
And try not to bruise your head,
Or fall and break your hand.
If you are hungry,
Ask it to let you eat in plenty;
If you are thirsty,
Ask it to let you drink water heartily;
If your hands are shaky,
Ask it to walk slowly;
If you feel dizzy,
Ask it to stop to wait for your recovery.
The monster tiger's teeth are edgy;
The monster tiger's mouth is dirty and smelly.
You should not touch its teeth;
You should not get close to its mouth.
If it is impatient,
You should not offend it;
If it is irritated,

你不要去斗。	The tone of your voice should not be acid.
不管有多少苦楚，	No matter how much misery you're suffering presently,
你都暂时忍受。	Please, do endure it temporarily.
等我追着了，	When I catch up with the tigers,
你就会得救。	You'll be rescued from the evil animals.
杀虎的日子呀，	The day to kill the tigers, my lass,
不会等很久！	Won't be long in coming, I promise!

扎董丕冉想了很多，	Zhadong Piran thought, thought and thought,
脚步也走得很快。	And his footsteps became faster and faster.
翻过彝家山，	He climbed over the Yi people's mountains,
又过仡佬寨。	And passed through the Gelao people's stockade villages.
为了追魔虎，	In order to catch up with the monster tigers,
大步朝前迈。	He strode forward, climbing mountains and crossing rivers.

第八章　沉睡

Canto 8　Sunk Deep in Sleep

二十四

不知追了多少天，
九双草鞋也磨穿。
不知追了几个月，
三件衣裳也扯烂。
爬到一座高山顶，
石多林又密呀，
道路被隔断。

扎董丕冉抬眼望，
魔虎踪迹看不见；
扎董丕冉侧耳听，
魔虎声音听不见。
他想拿起金笛吹，
探问情人在哪边；
可是肚子饿得慌，
手脚瘫软眼皮酸。
拿起金笛吹不动，
只会喘气淌冷汗。
他在地上坐下来，

XXIV

Not knowing how many days he had chased the tigers,
Zhadong Piran had worn out nine pairs of straw shoes.
Not knowing how many months he had chased the tigers,
Zhadong Piran had worn out three sets of clothing.
He climbed onto a high mountain top;
There, stones were thick, trees densely soaring up.
The path was cut off, so he had to stop.

Zhadong Piran raised his eyes and looked around the place;
The monster tigers disappeared without a trace.
Zhadong Piran strained his ears and listened attentively;
No sound of the tigers could be heard, really.
He wanted to take out the gold flute to play,
Inquiring where his love was right away.
But he felt famished,
His four limbs were weak and eyelids drooped.
He took the gold flute up and failed to play it;
He was simply panting and breaking out in a cold sweat.
He sat down on the ground,

想歇一会儿，	And wanted to rest for a second,
再把虎追赶。	And then chase the tigers as energetically as ever.
可是屁股一落地，	The moment his bottom touched the ground, however,
立刻睡倒了，	He fell asleep immediately,
呼呼就打鼾。	And began to snore thunderously.
扎董丕冉睡不久，	Soon after Zhadong Piran fell asleep under the blue sky,
十只魔虎就走过。	The ten monster tigers passed by.
只因他把山路走岔了，	Just because at a fork, he took the wrong road,
没把虎追着。	So, to catch up with the tigers he failed.
这时他在路边睡倒了，	Right then, he was sunk in sleep by the roadside,
反让魔虎撵上他，	And the monster tigers caught up with him instead;
差点碰着他的脚。	They almost trampled on his feet when running forward.
大魔虎闻见生人味，	First monster tiger smelled a living person;
转动眼睛在搜索。	It rolled its eyes and hunted for the man.
忽见地上躺着一个人，	On the ground, it saw a man lying, suddenly;
它就张开大嘴笑呵呵：	It opened its big mouth and smiled happily:
“这回走路走得多，	“This time, we’ve covered a long distance;
就是铁打的肚子呀，	Even if a belly that is made of an iron substance
这时也饥饿。	Would be hungry now and needs to eat to keep fresh.
这人皮嫩肉又厚，	This man has delicate skin and is rich in flesh;
真是打起灯笼难找着。	Such a man, even with a lantern, is hard to find, really.
瞌睡来了遇着花枕头，	As if one runs into an embroidered pillow when he gets

这是老天把他送给我！”
它气势汹汹扑过去，
就要去咬他的后颈窝。

sleepy,
The man has been sent to me by fate!”
Fiercely, towards the man on the ground it rushed straight,
About to bite him by the scruff of the neck, waiting for no mate.

蒙诗彩奏仔细看，
不禁吓得心胆寒。
这是扎董丕冉呀，
怎么睡倒在荒山？
眼下自己受苦又受难，
半路遇着情人更心酸。
她从魔虎背上跳下来，
立刻奔到他身边。
伸出双手护住他，
责备魔虎太凶残：
“他跟你们一无仇，
他跟你们二无冤。
如今你们要吃他，
真是害理又伤天！”

Mengshi Caizou looked at the man carefully;
She couldn’t refrain from feeling terror-stricken, really and truly.
“O, this is Zhadong Piran, my goodness!
Why does he sleep in the wilderness?”
Right then, she was having her fill of suffering,
And halfway, she met her sweetheart, evoking a sadder feeling.
From the tiger’s back she jumped down hurriedly,
And ran to him quickly.
She held out her hands to protect him,
And scolded the monster for being cruel and grim:
“You don’t have a score to settle with him, firstly;
He didn’t do anything wrong to you, secondly.
Now, you are going to eat the young man,
Which is really against Heaven and reason!”

大魔虎冷冷笑一声，

First monster tiger laughed grimly, and in surprise,

瞪起一双铜铃眼：	It glowered at her with its bell-like eyes:
“我们生来就吃人，	“We're born to eat human beings,
连肉带骨一齐咽。	Swallowing their flesh and bones and all things.
要咬要吃随我意，	I'll bite and eat as I please;
这事不要你来管！”	Stay away from this and leave it alone as it is!”
蒙诗彩奏不害怕，	Mengshi Caizou wasn't afraid, indeed;
指着魔虎大声骂：	Pointing at the tigers, in a loud voice she scolded:
“你们吃了彝家独儿子，	“You've eaten the only son of the Yi family,
如今又要来吃他，	And now you will eat him readily.
要是你们吃了他，	If you eat him today,
我就死在大树下。	I'll die under the big tree right away.
不再跟着你们走，	I won't go with you any longer;
你们连我一齐吃了吧！”	You just eat me and him together!”
三魔虎生来最狡猾，	Third monster tiger was born the most cunning;
立刻开口就问话：	It opened its mouth at once, asking:
“他是你的什么人，	“What is he to you, woman?
为何帮他说好话？	Why do you put in a good word for the man?
你要老实告诉我，	You have to tell me the truth;
不然就要吃了他！”	Otherwise, I'll eat him with my big mouth!”
蒙诗彩奏最机灵，	Mengshi Caizou was most quick-witted;
振振有词来回答：	Plausibly and volubly, she answered:

“他不是我的什么人，	“He is no one of mine,
无亲无故无缘法。	No relative or friend, nor my predestined valentine.
数遍苗山千万人，	Among all the people in the Hmong mountains,
我从来没有见过他。	I've never met him, one of the millions.
只因你们太残忍，	Just because you are too cruel and grim,
我才为他说句话。	So I put in a word for him.
害人之心不可有，	Harbor no evil intentions to harm other people;
对人不可太毒辣。	Don't be too ruthless and baleful.
我说的句句是实话，	Every word I said is truth;
你们莫要伤害他！”	You shouldn't harm the youth!"
大魔虎慢慢鼓起眼，	First monster tiger's eyes bulged out gradually,
认真辨认细观察：	And it looked at the young man carefully:
“咦，这人像在哪里见过面，	"Why! It seems that somewhere before, I've met this guy.
像是那回斗过我的扎董丕冉嘛！	He looks like Zhadong Piran, who fought me once, in my eye!
不，不会是扎董丕冉，	No, he can't be Zhadong Piran, my bitter foe;
扎董丕冉出门没回家。	Zhadong Piran is still away from home, I know.
嘿，不管他是哪一个，	Hey, no matter who he is,
先把他吃了再说话！”	I'll eat him first as I please!"
蒙诗彩奏奔到大树下，	Mengshi Caizou ran to a great big tree;
哭着喊着要往树上撞：	Crying and shouting, she was to bump against it immediately:
“你们吃人不眨眼，	"You kill people without blinking an eye;

我也不想再活啦！
我就撞死在这里，
你们连我也吞下。”

I don't want to live and I just want to die!
I'll bump against the tree and die here;
You can also swallow me; is that clear?"

三魔虎见状急上前，
紧紧拖住她：
“要是真的撞死了，
那就丢了一枝花。
大哥没妻我们没嫂子，
十个光棍做一家。
操心操肝白费力，
这样就不合算啦。
大哥呀，
不如这就依了她。
肚子饿了忍着点，
这人一定要留下。”

Seeing that, Third monster tiger stepped forward hurriedly;
And it dragged her firmly:
"If you bump against the tree and really kill yourself,
It's like a beautiful flower withering away itself.
My big brother will have no wife, we no sister-in-law; pitifully!
We ten bachelors will make a family.
It's in vain for us to have taken so much trouble and pains;
So, it isn't worthwhile if what we've done brings no real gains.
O big brother!
It would be better to yield to her.
Just endure it when you feel hungry;
We must leave the man alive, really."

大魔虎听听有道理，
立刻收住爪和牙。
蒙诗彩奏一颗心，
啪哒一声才落下。
扎董丕冉得救了，
全靠蒙诗彩奏几句话。

Hearing that, First monster tiger felt it reasonable
And at once, withdrew its claws and teeth from doing evil.
Mengshi Caizou's fearful heart,
With a sound of patter, fell back into her chest.
Zhadong Piran's life was saved
Because of all Mengshi Caizou had said.

蒙诗彩奏呀，	O Mengshi Caizou, an unfortunate lovely lady!
看见扎董丕冉正酣睡，	She saw Zhadong Piran sleeping soundly,
很想大声喊醒他。	And wanted eagerly to wake him up from his sleeping.
跟他诉说离别苦，	She was eager to relate to him the suffering of parting,
向他倾吐贴心话。	And pour out to him her innermost feelings.
多少情意多少话，	All her tender affection and sweet nothings,
尽在心中翻浪花。	Like waves, were surging up in her heart.
但是如果喊醒他，	But, if she had awakened him, her sweetheart,
多少事情就坏啦！	Too many things would have gone wrong!
魔虎将他认出来，	If First monster tiger had identified him before long,
定会一口吞掉他。	It must have devoured him in one gulp.
自己也会遭毒害，	She herself would have been beaten to a pulp;
落得双双难归家。	They would never return home shoulder to shoulder.
她定下心来想一想，	She calmed down and thought it over;
想出一个好办法；	Soon, she came up with a good idea, and
立刻取下银项圈，	All at once, she took off her silver neck band.
悄悄放进石旮旯。	She put it in a nook between stones secretly,
后跳上魔虎背，	And then jumped onto First monster tiger's back hurriedly.
跟着魔虎又出发。	The tigers, along with her, headed again for their cave unwillingly.

二十五　XXV

蒙诗彩奏骑在虎背上，	Mengshi Caizou was on the back of the tiger,
走了一程又一程。	And league after league, they were farther and farther.
想起扎董丕冉来，	She thought of Zhadong Piran, her sweetheart,
不觉泪水湿衣襟。	And before she knew it, tears wet her coat's front part.
眼泪落在虎背上，	Her tears fell down onto the back of the tiger,
一串一串往下淋。	And one string after another, they streamed down like a river.
大魔虎慢慢停下来，	First monster tiger slowed down and stopped completely;
张开嘴巴大声问：	Opening its mouth, it asked loudly:
“为何伤心流眼泪，	“Why do you feel so sad and shed tears?
出了什么大事情？”	What's the big deal? I'm all ears!”
蒙诗彩奏有心计，	Mengshi Caizou was intelligent and calculating;
边哭边答应：	She replied to the tiger while crying:
“刚才跳下你的背，	“I jumped down from your back just now;
也是怪我不机灵。	I'm to blame for not being smart, anyhow.
丢了一副银项圈，	I have lost a silver neck band;
叫我怎么不伤心？”	How could I not feel sad?”

大魔虎朝她脖颈看，	First monster tiger looked at her neck;
项圈确实没踪影：	True, the neck band was gone; no need to double check:
“项圈掉在哪一处，	“Where did you lose the neck band?
你可还能记得准？”	Can you remember exactly, the woodland or wasteland?”
“就在那个人身旁，	“Just around that sleeping young man;
明明白白记得清。”	I think I remember clearly, and I can.”
大魔虎听了哈哈笑，	Hearing her words, First monster tiger laughed loudly;
笑得眯起大眼睛：	It laughed and laughed, narrowing its eyes amusedly:
“这有什么了不起，	“There’s nothing so terrific about it,
何必气得泪沾襟。	And there’s no need to cry your heart out.
我去帮你拿回来，	I’ll go and get it back for you;
叫你见着就高兴。”	You’ll be happy when you see it anew.”
蒙诗彩奏抹抹泪，	Mengshi Caizou dried her tears;
假心假意诉苦情：	With her tongue in her cheek, she spoke of her fears:
“要是你去帮我拿，	“Suppose you go to look for it for me,
我也有点不放心。	I can’t rest assured and will feel uneasy.
你的本性难得改，	It’s too difficult for you to change your nature;
怕你害了他的命。	I’m afraid you may kill him for dinner.
看他孤孤单单出远门，	He is far away from home, alone and friendless;
睡在荒山野岭好可怜。	How pitiful he is to sleep in the wilderness!

你若害了他的命，	If you murder him and take his life away,
叫我怎忍心？	How can I be so hardhearted? O, nay!
你们放心等着我，	Trust me and wait for me, all of you, in the woodland;
让我一人去找寻，	Just let me alone look for the silver neck band.
找着项圈就回来，	When I find it, I'll come back promptly;
一定不会误时辰！”	I promise I won't hold up the journey!"
三魔虎摇头冷冷笑：	Third monster tiger laughed scornfully, shaking its head:
“大哥莫听她的话，	"Big brother, don't believe what she said.
她的话语不可信。	Her words should never be trusted even if they're sweet.
前回让她去摘果子吃，	Last time, we let her pick wild fruits to eat,
差点误了大事情。	Which almost bungled the matter.
要不是我追得快，	If it hadn't been for the reason that I ran faster,
她早就远走高飞无踪影。	She would have left without any trace.
还是让我去找项圈吧，	Better to let me look for the neck band, and in that case,
这样事情才把稳。”	Everything will be in the bag and in place."
大魔虎听罢点点头：	Hearing its words, First monster tiger nodded its head:
“就让三弟去找寻。	"Just let third younger brother do as he said.
可要记住一件事，	However, you should keep this in your mind;
莫要伤害那个人。”	Don't do harm to that man and be kind."
三魔虎顺着原路转回去，	In the mountains, Third monster tiger retraced its steps;
为找项圈脚不停。	To find the neck band, it didn't stop its footsteps.

来到扎董丕冉的身边，	When it came to Zhadong Piran's side,
睁大眼睛瞧，	The tiger looked around, opening its eyes wide,
又用鼻子闻。	And then it smelt with its sharp nose.
项圈藏在石旮旯，	The neck band was hidden in a nook between stones;
左寻右找白费心。	The tiger searched everywhere, only to catch at shadows.
三魔虎垂头丧气跑回来，	Third monster tiger ran back dejectedly;
蒙诗彩奏好高兴：	Seeing it, Mengshi Caizou was very happy:
"还是让我去找吧，	"It would be better to let me go.
你们莫要起疑心。"	You shouldn't become suspicious and treat me as a foe."
二魔虎忙插嘴：	Second monster tiger was in a hurry to get in a word:
"让她去找也要得，	"It's desirable to let her go as she preferred,
免得我们费精神。	Which can save us much trouble and energy.
来到这里离家远，	This place is far away from her family;
谅她不敢再逃奔。"	I don't think she dares once again to flee."
大魔虎瞅瞅二魔虎：	First monster tiger cast a look on Second monster tiger:
"二弟的主意不可靠，	"Your ideas are unreliable, my second younger brother'
常常坏事情。	And they make things worse very often.
这事由我来安排，	I'll see to this matter in person,
你们莫操心。"	And don't worry about it any longer, all of you."
回头又对蒙诗彩奏说：	Turning around, it said to Mengshi Caizou:
"让我陪你一同去，	"Let me go together with you, and

找着项圈就回程。”	We'll come back after finding the neck band."
蒙诗彩奏暗叫苦：	In her heart, Mengshi Caizou complained bitterly:
“这家伙跟我一同去，	"That devil will go with me,
麻烦可就多得很。”	And there will be more trouble to come."
她又思量一阵子，	She considered it in her mind for some time,
扑哧一下笑出声：	And suddenly, she snorted with laughter:
“有你陪我一同去，	"If you are going with me as a partner,
我也不觉孤零零。	I won't feel lonely on the way.
现在我俩就走吧，	Let's go right away.
找着项圈就回程。”	Finding the neck band, we'll return without delay."
蒙诗彩奏带着大魔虎，	Mengshi Caizou, together with First monster tiger,
停停又走走，	In fits and starts, was on the way towards her lover;
走走又停停。	In starts and fits, she was not in a hurry.
她故意领它四处转，	She led the way and wandered around purposely;
转得它四只脚掌酸又疼。	First monster tiger's four paws ached badly.
大魔虎说：	First monster tiger said wearily:
“找不着项圈就算了，	"If the neck band can't be found, just let it be.
莫在这里瞎转圈圈白费劲。”	Don't wander around blindly and waste your energy."
蒙诗彩奏说：	Mengshi Caizou replied firmly:
“就是十天半月也要找，	"Even if I have to spend ten or fifteen days, I'll find it.
这项圈是我的命根根。”	The neck band is my very life and spirit."

大魔虎说：	First monster tiger said:
“那你自己去找吧，	“Then, look for it yourself and just go ahead;
我在这棵树脚打个盹。”	I’ll have a nap under this tree instead.”
蒙诗彩奏心欢喜，	Mengshi Caizou felt happy inwardly,
两步并作一步行。	And headed for her honey hurriedly.
又来到那片草地上，	She came back to the grassy level ground,
扎董丕冉还没醒。	Where Zhadong Piran was still in a sleep so sound.
这回她也不想再逃跑，	This time, she didn’t want to run away again;
她知道要是自己逃跑了，	She knew even if she escaped successfully,
扎董丕冉也会没性命。	Zhadong Piran would yet be killed inevitably.
她想大声喊醒他，	She wanted to wake him up with a loud voice presently,
又怕大魔虎暗中观动静。	But she feared that the tiger might be watching her secretly.
只好假装兜个大圈子，	So she had to circle around the mountains falsely.
又回到大魔虎耳边说几声：	Returning to First monster tiger, she whispered in its ear:
“这项圈一下难找着，	“It’s hard to find the neck band, and I fear
我怕你等得太焦心。	A long time waiting may make you terribly worried.
回来跟你说句话，	I came back to have a word with you, indeed;
也好让你定定神。	I just want you to pull yourself together.
你在这里安心等着我，	Please, feel at ease and wait for me a bit longer;
我再去找找就回程。”	I’ll go to look for it again and return shortly after.”
大魔虎也是假装在打盹，	Pretending to have a nap was First monster tiger,

暗中盯着她身影。	And in secret, its eyes were fixed on her.
它怕她这回又逃跑，	Afraid that for a second time, she might flee,
心中总是难平静。	It couldn't calm down, always feeling uneasy.
这时见她又回来，	Now, it saw that she had returned;
这才放了心：	First monster tiger finally felt relieved:
“你再回去找找吧，	"Look for it once more and just go ahead.
你的话语我相信。”	I believe what you said."
说罢慢慢闭起眼，	With that, it closed its eyes slowly,
鼻洞里头打哼哼。	And began to snore loudly.
蒙诗彩奏见它睡着了，	Mengshi Caizou, seeing the tiger sleeping,
赶忙拔脚朝前奔。	Hurried to make her way as if on the wing.
跑到扎董丕冉的身边，	She ran to Zhadong Piran rapidly;
又喊又推催他醒：	Crying and pushing, she tried to awake him eagerly:
“阿哥你快睁开眼，	"Brother, open your eyes quickly!
蒙诗彩奏已来临。	Mengshi Caizou has arrived, finally;
快快起来杀魔虎，	Get up soon to kill the monster tigers completely;
救我回去好成亲。”	Save me, take me home and marry me."
喊一阵，	She cried for a while;
推一阵，	She pushed him for a while;
哭一阵，	She wept for a while;
催一阵，	She hurried him for a while.
喊得嗓子发了哑，	Mengshi Caizou cried and cried till her voice became hoarse;

扎董丕冉还没醒。

Zhadong Piran, sunk deep in sleep, was like a dead horse.

那边树下魔虎叫，
催她快快转回程。
一声更比一声高，
一声更比一声紧。

Over there, under the tree, First monster tiger called her loudly,
Urging her to make the return journey rapidly.
Its voice became louder and louder;
Its voice became tighter and tighter.

她忙拣起银项圈，
将它挂在脖子上；
脱下一件花内衣，
流着眼泪盖情人。
又去摘下一兜花，
匆匆忙忙转回程。

She picked up the silver neck band hurriedly,
And put it around her neck promptly.
She took off her floral underclothes,
And put it over her honey, drowning in tears.
She then picked a bunch of flowers swiftly,
And hurriedly made her return journey.

大魔虎见她走过来，
扯起嗓子大声问：
“你的项圈可找着？
叫我等得心烦闷。”
她把衣领掀开来，
一副项圈挂脖颈。
大魔虎这才没话说，
驮着她又往前奔。

Seeing her coming back, First monster tiger
Shouted at the top of its voice and asked her:
“Have you found the neck band yet?
You’ve made me impatient and upset.”
She lifted the collar of her coat, and
Around her neck hung a silver neck band.
Seeing that, First monster tiger said nothing,
And with her on its back, it was running.

二十六

扎董丕冉睡得甜，
不知睡了多少天。
天上打响大闷雷，
他才醒来揉揉眼。
他想翻身翻不动，
睁大眼睛仔细看：
茅草长起将他盖，
青藤长起将他缠。
盖得严实缠得紧，
叫他怎么能动弹？
他慢慢抽出长刀来，
上上下下割一遍。
丛丛茅草已割倒，
条条青藤已割断。
他转动身子爬起来，
一件花衣在眼前。
凭着花衣细判断，
蒙诗彩奏来过他身边。
只觉一阵眼睛花，

XXVI

Zhadong Piran had a sweet sleep,
Not knowing how many days had passed when he was
asleep.
Till there came a rumble of dull thunder in the skies,
He finally woke up and rubbed his eyes.
He wanted to turn over but failed unexpectedly.
Opening his eyes wide, he looked carefully:
Cogon grass grew high, covering him up like a duvet;
Vines grew long, twining around him all over the
pathway.
Fully covered up and tightly twined,
How could he move out of such a bind?
With great difficulty, he drew out the long machete,
And cut from head to toe all the covering over his body.
One thicket after another, the cogon grass was cut down
entirely;
One stem after another, the vines were cut off completely.
Shaking his body, he rose to his feet,
And saw the floral underclothes with many a pleat

接着便是泪涟涟。

From the floral underclothes, he could decide
That Mengshi Caizou had been at his side.
He felt the world became blurred suddenly,
And then tears streamed down continuously.

他怪自己瞌睡大，
睡着就像死一般。
一觉睡得这么久，
不知情人来身边。
如今误了大事情，
怎能杀虎报仇冤？
他捧着那件红内衣，
前后左右转一圈。
踏遍青山找情人，
哪里能见情人面？
他又取下金笛吹，
忙将情人来呼唤：

He blamed himself for sinking deep in sleep
And for sleeping like a log when he was sound asleep.
He had slept for such a long time,
Not knowing his sweetheart had come to him.
Now he had bungled the most important matter;
How could he get revenge and kill many a tiger?
He held the red floral underclothes in both hands,
And searched everywhere around the woodlands.
All over the green mountains he searched for his sweetheart;
Where could he find the lass in his heart?
He then took out the gold flute to play,
And tried hard to call his sweetheart without delay:

“布哩布哩布哩噜，
怪我大意又疏忽。
一觉睡去不会醒，
错过良机杀魔虎。
我的蒙诗彩奏呀，

“Boo-lee-boo-lee-boo-lee-lu,
I’m to blame for being careless, and heedless, too.
In a deep sleep, I couldn’t be awakened by thunder,
And missed a good opportunity to kill the tigers.
O Mengshi Caizou, my lass!

你究竟到了哪一处?	Where actually are you now, alas?
你若听到金笛声,	If you have heard the gold flute,
赶忙回答莫迟误!	Reply right away and let me know your route!
看见你的红内衣,	At the sight of your red floral underclothes,
我的心中就痛苦。	My heart aches as if pierced by arrows.
只见衣裳不见人,	I can see only the clothes, not my darling;
叫我怎能不啼哭?”	How can I keep myself from crying?”
吹罢金笛仔细听,	Having finished playing the gold flute, he listened carefully;
深山处处无回音。	In the deep mountains, no echoes came to him simply.
只有风吹草动呼呼响,	He heard only the wind whistling and the grass rustling;
只有鸟叫虫鸣唧唧声。	He heard only birds warbling and insects chirping.
扎董丕冉心焦急,	In Zhadong Piran's heart, anxiety surged up like a tide
睁大一双亮眼睛。	And he opened his bright eyes wide.
扒开草棵细细看,	Pushing aside the cogon grass, he searched carefully,
沿着小路慢慢行。	And walked along the footpath slowly.
魔虎脚迹一个连一个,	One after another, the tigers' footprints, clearly seen,
一直伸进大森林。	Stretched into the big forest, deep and green.
脚迹窝里浸满水,	The footprints were filled with water,
长出青苔一层层。	And in them, moss grew layer by layer.
扎董丕冉很失望,	Zhadong Piran felt utterly disappointed,
心头罩上一团云。	And in clouds was his heart shrouded.
他从脚迹来判断,	Judging by the tigers' footprints, a conclusion he drew
魔虎远去难追寻。	That they'd gone far and were hard to pursue.
到了这个时候呀,	Now, under the circumstances,
就要忍耐受艰辛。	He would endure all the hardships and difficulties.

难得追呀也要追，	He would chase though it was difficult;
难得寻呀也要寻！	He would search regardless of the result.

二十七　　XXVII

顺着魔虎脚迹走，	Following the monster tigers' footprints closely,
日夜兼程往前赶。	Day and night, he pressed forward firmly.
跨过浑水河，	He crossed Muddy Water River,
翻过太阳山；	And Sun Mountain he climbed over;
穿过刺竹坝，	He passed through Thorny Bamboo Basin, and beyond,
绕过烂泥潭；	He made a detour around Mud Pond;
钻过大黑箐，	He went through Big Dark Wooded Valley,
越过要命在。	And climbed over Yaomingzai ridge successfully.
越是往前赶，	Zhadong Piran chased farther and farther,
魔虎脚迹越新鲜。	And the tigers' footmarks became fresher and fresher.
不知走了多少路，	Not knowing how many roads he'd walked down,
登上一座大山岭。	Zhadong Piran climbed onto a big mountain.
看见路边有堆灰，	He saw a pile of wood ashes by the roadside,
扎董丕冉很高兴。	And Zhadong Piran felt very happy inside.
赶忙取出牛干巴，	Hurriedly, he took out the dried beef,
放进灰堆焐一阵。	And warmed it up in the ashes for a time brief.

这时肚子饿得慌，
烧块干巴吃一顿。
可是干巴烧不熟，
想吃也是吃不成。
伸手进去摸一摸，
灰堆已经冷冰冰。
魔虎还在离得远，
收起干巴赶路程。
不知走了多少天，
来到一条大河边。
河边又有一堆灰，
扎董丕冉心喜欢。
他又取出牛干巴，
放进灰堆焐半天。
肚子饿得难忍受，
烧块干巴吃一餐。
可是干巴烧不熟，
又冷又硬难得咽。
伸手进去试一试，
炭熄灰冷无火烟。
魔虎还在离得远，
收起干巴把路赶。

Then, he was feeling utterly hungry,
So he tried to bake a block for a meal promptly.
However, the dried beef remained underdone;
Though wanting to eat it eagerly, he actually had none.
With his hand, he felt the wood ashes,
And they had already become cold in the cool breezes.
The monster tigers were still far away,
So he picked up the dried beef and made his way.
Not knowing how many days he had walked to save his lover,
Zhadong Piran, one day, came to a big river.
There was again a pile of wood ashes by the riverside;
Zhadong Piran felt extremely happy inside.
He again took out the dried beef hurriedly,
And warmed it up in the ashes for a long time eagerly.
Feeling utterly hungry and finding it hard to beat hunger,
He wanted to bake a block for a dinner.
However, the dried beef remained underdone;
It was cold and hard, and he swallowed none.
With his hand, he touched the wood ashes;
Charcoal fire dead, ashes cold, no smoke rose.
The monster tigers were still far away,
So he picked up the dried beef and made his way.

扎董丕冉呀，	O, Zhadong Piran, the young lover,
为了搭救蒙诗彩奏，	In order to save Mengshi Caizou from danger,
不知翻过多少大山头，	Had climbed over many a mountain.
白天顶着烈日行，	In the daytime, he walked under the burning sun;
晚上戴着月亮走。	At night, bathed in moonlight, he hurried in spite of the dangers.
不怕山高水又长，	He was neither afraid of high mountains nor long rivers;
不惧林密和坡陡。	He was neither fearful of a dense forest nor a steep slope.
这天刚过晌午后，	One day, right after the noon, filled with hope,
他钻进一条大山沟。	He went into a big mountain valley,
又见树脚有堆灰，	And saw again a pile of wood ashes at the foot of a tree;
扎董丕冉心甜透。	Zhadong Piran felt happy thoroughly.
他又取出牛干巴，	He took out again the dried beef immediately,
赶忙焐进灰里头。	And hurriedly, he put a block into the wood ashes.
他在旁边等一阵，	He waited nearby for quite a while in the bushes;
掏出干巴咬一口。	Then, he picked it up and had a bite;
干巴焐得热乎乎，	The dried beef had been warmed up a bit;
也还勉强咽下喉。	Zhadong Piran swallowed it down, though with difficulty
伸手进去探一探，	He put his hand into the ashes and felt it quickly;
灰堆冒烟正烫手。	Smoke rising, the ashes were hot.
他想魔虎已不远，	The tigers couldn't be far away, he thought;
信心百倍朝前走。	Blooming with confidence, he set out like a shot.

跨过一座天生桥，	Crossing a natural bridge,

登上一个小山包。	Mounting a small mound and standing on the ridge,
扎董丕冉擦把汗，	Zhadong Piran wiped the sweat off his face,
放开眼睛四处瞧。	And looked around to search for the tigers' trace.
路边又有一堆灰，	There was again a pile of wood ashes by the roadside;
扎董丕冉呵呵笑：	Zhadong Piran chortled merrily, a smile so wide:
“这灰堆定然有来历，	"There must be a cause for the wood ashes;
定是情人设下的指路标！”	They must be guide signs left by my honey in those places!"
心头高兴手脚快，	Immensely pleased, he acted swiftly,
赶忙打开麻布包。	And opened the linen bag quickly.
拿出一块干巴来，	Taking out a block of dried beef,
把它放在灰上烤。	He baked it on the ashes in the mountain massif.
灰里火炭还发红，	In the ashes, charcoal was still burning red;
烤得青烟往外冒。	The dried beef let out light smoke, spreading overhead.
这块干巴肥又大，	Fat and big was this block of dried beef;
又宽又厚难得烤。	Wide and thick, it was hard to bake in a time brief.
可是因为火炭红，	However, as the charcoal was still burning,
咂袋辣烟就熟了。	The dried beef was well done after a short time waiting.
又香又软很好吃，	Scented and soft, the dried beef was so tasty;
越吃越觉有味道。	The more he ate, the more delicious it seemed to be.
大口嚼来大口咽，	He chewed every mouthful of dried beef and devoured it;
津津有味吃个饱。	With great relish, he had eaten his fill, leaving not a bit.
灰堆旁边布满虎脚迹，	Tigers' footprints were seen everywhere around the ashes;
魔虎定然离得很近了。	The monster tigers now must be very close.
吃完干巴赶路程，	Finishing the dried beef, he hurried to make his way;

杀虎的日子快到了!	The day to kill the tigers wouldn't be far away!

扎董丕冉呀,	O, Zhadong Piran, full of energy,
抽出那把大长刀,	Drew out the long machete,
迈开双脚大步跑。	And ran with a long loping stride.
步步踩着虎脚迹,	Following the tigers' footmarks closely, he tried,
沿着小路上山腰。	Along the path, to climb halfway up the mountain.
穿过芭蕉林,	He went through Chinese Banana plantation,
走过野猪坳,	Walked past the Wild Boar Col fearlessly,
来到魔虎山,	And reached the Monster Tiger Mountain finally;
山高岩陡峭。	Rocks abrupt and steep, the mountain was high.
千个石峰拔地起,	Thousands of stone peaks soared into the sky;
巍巍峨峨冲云霄;	High above the clouds, they were impressively towering.
万棵树木倚天立,	Millions of trees, like pillars of heaven, were erectly standing;
摇摇晃晃起林涛。	Trees swaying and swinging, winds were whistling.
听见一声吼,	Suddenly, Zhadong Piran heard a burst of roaring;
呼呼啦啦似虎啸;	Growling and rumbling, it sounded like tigers' voices.
看见一堆火,	Then, he saw a huge bonfire and wood ashes;
噼里啪啦在燃烧。	Crackling and spluttering, the bonfire was brightly burning.
扎董丕冉心里想,	In his heart, Zhadong Piran was thinking:
魔虎刚刚过山腰。	"The monster tigers have just left the bonfire place;
附近深山密林里,	The deep dense forest nearby is a good dwelling space;
定是它们的窝巢。	There, the monster tigers must live someplace."

二十八　XXVIII

扎董丕冉呀，
爬上一棵大古树，
取出金笛吹起来，
笛声阵阵绕山谷：

“布哩布哩布哩噜，
我恨透那十只虎。
抢我情人进深山，
不知藏在哪一处。
幸好灰堆来指路，
我爬山过水不迷途。
只因我疏忽又大意，
贪睡竟把良机误。
蒙诗彩奏呀，
我的笛声你可听清楚？
请你快快回答我，
好把魔虎尽铲除！”

O Zhadong Piran, miserable and merry,
Climbed up a huge ancient tree,
And took out the gold flute to play.
In the mountains, the sound of the flute spread away:

“Boo-lee-boo-lee-boo-lee-lu,
I hate the ten tigers to death and I really do.
They kidnapped my honey and took her to deep mountains;
I don’t know where I can find the villains.
Luckily, the wood ashes guided me the right way;
Climbing the mountains and crossing the rivers, I didn’t stray.
Because of my carelessness and negligence,
I overslept and missed the best chance.
O Mengshi Caizou, my sweetheart,
Have you heard my gold flute?
Answer me as soon as you can, please.
So I can get rid of all the monster tigers!”

笛声飞过高山岭，
满山满谷起回音。
林中传来木叶响，
声音悠扬听得清：

“布哩布哩布噜哩，
误失良机不怪你。
我拿灰堆给你指方向，
你来到虎山路不迷。
现在杀魔虎，
也还来得及。
沿着花路来找我，
我在山洞等着你。
十只魔虎太凶恶，
将我困在山洞里。
快来呀快来吧，
莫再失良机！”

扎董丕冉听到木叶声，
心中焦急如火焚。
虽说情人有下落，
可是被虎缠了身。
抬眼顺着山上望，
小路伸进半山中。

The sound of the flute flew over ridges;
All over the mountains and valleys, there arose echoes.
From the forest, the music of the tree leaf was heard;
So melodious and distinct was the sound:

“Boo-lee-boo-lee-boo-lu-lee,
You are not to blame for missing the opportunity.
I left the wood ashes to guide your way;
So, in the Monster Tiger Mountain, you won't stray.
Now, to kill the tigers for their crime,
There's still time.
Follow the flower path to look for me;
I'm right here in the cave waiting for thee.
The ten monster tigers are so ferocious
That they keep me in their living place.
O, hurry, my love, hurry!
Don't miss again the opportunity!”

Zhadong Piran heard the tree leaf sound;
As if burned by a fire, he felt greatly worried.
Though his sweetheart's whereabouts he had gotten to know,
Wherever she went, the tigers would follow.
He lifted up his eyes to the mountain, and

路上撒满小红花，
这是情人把路引。
他从树上跳下来，
踏着花路往前行。

Halfway, the path disappeared from the forestland.
The path was covered with little red flowers,
Which were to guide her lover to where she was.
He jumped down from the huge ancient tree,
And along the flower path, he marched upwards bravely.

第九章 血溅魔窟

Canto 9 Bloodshed in Monsters' Cave

二十九

花路左盘右转，
一直通到山巅。
你看扎董丕冉呀，
顺着花路猛追赶。
当他爬到山顶上，
花路突然就中断。
来到这里没有路，
眼前尽是荒草滩。
“蒙诗彩奏在何处？
蒙诗彩奏在哪边？”
扎董丕冉问苍天，
苍天泛起云片片；
扎董丕冉问大地，
大地默默不开言，
问遍四方无回音，
扎董丕冉心烦乱。
就在路断心急时，
一个奇迹突然现：

XXIX

Like a snake, the flower path zigzagged in the sun,
And it stretched upwards to the top of the mountain.
O, look at Zhadong Piran, the lad!
He chased along the flower path as if mad.
When he climbed onto the mountain top,
The flower path suddenly ended and he had to stop.
On the mountain top, the path disappeared, and
Before him, there was only wild grassland.
“In what place are you, Mengshi Caizou?
In what direction are you, Mengshi Caizou?”
Zhadong Piran asked the blue sky,
And in the blue sky, clouds came to his eye.
Zhadong Piran asked the great earth,
And the great earth kept silent, not opening its mouth.
He asked all sides and got no reply;
Zhadong Piran felt perplexed and began to sigh.
Just when he found no path and felt saddened,
A miracle suddenly happened:

一只小蜜蜂，	A little bee
飞到面前打转转；	Flew to him and revolved merrily.
一只小蝴蝶，	A little butterfly
飞到身边绕圈圈。	Flew to his side and circled, catching his eye.
蜜蜂蝴蝶说了话，	The bee and the butterfly spoke to him happily;
句句话语赛蜜甜：	Each word was much sweeter than honey:
“扎董丕冉别忧愁，	“Zhadong Piran, please don't worry!
有心杀虎莫怕难。	When you're determined to kill the tigers, fear no difficulty.
请你扒开苦刺窠，	Please, push the sophora davidii shrubs aside;
跟着我们上高山。	Follow us to the high mountain and we'll be your guide.
等到爬上悬岩头，	Climb onto the high cliff;
定会见你情人面。”	You're sure to meet your sweetheart and future wife.”
蜜蜂蝴蝶前面飞，	The bee and the butterfly flew ahead,
扎董丕冉在后撵。	And Zhadong Piran followed behind and sped.
钻过刺窠一丛丛，	He went through thorny bushes,
攀过藤萝一串串。	And climbed up rattan tangles.
看两手，	He looked at his two hands momentarily,
十个指头都划烂；	And the ten fingers were scratched completely;
摸脸上，	He touched his face lightly,
满脸戳得血斑斑。	And his whole face was jabbed bloody.
浑身上下是伤痕，	From head to toe, there were cuts and bruises;
忍痛赶路咬牙关。	Despite the pain, gritting his teeth, he hurried through

为了杀魔虎，	bushes.
不怕受苦难；	In order to kill the monster tigers,
为了救情人，	He was not afraid of difficulties and dangers;
敢去闯龙潭。	In order to rescue his lady fair,
可是道路不平坦，	He dared to break into the dragon's lair.
忽明忽灭多变幻。	However, the path was tortuous;
来到一座悬岩上，	Now in view, now hidden, it was capricious.
蜜蜂蝴蝶已不见。	Then, he came to a high cliff, and
	The bee and the butterfly had disappeared from the highland.

扎董丕冉喊蜜蜂，	Zhadong Piran called the bee,
不知蜜蜂在何处；	But where it was he didn't see.
扎董丕冉唤蝴蝶，	Zhadong Piran called the butterfly,
不知蝴蝶在哪边。	But it couldn't be seen in the sky.
千声喊来万声唤，	After a thousand calls and a million entreaties,
蜜蜂蝴蝶不露面。	The bee and the butterfly didn't show up, only the breeze.

扎董丕冉站在岩顶上，	Standing on the cliff, Zhadong Piran frowned,
举目四处看。	And raised his eyes to look around.
向左看，	He looked to the left instantly;
绵绵大山一架接一架，	Mountains stretched away continuously;
灰灰蒙蒙连着天；	Grey and misty, they melted into the sky gradually.
向右看，	He looked to the left presently;

茫茫林海一片连一片，	A vast sea of trees rolled away into the distance;
一眼难得望到边；	The boundless view was beyond his eyes at a glance.
向后看，	Turning his head, he looked backwards;
万丈峭崖一层叠一层，	The ten thousand foot cliff descended downwards;
叫人头晕目又眩；	So dizzy and dazzled was his head.
向前看，	Zhadong Piran looked straight ahead;
照妖河里一浪推一浪，	The waves pushed forward in Monster-revealing River;
波光粼粼亮闪闪。	The light on them competed to glisten and glister.
顺着岩石往下看，	Looking downward, he searched the lass he came to save;
一个大洞悬在半岩间。	Halfway up the cliff, there was a big cave.

蒙诗彩奏坐在岩洞口，	At the mouth of the cave, Mengshi Caizou was sitting;
低头绣花手不闲。	Bending her head down, she was busy embroidering.
扎董丕冉见了她，	Zhadong Piran, seeing his sweetheart,
又惊又喜又心酸。	Felt surprised, happy and sad in his heart.
路行千里历艰险，	Having covered thousands of miles and faced many a difficulty,
终于见着情人面。	He finally saw his love and honey.
一股激情涌心头，	A surge of passion welled up suddenly,
不觉两眼泪涟涟。	And tears streamed down unwittingly.
滴滴泪水往下落，	Teardrops fell down from his face,
一直落到岩洞前。	And they fluttered straight to the cave place.
正好落在花帕上，	They fell down onto her floral handkerchief by chance,
打湿花帕一片片。	And wet the handkerchief at the cave's entrance.

蒙诗彩奏很奇怪，	Mengshi Caizou felt quite surprised;
赶忙丢下针和线。	Hurriedly, she put aside her needle and thread.
提起花帕抖一抖，	Picking up the floral handkerchief, she promptly shook it,
满心狐疑独自言：	And said to herself in puzzlement:
“今天是个大晴天，	“Today, it is bright and sunny;
为何半空落雨点？	Why do raindrops fall suddenly?
淋湿我的摆喳喳[1]，	My newly embroidered floral cloth they wet,
叫我心中很不安！”	And made me greatly worried and upset!”
说完又坐下绣花帕，	With that word, she sat down again to embroider;
绣的花帕更鲜艳。	The floral handkerchief became more colorful than ever.

扎董丕冉有心计，	Zhadong Piran was a young man of intelligence;
摘兜野花撒下去。	Picking a bagful of wild flowers, he sprinkled them at once.
一把撒在岩洞口，	A handful of them were sprinkled at the cave's mouth;
一把撒在她的衣兜里。	A handful of them were sprinkled onto her coat's front cloth.
一把一把往下撒，	One handful after another, he sprinkled them down hopefully;
花朵纷纷落满地。	In profusion, the flowers fell onto the ground before his honey.

她看着花朵落下来，	Seeing the flowers falling down unceasingly,
心中不禁又猜疑：	In her heart, she couldn't help thinking suspiciously:

① 摆喳喳：苗语，指新刺绣的花布。

"今天没有刮大风，	"Today, there is no strong wind around;
为何花朵飞满地？	How can flowers flutter onto the ground?
究竟花朵从哪来？	Where have all the flowers come from, actually?
这事看来很稀奇！"	The situation was evidently rather strange, really!"
说完抬头往上看，	Thinking this, she looked up instinctively,
心中顿觉惊又喜。	And in her heart, she felt surprised and happy.
在那高高岩顶上，	On the top of the high cliff, up in the air,
扎董丕冉在站立，	Zhadong Piran was standing there,
向她点头微笑，	Nodding at her and smiling,
向她挥手示意。	Waving at her and signaling.
蒙诗彩奏呀，	O, Mengshi Caizou, full of happiness,
丢下手中活，	Put aside her needle work at once;
对着岩顶轻轻唱起歌：	Facing the cliff top, she began to sing:
"抬头见亲人，	"Looking up, I see my darling;
心里真快乐。	I feel so happy to see my sweetheart.
多少贴心话，	There're too many sweet words in my heart,
不知从何说。	And I don't know where to start.
魔虎出外去找食，	The monster tigers are out looking for food,
要到天黑才回窝。	And won't come back till the sun sets in the wood.
请你快点下山岩，	Please, come down from the cliff top right away;
商量办法斩妖魔！"	To kill the monsters, we have to think out a way!"
扎董丕冉听见这歌声，	Zhadong Piran heard her singing;

心绪如潮猛翻腾。
恨不得身上长翅膀，
立刻飞下悬岩去。
可是眼前没有路，
怪石林立好吓人。
刀削斧劈大岩子，
真是寸步也难行！
他对着岩下轻轻唱，
唱出忧伤和苦闷：

His state of mind, like the tide, was rising and rolling.
He craved for a pair of wings eagerly
To fly down from the cliff immediately.
However, there was no path available;
Strange stones stood like a forest and looked terrible.
They seemed to be peeled by a knife or chopped by a hatchet;
To move a single step was thus so difficult!
Looking downwards, he sang gently;
He was singing about his anguish broken-heartedly:

“找到阿妹我高兴，
追上魔虎我痛恨。
只是脚下无路走，
难与阿妹在一起！”

“Having found you, sister, I feel buoyant;
Having caught up with the tigers, I am indignant.
However, there's no path leading to you,
And it's difficult for me to come to your rescue!”

蒙诗彩奏忙回答，
句句话语寄深情：
“岩上有根葛麻藤，
一直挂到石洞门。
顺着藤子梭下来，
就可杀死魔虎雪仇恨。”

Mengshi Caizou hurried to answer her darling,
And each word conveyed her deep feeling:
“On the rock, there's a kudzu vine, and by chance,
It hangs down straight to the cave's entrance.
Hold fast to the kudzu vine, just slide down;
You can kill the tigers to avenge all they've done.”

扎董丕冉仔细瞧，

Zhadong Piran looked at the vine carefully,

果然有根葛麻藤。	And there was a kudzu vine, really.
悬空挂在陡岩上，	Down from the steep cliff, it hung in the air,
随着微风在摆动。	And in the breeze, it was swinging here and there.
这藤足有九丈长，	The vine was more than thirty meters long;
叶子长得翠生生；	Its leaves were fresh, green and oblong.
这藤只有拇指粗，	The vine was only thumb-thick, hung from the cliff stone,
无杈无蔓孤零零。	And with no branches and tendrils, it was all alone.
要想顺藤往下梭，	To slide down the vine he did eagerly want,
又怕藤断会伤身；	But feared that it might break and he'd be hurt.
若不顺藤往下梭，	If he didn't slide down for fear of being wounded,
前后左右无路径。	There was no path on any side.
望着葛藤想一阵，	Looking at the kudzu vine, he thought for a time brief;
下岩只有梭葛藤。	There was but the vine to go down the cliff.
为了杀虎报仇恨，	In order to kill the tigers and take their revenge finally;
哪管伤身不伤身！	How could he care about his own body!

他抓住藤子一蹬脚，	Grasping the vine, he pressed down with his feet hard,
身子下滑像腾云。	And his body slid down as if he was riding on a cloud.
离地还有三丈高，	When he was still ten meters from the ground,
葛藤咔嚓响一声。	The kudzu vine let out a cracking sound.
蒙诗彩奏抬头望，	Mengshi Caizou looked up at the lad,
真是吃了一大惊。	And she was really frightened.
扎董丕冉往下落，	Zhadong Piran was falling down toward her
好像鹞子在翻身。	As if a northern sparrow hawk was turning over.

要是高高摔下地，
定会折骨又断筋。
蒙诗彩奏心一急，
连忙扯开长褶裙。
长裙张开像把伞，
她把两边抓得紧。
稳稳撑在地面上，
情急生智救情人。
说时迟呀那时快，
一团黑影晃眼睛。
扎董丕冉落下来，
正好落在长裙里。
长裙将他接住了，
没伤骨头没伤筋。

If he fell down from such a high place,
He would break bones and injure tissue in that case.
Mengshi Caizou was extremely anxious in her heart;
So, hurriedly, she spread her long pleated skirt apart.
The long skirt spread like an umbrella in daylight,
And she held the two edges of the skirt tight.
As if rooted, she stood on the ground firmly;
At a critical moment, she hit on a good idea to save her honey.
In the twinkling of an eye,
A shadowy figure flashed down from the sky.
Zhadong Piran fell down swiftly,
And he fell into her long skirt luckily.
The long skirt caught him just right;
No bones breaking, no tissues injuring, he fell from that height.

扎董丕冉走下地，
蒙诗彩奏放了心。
情人相逢惊又喜，
哽哽咽咽诉苦情。
她对着他细讲述，
被虎侮辱仇恨深。
他向着她细诉说，

Zhadong Piran rose to his feet promptly;
Mengshi Caizou felt relieved finally.
Reunited, the two lovers felt surprised and happy;
Groaning in tears, they spoke of painful longing sorrowfully.
In great detail, she told the lad
The tigers' insult and her deep hatred;

追赶魔虎受苦辛。
哭一阵啊讲一阵，
越讲越觉更伤情。
大树听了垂下头，
小河听了放悲声。
这时魔虎没回来，
洞里显得很寂静。
他俩走进石洞里，
仔仔细细来谈心。
蒙诗彩奏瘪瘪嘴，
痛哭流涕不成声：

In great detail, he told the lass,
To catch up with the tigers, he had suffered great hardships.
They cried a while and a while they recounted;
The more they recounted, the more they felt afflicted.
Hearing what they had suffered, big trees hung their heads;
Hearing what they had endured, brooks let out painful
sounds.
Then, as the monster tigers hadn't come back yet;
The cave seemed to be so quiet.
Into the cave did they two walk;
In great detail, they then had a heart-to-heart talk.
Mengshi Caizou pursed her lips;
Tears streaming down, she choked with sobs for the hardships:

“魔虎施计我落井，
从此落进虎掌中。
起先我也曾逃走，
魔虎奸诈没逃成。
后来想逃没有逃，
山高水远路难认。
又怕你来不见我，
误了杀虎大事情。
忍辱含悲过日子，
等你杀虎雪大恨。

“The monster tigers set a trap and pushed me down the well;
Ever since, I was kidnapped and lived in hell.
At first, I tried once to run away;
However, the tigers were crafty and I failed halfway.
Later, I wanted to escape but didn't try,
'Cause I would get lost with the distance far and mountains
high.
When you're here, without meeting me, I also feared,
The important matter of killing the tigers might be spoiled.
Suffering and enduring humiliations, I frittered away my

顺从魔虎是假意，
等你报仇是真心。
这事你别错怪我，
我说的话是真情。”

time,
Waiting for you to kill the tigers and get revenge on them.
To be obedient to the tigers I was pretending;
To wait for you to get revenge is my true feeling.
Don't blame me for this due to misunderstanding;
What I said is my real thinking."

扎董丕冉听完话，
心中更觉痛难忍：
“你的遭遇最悲惨，
木叶声里已知情。
是你叫我磨大刀，
磨快大刀除祸根。
我将大刀磨快了，
立刻追虎赶路程。
这事怎能怪罪你，
只怪魔虎太凶狠。
如今我俩得相会，
正好商量大事情。”

Zhadong Piran, having heard his sweetheart,
Felt even more heart-broken in his heart.
"Your sufferings are most tragic,
I've known it from the leaf music.
It's you who asked me to grind my long machete,
And sharpen it to uproot the evil completely.
I sharpened the long machete
And hurried to chase the tigers immediately.
How can I blame you for this, my honey?
The tigers should be blamed for their ferocity.
Now, we are finally together,
And it's time to discuss the important matter."

贴心的话说不完，
离别的苦难诉尽。
你一言呀我一语，
不觉太阳落山顶。

Intimate words flowed out ceaselessly,
And sufferings after departure couldn't be told fully.
They talked back and forth without stop.
Unconsciously, the sun set from the mountain top.

扎董丕冉摘朵花，
放在鼻尖闻一闻。
然后插在她鬓旁，
脉脉向她表深情。

Zhadong Piran picked a flower,
Smelled it and took in its fragrant odor.
He then placed it in her hair around the temple tenderly,
And expressed to her his deep feelings lovingly.

蒙诗彩奏抬头看，
照妖河里现魔影。
十只魔虎排成队，
吼吼叫叫转回程。
魔虎虽然离得远，
照妖河里看得真。
这条河叫照妖河，
能使魔虎现身形。
就靠这条照妖河，
蒙诗彩奏观动静。
魔虎出门瞧得准，
魔虎回来看得清。
魔虎背上驮牲口，
一定又去糟害人！
扎董丕冉也来看，
越看心中越愤恨。
唰啦抽出那金笛，
凑到嘴边吹几声：
“布哩布哩布哩噜，

Mengshi Caizou raised her head;
In the Monster-revealing River, reflections of monsters spread.
The ten monster tigers walked single file;
Roaring and huffing, they were on their way back for a while.
Though they were still far away,
In Monster-revealing River, they were seen clearly in the day.
The river was named Monster-revealing River,
And it could reveal the figure of a monster tiger.
Depending on the Monster-revealing River,
Mengshi Caizou could know the activities of any monster.
When the monster tigers went out, she knew precisely;
When the monster tigers came back, she knew clearly.
When the monster tigers carried livestock on their backs,
They must have made havoc for people in packs!
Zhadong Piran also looked in the river;
The more he looked, the angrier he felt more than ever.
Swish! He took out the gold flute,

看见魔虎我愤怒。	Putting it close to his mouth, he played it:
它们扰乱村和寨，	“Boo-lee-boo-lee-boo-lee-lu,
抬走牛马又吃猪。	Seeing the monster tigers, into a rage I flew.
糟害牲口又伤人，	They disturbed villages and stockade villages,
蒙诗彩奏受侮辱。	Robbing them of cattle and horses, and eating pigs.
为救阿妹我今入虎穴，	With livestock they played havoc and people they wounded;
历尽人间千般苦。	Mengshi Caizou has been humiliated.
今天我要拼一场，	To rescue my honey, I entered the tigers’ lair
杀死十只大魔虎！	After countless hardships that were hard to bear.
我要剥它们的皮，	I’m going to fight hard today
我要吃它们的肉！”	To kill the ten monster tigers anyway!
	I’ll flay them bit by bit;
	I’ll eat their meat!”

扎董丕冉一吹完，	Zhadong Piran, the minute he finished playing the flute,
抽出大刀舞起来。	Took out and wielded the long machete.
大刀舞得呼呼响，	The long machete whirred violently
好像蛟龙闹大海。	As if a flood dragon was rolling in the sea.
只见刀光不见人，	Man invisible, only the glint of the machete was seen;
蒙诗彩奏看着发了呆。	Looking at that, Mengshi Caizou stood frozen.
两只眼睛眨不下，	Eyes wide open, she was breathless;
半天她才醒过来。	Half a day passing, she regained consciousness.
赶紧拿起木叶吹，	Hurriedly, she picked up a leaf to play.
对着阿哥表心怀：	Facing her honey, she expressed her feelings without delay:

“布哩布哩布噜哩，	“Boo-lee-boo-lee-boo-lu-lee,
魔虎作乱人焦急。	The monster tigers are creating havoc and anxiety.
叫声阿哥听我讲，	O brother, please listen to me;
阿妹有话告诉你。	Your sister has a few words for thee.
十只魔虎威力大，	The ten monster tigers are all mighty;
四方猎人也难敌。	Hunters around are no match for them, rarely!
多少猎人来打虎，	Too many hunters came to hunt the tigers,
个个死在虎口里。	But each of them was killed by the monsters.
单人独手难对付，	It's hard to fight the tigers singly;
杀虎还需施巧计。	To kill them, we need to act cleverly.”
“四方猎人没本事，	“The hunters around are useless;
个个死在虎口里。	Those who came were killed, thus.
我的本事最高强，	I'm the most skillful huntsman, honey;
不杀魔虎不见你！”	Without killing the tigers, I won't come to thee!”
“你的本事我知晓，	“You have great abilities, I know;
千人万人不如你。	No one can be your match high and low.
可是魔虎法力大，	However, the monster tigers have almighty power,
不可粗心和大意。	So you shouldn't be careless of the danger.
我也有点小本事	I have some basic skills as well,
也想设法逃出去，	And had planned to run away from the cell,
怎奈魔虎太凶恶，	But the monster tigers are too ferocious,

只得忍下这口气。” So I had to swallow the insult and bitterness.”

吹完就往前面看， Having finished playing, at the river she had a good look;
魔虎已经过小溪。 The monster tigers had crossed the small brook.
眼看魔虎要回窝， Very soon, the tigers would be back to the cave;
蒙诗彩奏拿主意。 Mengshi Caizou had decided on the next move.
事事赶紧准备好， Everything should be well prepared;
慢了一步来不及。 One step late, things would get messy.
夺下阿哥手中刀， From his hand she wrested the machete,
将它插进刀鞘里。 And inserted it into the sheath promptly.
把嘴凑在他耳边， Putting her mouth close to his ear,
悄悄讲了好几句。 She whispered a few words to her dear.
扎董丕冉点点头， Zhadong Piran nodded his head,
暗夸阿妹有心计。 And inwardly, admired her for what she had said.

三十 XXX

蒙诗彩奏的话呀， O, what Mengshi Caizou had designed
扎董丕冉记心上。 Zhadong Piran bore deeply in mind.
瞧他一点不作声， Look! He kept silence and said nothing;
蹲在岩洞石壁旁。 Close to the rock face he was squatting.
蒙诗彩奏拿长裙， Mengshi Caizou held her long pleated skirt,

紧紧盖在他身上。	And covered him tight with the makeshift covert.
她又搬块大石头，	Then, a big stone she managed to move,
支在石洞正中央。	And set it in the center of the stone cave.
坐在石上绣花帕，	Sitting on the stone, the handkerchief she was embroidering;
一针一线绣得忙。	One stitch after another, she was busy working.
洞里显得很平静，	The cave seemed to be peaceful;
她也显得很安详。	She also seemed composed and graceful.
只听一阵嗷嗷叫，	Suddenly, bursts of howls came to their ears;
叫声震山冈。	The howls shook mountains and caused fears.
大魔虎一纵进了洞，	First monster tiger jumped into the lair;
驮来一匹青骒马。	And on its back it carried a green mare.
它拿鼻子四处闻了闻，	Here, there, and everywhere, the tiger smelled;
张开大口说了话：	It opened its big mouth wide and yelled:
“怎么有股甜酒[①]味？	"How come the cave smells of sweet wine[①]?
你吃了甜酒才绣花？”	Did you start embroidering after eating food so fine?"
蒙诗彩奏不惊慌，	Mengshi Caizou was not horrified;
若无其事把话答：	As if nothing had happened, she replied:
“你在外面吃甜酒，	"You ate sweet wine outside,
吃得满嘴冒油花。	And oil smeared your mouth inside.

① 甜酒：苗族传说中，说老虎吃人是吃甜酒，吃狗是吃白酒。

① In Hmong legends, "eating sweet wine" means the eating of human beings by tigers; "eating liquor" means the eating of dogs by tigers.

你把鼻孔张大点，	Just open your nostrils wide,
闻闻你的大嘴巴。	And smell the breath from your mouth inside.
我在家里不出门，	I stayed at home without going outside;
哪有甜酒来吃呀？”	How could I have sweet wine to eat and get satisfied?"
大魔虎放下青骒马，	First monster tiger put down the green mare;
喘着粗气又说话：	Panting heavily, it did flare:
“就算你没有吃甜酒，	"Granted you haven't eaten sweet wine,
总是有人来过啦。	Somebody must have been here, judging by the sign.
满洞都是生人味，	The cave is filled with smell of a living person;
我说的话不会假。”	What I said can't be false, I'm certain."
“劝你莫要瞎猜想，	"You'd better not make a wild guess;
劝你莫要说胡话。	You'd better not talk nonsense.
这个洞里只有我，	In the cave, there is only one me;
你说哪个来过嘛？”	How can you say somebody has been here already?"
“要是没有人来过，	"If nobody has been here,
你又为何戴朵花？”	Why do you wear a flower in your hair?"
蒙诗彩奏吃一惊，	Mengshi Caizou felt appalled;
想起头上有朵花。	There was a flower in her hair, she recalled.
但她立刻就镇静，	But she calmed down immediately,
冷言冷语回答它：	And replied to the tiger coldly:

"我的脾气有点怪,	"I have a strange temper,
生来就是爱戴花。	And I'm a born flower lover.
风一吹来花就落,	Flowers fall down when wind blows;
你看满地都是花。	You can see the ground covered with flowers.
其中一朵最鲜艳,	One of them has the brightest color;
我就拣来戴上啦!"	Picking it up, I wore it in my hair to look better!"
大魔虎听了没话说,	Hearing that, First monster tiger said nothing;
倒在一旁就睡下。	Lying on the ground, it was dozing.
忽听一阵树叶响,	Suddenly, leaves were heard whistling;
条条树枝在发抖。	Branches and twigs were trembling.
二魔虎唰地跳进洞,	Second monster tiger flashed into the cave like lightning,
驮来一头大牯牛。	A big bullock on its back, dying.
它向四周看了看,	The tiger looked around,
粗声粗气问情由:	And asked in a deep, gruff sound:
"甜酒味道这么香,	"The smell of sweet wine is so fragrant;
莫非大嫂吃甜酒?"	Could it be that my sister-in-law ate one when we were out?"
蒙诗彩奏不惊慌,	Mengshi Caizou wasn't terrified;
大大方方又开口:	Naturally and unaffectedly, she replied:
"二弟你别说昏话,	"Second brother, don't drool; do talk fine!
你到外面吃甜酒,	You went outside to eat sweet wine,

吃在肚子里，	And ate it down into your belly.
香在鼻洞头。	In your nostrils, the flavor lingered faintly.
我在家中坐，	I stayed at home,
不到外面走，	And didn't go outside to roam.
白酒难吃上，	I have no chances to eat liquor.
哪能吃甜酒？	How can I have the chance to eat sweet wine, brother?"
二魔虎放下大牯牛，	Second monster tiger put down the bullock in the cave;
瞅着地面不肯走：	Staring at the ground, he had no intention to leave:
"满地都是人脚印，	"On the ground, there're numerous footprints of a man.
这事一定有来头。	For this, there must be a certain reason.
就算你没吃甜酒，	Even if you didn't eat sweet wine as you said,
也引生人来洞头。"	A stranger to the cave you must have led."
蒙诗彩奏冷冷笑，	Mengshi Caizou smiled grimly;
说话滴水也不漏：	Her logic irrefutable, she spoke deliberately:
"我整天都在洞里走，	"The whole day, in the cave I walked around;
我的脚迹处处留。	My footprints covered every inch of the ground.
疑心疑肝生暗鬼，	Suspicions create fantastic fears;
二弟真是没理由！"	Second brother, there're no reasons for your sneers!"
二魔虎一听没话说，	Hearing that, Second monster tiger became speechless;
只得讨个没趣头。	Feeling put out, the tiger was listless.
倒在地上睡着了，	Lying on the ground, it fell asleep;

鼾声呼呼响不休。	It snored loudly without a stop.
又听刮起一阵风，	Again, a sudden gust of wind was heard blowing;
山间四处如响雷。	Everywhere in the mountains, it seemed to be thundering.
三魔虎倏地蹿进洞，	Third monster tiger dashed into the cave suddenly.
背上驮着一个人。	On its back, there was a man, clearly.
这人已经被咬死，	The man had been bitten to death already.
浑身上下血淋淋。	He was bloody all over his body.
三魔虎一进洞里来，	The moment Third monster tiger got inside,
就用鼻子四处闻，	It smelled with its nose from side to side.
阴阳怪气打哼哼：	Cryptically and sarcastically, it taunted her:
"大嫂在家有福气，	"Sister-in-law, when at home, how lucky you were!
吃了甜酒香喷喷。	You ate sweet wine and it smelled appetizing.
咋不留点给我呀，	Why don't you leave some for me to ease my longing,
让我也来开开荤？"	And let me resume meat-eating?"
蒙诗彩奏盯住它，	Mengshi Caizou stared at the tiger,
直起嗓子骂出声：	And strained her throat to curse the monster:
"三弟背上驮着人，	"Third brother, you are carrying a man on your back;
满洞甜酒味正浓。	In the whole cave, the smell of sweet wine is so thick.
你吃了甜酒不认账，	You've eaten sweet wine and are now pretending otherwise;
还要血口来喷人！	You're smiting me with your malicious tongue, to my surprise!
你不说话我不气，	You don't talk and I won't feel angry;
你一说话我生恨。	

世间数你无道理，	Once you talk, you drive me crazy.
吃人害人没良心！”	In the world, you're the one who is the most ruthless;
	You eat people, harm people and are heartless!"

扎董丕冉在裙下，	Under the skirt Zhadong Piran was hiding,
听说魔虎又掩人。	And heard the tiger had carried out a killing.
牙齿咬得格格响，	He ground his teeth;
一腔怒火胆边生。	His heart burned up with wrath.
气得伸手抽长刀，	Furious, he tried to take out the machete,
要跟魔虎来厮拼。	Ready to fight the monster tiger bravely.

蒙诗彩奏好机灵，	Mengshi Caizou was so smart;
看见裙下有响动，	When she saw the motion under the skirt,
轻轻咳了一声嗽，	She coughed slightly,
又去按按长褶裙。	And then pressed the long pleated skirt lightly.
暗示阿哥别动手，	She was hinting that her honey shouldn't take action
免得坏了大事情。	So as not to spoil the great mission.
扎董丕冉忍住性，	Zhadong Piran controlled his temper,
强压怒火不吱声。	Maintaining a stony silence, he suppressed his anger.

三魔虎生性最狡猾，	Third monster tiger was born cunning;
看见长裙起疑心：	It saw the long skirt, suspicions arising:
“大嫂洗的长褶裙，	"Sister-in-law, when you washed your long pleated skirt,
常常晾在洞外小树丛；	Very often, on bushes outside, under sun you dried it.

今天却是有点怪，
为何晾在石洞中？
大嫂不要再瞒我，
长裙底下定有人！”
说罢就要掀长裙，
蒙诗彩奏好心惊，
火焰舔着眼眉毛，
急中生智解危境。
她忙丢下针和线，
哎哟哎哟叫几声。
三魔虎赶紧缩回爪，
“大嫂为何叫出声？”

But today, it's a bit strange, I believe.
Why do you dry it inside the cave?
Sister-in-law, don't cheat me any more.
Under the long skirt, there must be somebody, I'm sure!"
With that word, it was ready to lift the long skirt
completely.
Mengshi Caizou felt terrified, utterly and inwardly.
Dangers and flames were coming to eyebrows;
In desperation, she hit upon an idea to deal with the dangers.
She put aside the needle and thread hurriedly;
As if in great pain, she groaned suddenly.
Third monster tiger drew back its paw hastily,
"Sister-in-law, why do you groan abruptly?"

“绣花针儿戳手掌，
赶快找药来止疼！”
说着伸出左手来，
手心果然有血印。
那血滴滴往下落，
落在地上红殷殷。

"I jabbed my palm with the embroidery needle;
Get herbal medicine to ease my pain as soon as possible!"
While speaking, she stretched out her left hand in pain;
Really, in the center of the palm, there was a bloodstain.
Drop by drop, blood kept dripping;
Dark red, it dripped onto the ground, glistening.

三魔虎用力耸耸肩，
放下背上那个人。
张着嘴巴喘口气，

Third monster tiger shrugged its shoulders hard;
Putting down the man on its back, it was caught off guard.
Its mouth wide open, the tiger breathed deeply;

几步蹿出石洞门。	Within steps, it jumped out of the cave rapidly.
钻进草窠去找药，	It went into grass to look for herbal medicine;
找了半晌无音信。	For a long time, there was no news of the demon.
蒙诗彩奏手脚快，	Mengshi Caizou was agile and nimble;
赶紧掀开长褶裙。	She lifted the long pleated skirt as soon as possible.
示意阿哥进后洞，	She hinted that her honey go to the back cave immediately,
大石背后暂藏身。	And hide behind a big rock temporarily.
扎董丕冉跳起来，	Zhadong Piran sprang to his feet promptly,
闪身跳进后洞中。	And flashed into the back cave swiftly.
蒙诗彩奏真伶俐，	Mengshi Caizou was quick-witted, really;
顺手抓个大竹笼，	She picked up a big bamboo cage randomly,
将笼放在裙底下，	And put it under the skirt quickly,
就跟原来一个样。	Which looked like it had originally.
三魔虎找药进洞来，	Having found herbal medicine, Third monster tiger returned;
看着长裙没变动。	Looking at the long skirt, the tiger saw it hadn't been moved.
裙下究竟有何人？	Who on earth was under the skirt?
疑团还在填心胸。	The doubts were still in his heart.
它一纵身蹿过去，	The tiger jumped forward in a stride,
用爪扒开长褶裙。	And used its paw to push the skirt aside.
裙下是个竹笼子，	Under the skirt a bamboo cage was right there;
这时它才放了心。	Not till then, did it finally calm down, free from care.

蒙诗彩奏包好手，	Mengshi Caizou bandaged her hand,
假意对它谢大恩：	Pretending to thank it for being kind:
“三弟心肠最慈善，	“Third brother, in the world, you're the kindest one.
愿你多福添寿命！”	May you live long and have all the luck under the sun!”
她的话是风凉话，	She was making wisecracks,
一字一句说得重，	And emphasized each word of her remarks.
哪是多福添寿命？	How could she wish the monster live well?
分明叫它命归阴！	She was praying that the tiger would go to hell!
三魔虎狡猾又愚蠢，	Third monster tiger was both crafty and silly.
听了反而很开心。	Hearing her words, it felt very happy.
四脚一伸倒下地，	Four limbs stretching, the tiger lay on the ground.
躺在洞里入梦境。	Sleeping in the cave, it quickly entered dreamland.
蒙诗彩奏咳声嗽，	Mengshi Caizou coughed lightly;
扎董丕冉出后洞。	Zhadong Pian emerged from the back cave quickly.
重又躲在长裙下，	He was hiding again under the skirt patiently.
等待时机报仇恨。	To have their revenge, he was waiting for the opportunity.
还有其他七只虎，	There were still seven other tigers.
也跟着陆续回洞里。	One after another, back to the cave came the monsters.
个个背上驮牲口，	On their backs, each carried domestic animals,
尽是羊狗猪鸭鸡。	Which were goats, dogs, pigs, ducks and chickens.
都说洞里来生人，	They all said there was smell of a strange living person.
个个心中犯猜疑。	Each, in its heart, had a sneaky suspicion.

蒙诗彩奏巧回答，	Mengshi Caizou replied cleverly,
将虎一一哄出去。	And coaxed each of them out of the cave successfully.
七只魔虎没话说，	The seven monster tigers had nothing to say.
个个伸腰躺下地。	On the ground each of them stretched and lay.

三十一 XXXI

月亮升到东山顶，	The moon rose up high above the top of East Mountain;
茫茫林海多寂静。	The endless sea of forests stood still as if frozen.
十只魔虎睡着了，	The ten monster tigers all fell asleep,
洞里处处起鼾声。	And were heard snoring all over the cave in their sleep.
蒙诗彩奏坐在石头上，	On a stone Mengshi Caizou was sitting;
细听细看察动静；	Listening carefully, she was watching what was happening.
扎董丕冉躲裙下，	Zhadong Piran hid under the skirt anxiously,
紧紧握住长刀柄。	His hand firm on the handle of the long machete.
黄昏过后夜深沉，	Dusk shaded into deep night;
蛐蛐蛤蟆歇了声。	Crickets and toads were silent, hidden from sight.
虎影斑斑满石洞，	The tigers' shadows filled the cave completely;
石洞里头阴森森。	Inside the cave, it was dismal and gloomy.
扎董丕冉举起刀，	Zhadong Piran raised his machete,
猛然掀开长褶裙。	And lifted the long pleated skirt abruptly.

呼地一声站起来，	He flapped all of a sudden,
瞪着一双大眼睛。	And stared, with his eyes wide open.
蒙诗彩奏心一动，	Mengshi Caizou's heart was slightly stirred,
想到这事要冷静。	Thinking that they needed to be cool-headed.
要是莽撞来行事，	If they were too rash in taking action,
魔虎定然杀不成。	It was certain that they wouldn't kill any demon.
杀虎不成不打紧，	It didn't matter much if they failed to kill the tigers,
惹来灾祸无穷尽。	However, their failure would lead to endless disasters.
赶忙将他强按下，	She hurried to press him down firmly,
叫他耐心等时辰。	Asking him to wait patiently for the opportunity.
扎董丕冉没奈何，	Zhadong Piran had no choice
只得躲进长褶裙。	But to hide under the skirt and drop his voice.
大约夜已到三更，	It was about the dead of night;
石洞门口月亮明。	Up above the entrance of the cave, the moon shone bright.
蒙诗彩奏站起来，	Mengshi Caizou rose to her feet,
试探老虎醒没醒。	And tried out whether the tigers were awake or not.
她拿一个大竹筒，	She picked up a big bamboo tube from the ground,
高高举起过头顶，	And raised it high above her head;
然后使劲砸下来，	She then threw it hard down on the ground;
嘭嘭咚咚发响声。	The bamboo tube banged, making a loud sound.
大魔虎睡得像死猪，	First monster tiger slept like a dead pig,
没有听见竹筒声，	And didn't hear the sound, though it was big.
二魔虎听了哼一哼，	Hearing the sound, Second monster tiger snorted.

翻个身就无动静；	Turning over, it no more acted.
三魔虎听了嚷起来，	Hearing the sound, Third monster tiger shouted.
粗声粗气最难听：	Deep and gruff, so terrible its voice sounded:
“这是哪样东西响，	“What is that noise all about?
吵得叫我睡不成！	I was roused; did a war break out?
半夜三更瞎胡闹，	In the dead of night, sister-in-law, you're making noises.
莫非大嫂生歹心？”	Can it be that you have malicious purposes?
蒙诗彩奏冷冷笑，	Mengshi Caizou laughed grimly,
伶牙俐齿说原因：	And talked about the reason readily:
“我拿竹筒去打水，	“I took the bamboo tube to fetch water;
竹筒落地发响声。	It fell on the ground and made a noise, however.
三弟不必生疑惑，	Third brother, don't get suspicious;
怪我做事不小心！”	I'm to blame for being careless!”
三魔虎听罢咂咂嘴，	Hearing her, Third monster tiger smacked its lips fretfully;
闭起眼睛入梦境。	Closing its eyes, it drifted into a sound sleep quickly.
过了一阵夜更静，	After a while, quieter became the night;
蒙诗彩奏又起身。	Mengshi Caizou rose again to her feet.
拿个土罐摔在地，	She took a clay pot and dropped it on the ground;
叭的一声碎片飞。	The pot broke into pieces with a cracking sound.
十只魔虎都没醒，	The ten monster tigers were not awakened;
呼呼大睡没吱声。	Voiceless, they were roaming in dreamland.
看来魔虎已睡熟，	The monster tigers were seemingly sleeping soundly,

可是她仍不放心。	But anxiety still lingered in her heart faintly.
这个时候最要紧，	That was the most critical moment,
更须沉着又冷静。	And she must be cooler in making a judgment.
要是稍稍有疏忽，	If she was a bit careless,
横生岔事理不清。	Unexpected difficulties arising, their efforts would be fruitless.
凝神沉思好一会，	Collecting herself, for quite a while, she was thoughtful;
她又拿起绣花针。	Again, she picked up her embroidery needle.
先去戳戳大魔虎，	With the needle, she first jabbed First monster tiger
看它会醒不会醒。	To see whether it was awake or still a dreamer.
大魔虎接连挨两针，	First monster tiger was jabbed twice,
也不听它哼一哼。	But it didn't groan even once.
看来它是睡熟了，	It appeared that the tiger was sleeping soundly;
蒙诗彩奏放了心。	Mengshi Caizou felt greatly relieved and easy.
再去戳戳二魔虎，	She then jabbed Second monster tiger,
二魔虎只是翻个身。	And it just turned over.
看来它也不会醒，	It seemed that the tiger wouldn't be awakened;
蒙诗彩奏又放心。	Mengshi Caizou again felt hugely relieved.
又去戳戳三魔虎，	She jabbed Third monster tiger for a third try;
三魔虎嗷地吼一声，	The tiger roared with a loud cry.
骨碌翻身跳起来，	It rolled and jumped to its feet instantly;
瞪着一双蓝眼睛：	With a pair of blue eyes, it stared at her angrily:
“大嫂为何来捣乱，	"Sister-in-law, why did you create such a disturbance?
可是出了大事情？	Has anything critical happened? What a nuisance!

我才刚刚睡着了，
你又将我来吵醒！”
说着张开血盆口，
样子凶恶又狰狞。

I just fell asleep,
And you woke me up from my sleep!”
With that word, it opened its bloody mouth;
So ferocious was its look, so hideous its teeth.

蒙诗彩奏忙回答，
假装跟它献殷勤：
“三弟也真太小气，
何必发怒吓唬人。
我跟你们来这里，
一无戚来二无亲。
你们整天出门去，
我在洞里孤零零。
要想说话没说处，
要想唱歌没人听。
整天低头绣花朵，
没有趣头心烦闷。
现在看你没睡着，
跟你说话散散心。
谁知你竟不通情，
发威逞凶现兽性！”

Mengshi Caizou hurried to answer,
Pretending to do her utmost to please the tiger:
“How narrow-minded you are, Third brother!
Why should you be frightening and lose your temper?
I followed you all to this cave;
Here, I have neither a family member nor a relative.
Every day, you all go outside,
And I am alone inside.
I want to talk, but I have no company;
I want to sing, but there’s no one to listen to me.
Every day, I bend my head over embroidery;
Life is so boring that I feel unhappy.
Now, seeing that you were still awake;
To relieve my boredom, with you I wanted to talk.
Who would have thought you were poor in
understanding!
You lost your temper and became so intimidating!”

蒙诗彩奏一番话，

What Mengshi Caizou had said indignantly

三魔虎听了很高兴：
“叫声大嫂莫见怪，
我的脾气生来愣。
得罪大嫂好多回，
还望大嫂莫认真。
大嫂好意我认得，
怪我身子太疲困。
整天串村又串寨，
累得腰酸脚又疼。
无力跟你款白话，
有话明天再慢叙。”
说完倒下又睡着，
戳它几下不会醒。

Made Third monster tiger glad and happy:
“O, sister-in-law, don't feel offended and angry!
I was born reckless and foolhardy.
Several times, I've offended sister-in-law recklessly.
I do hope sister-in-law doesn't take it seriously.
Sister-in-law's good intentions I know.
I'm to blame for being fatigued and slow.
Every day, from villages to stockade villages, I wandered.
My waist is sore, my feet hurt, and I'm extremely tired.
I'm too exhausted to chat with you;
Let's wait till tomorrow and chat anew.”
With that, the tiger lay on the ground and fell asleep.
Jabbed several times, it didn't wake from its sleep.

三十二　XXXII

十只魔虎都戳过，
戳弯一颗绣花针。
有的被戳醒来了，
有的再戳也不醒。
不会醒的别管它，
让它各自去做梦。

The ten tigers had all been jabbed one after another;
The embroidery needle bent when she did the last monster.
Some were roused when jabbed;
Some, though jabbed several times, weren't disturbed.
Leave those who were sleeping soundly in peace,

对于醒的怎么办？
就用巧语将它哄。
等到过了许多时，
她又挨个戳几针。
魔虎睡得更昏沉，
从大到小戳不醒。

And just let each tiger dream in its sleeping place.
What could she do to those who were roused already?
She used sweet words to coax them to take it easy.
For quite a long time, she waited;
Several times, each of the tigers she jabbed.
The monster tigers slept even more soundly;
In birth order, the tigers, when jabbed, still slept deeply.

杀虎时机来到了，
赶忙掀开长褶裙。
扎董丕冉跳起来，
站在洞里抖抖身。
长刀舞得像闪电，
双脚跳得旋风生。

The opportunity to kill the tigers came, eventually;
She lifted the long pleated skirt hurriedly.
Zhadong Piran jumped to his feet promptly;
Standing in the cave, he stretched his body.
The long machete was wielded like lightning;
He quickened his footsteps, a whirlwind arising.

像进地里砍南瓜，
像上山去割麻秆，
左砍右剁呼呼响，
杀得魔虎遍地滚。
地上淌满魔虎血，
石壁溅满虎脑髓。
钢刀捅出虎肠子，
手指抠烂虎眼睛。
刀光闪闪石岩抖，

He seemed to be cutting watermelons in the field;
He seemed to be cutting hemp stalks on the mountainside;
Left or right, he was chopping tigers, making many a sound;
The tigers were chopped up, rolling on the ground.
The cave streamed with tigers' blood all over the place;
The tigers' brains splashed everywhere on the rock face.
The tigers stabbed, their intestines came out of bellies;
Zhadong Piran's fingers dug into the tigers' eyes.
The machete flashed bright, rocks trembling;

血肉横飞天地惊。
一刀捅死十魔虎，
九魔虎又丧了命。
刚刚剁了八魔虎，
七魔虎又归了阴。
从小到大杀过来，
一刀一个不落空。
当他杀死四魔虎，
不慎绊着长褶裙。
连人带刀跌在地，
正好把三魔虎碰醒。
它嗖地一下跳起来，
气势汹汹要拼命。
扎董丕冉不惊慌，
故意躺着不动身。
等到魔虎扑过来，
他才使出好本领。
刀把支在地面上，
刀尖直指虎喉咙。
任这魔虎再狡猾，
也难逃脱这一招。
三魔虎朝他一扑下，
脖颈截个大窟窿。
它仰天伸伸脚，

Flesh and blood flew everywhere, the sky and the earth
shaking.
In one strike, he stabbed Tenth monster tiger to death.
Ninth monster tiger very soon stopped its breath.
He just chopped up Eighth monster tiger,
And Seventh monster tiger followed closely his eighth
brother.
In reverse birth order, he managed to kill tigers one after
another;
One strike and one tiger, he didn't miss any monster.
After he killed Fourth monster tiger,
He accidently stumbled over the long pleated skirt, however.
He fell on the ground, together with the long machete;
He bumped against Third monster tiger and woke it,
unfortunately.
With a swish, it jumped to its feet instantly,
And was ready to fight him to death aggressively.
Zhadong Piran was not in the least scared inwardly;
He lay on purpose on the ground motionlessly.
He was waiting for the tiger to spring on him patiently,
So he could put to good use his ability.
With the handle standing on the ground, he set up the
machete,
The tip of which pointed directly at the tiger's throat.

滚在一旁丧了命。

No matter how cunning Third monster tiger was,
It was impossible for it to survive the coming fatal blow.
The moment the tiger sprang on him brutally,
Into its neck, a big hole was poked immediately.
The monster fell flat on its back, its four limbs stretching;
It rolled aside dead, ending its evil life of killing.

大魔虎和二魔虎，
这时一齐被惊醒。
它们弹腿翻起身，
一只左边扑，
一只右面攻，
齐向扎董丕冉扑过来，
又吼又咬又撕蹬。
扎董丕冉沉住气，
力敌二虎显威风。
大刀舞得团团转，
前三后四使劲挡，
左五右六奋力拼，
两只魔虎难招架，
被杀得遍地乱打滚。
扎董丕冉一弹腿，
身子腾在半空中，
奋力一刀劈下来，

First monster tiger and Second monster tiger,
With a start, were then awakened together.
They sprang to their feet,
One attacking from the left,
One attacking from the right,
They sprang together on Zhadong Piran with all their might;
They roared, bit, kicked and tried to tear him.
Zhadong Piran kept calm and grim;
He fought the two tigers, showing his power and bravery.
The long machete was wielded with great facility;
He was fighting bitterly backward and forward;
Left and right, he was fighting hard;
The two tigers couldn't hold their own in the fight;
They rolled about on the ground in the dark night.
Zhadong Piran sprang from the ground;
Up in midair, he was found;
With great might, he struck downward;

二魔虎刀光闪处丧了命。	The machete flashing past, Second monster tiger got killed.
大魔虎见十个弟兄死九个，	First monster tiger saw each younger brother's death;
气得头发晕。	It felt faint and short of breath.
眼睛鼓得像尿泡，	Its eyes bulged out like bladders,
大吼一声如雷鸣。	And it roared like a clap of thunder.
大口张得像铜盆，	Its wide open mouth was as big as a basin;
牙齿尖得像铁钉。	Its teeth, like iron nails, were pointed and keen.
拼着老命撞过来，	Risking its life, First monster tiger bumped into him;
扎董丕冉一时站不稳，	Zhadong Piran, for a short while, couldn't stand firm.
又脚一滑扑下地，	He slipped and fell due to losing his balance;
躺在地上打个滚。	Ha lay on the ground and rolled about once.
他不立刻爬起来，	Zhadong Piran didn't rise to his feet instantly;
伏在地上养精神。	Instead, on his hands and knees, he was boosting energy.
大魔虎以为得手了，	First monster tiger thought it had killed him successfully;
张开嘴巴想咬他的后脖颈。	Opening its mouth, it aimed at the back of his neck ruthlessly.
这时扎董丕冉一躬腰，	Then, Zhadong Piran doubled up quickly,
来个岩鹰巧翻身。	And turned over like an eagle skillfully.
呼的一声跃起来，	Swish! He jumped to his feet,
一步蹿出石洞门。	And in a stride, out of the cave he dashed.
大魔虎一嘴咬下去，	First monster tiger bit down, and in the same breath,
咬着那个大石墩。	A big stone block came into its mouth.
嘴巴哪有石头硬，	How could its mouth be as hard as a stone?
磕得满嘴血淋淋。	The tiger's mouth was bloody and it made a groan.

这下蒙羞更恼怒，
四脚一纵出洞追。

Then, it felt humiliated and even became angry;
It jumped out of the cave to chase the lad wildly.

扎董丕冉不慌乱，
舞起长刀又来拼，
忽左忽右进又退，
忽高忽低捷如飞。
瞧他越斗越勇猛，
各路刀法学得精。
头上三刀光闪闪，
脚下三刀冒火星；
身前三刀龙现爪，
身后三刀凤翻身；
东西三刀鬼也哭，
南北三刀神也哼。
大魔虎哪里能招架？
跌跌撞撞乱扑腾。
死到临头心不甘，
狠命一扑山压顶。
扎董丕冉被压着，
只觉眼花头发晕。
因他连杀九只虎，
力气也就减几分。
他想挺胸鼓鼓劲，

Zhadong Piran didn't lose his head;
Waving the machete, he fought again bravely instead;
He fought left or right, or forward, or backward;
He fought high or low, as swift as a bird.
Look! The more he fought, the braver he was!
In different skills of machete fighting he had no flaws.
High above the tiger's head, the machete flashed brightly;
Before the tiger's paws, the machete flickered quickly;
He fought forward bravely;
He fought backward swiftly;
He fought east or west, which made a ghost frightened;
He fought south or north, which made a god stunned.
How could First monster tiger hold its own!
It stumbled and let out a great groan.
The tiger was unwilling to drop out when facing death;
Like a mountain, it threw itself on him, using all its
strength.
Zhadong Piran was pinned under the tiger;
He felt dizzy and his vision began to blur.
Since he had killed nine tigers consecutively,
His strength was ebbing away, naturally.

可是双脚站不稳。
身子一晃要跌下，
刀法也就不严谨。
魔虎看到这空隙，
拼命一扑力千钧。
蒙诗彩奏心一震，
急得冷汗湿手心。
危急之中强镇定，
连忙抓起长褶裙。
她把长裙甩过去，
紧紧罩住魔虎身。
魔虎被罩动不得，
晕头转向乱打滚。
扎董丕冉举起刀，
照准虎心狠使劲，
只听魔虎一声嚎，
褶裙下面血水喷……

He wanted to straighten and pep himself up eagerly,
But his two feet couldn't stand up steadily.
His body shook and he was about to fall down,
So his skills weren't as precise as they had been.
The monster tiger noticed the loophole very soon,
And risking its life, it sprang on him like a mountain.
Mengshi Caizou was greatly shocked by the fighting;
Her palms were cold with sweat, and anxious she was
feeling.
At the critical moment, she managed to keep her head;
Hurriedly, the long pleated skirt she grabbed.
She threw the long skirt towards the tiger,
And it tightly covered the monster.
The monster tiger was covered and couldn't move;
Confused and disoriented, it rolled about outside the cave.
Zhadong Piran raised the machete,
Targeting the tiger's heart, he struck forcibly;
The monster tiger was just heard howling,
And under the pleated skirt, blood began spurting…

第十章　苦守坟台

Canto 10　Keeping the Grave Faithfully

三十三　　XXXIII

十只魔虎被斩除，	He had killed the ten monster tigers;
灾难过去得幸福；	Happiness came after disasters.
黑夜之后是黎明，	After the dark night came the dawn,
朝霞朵朵映山林。	And rosy clouds floated over the mountain.
扎董丕冉拿起刀，	Zhadong Piran picked up the machete,
十张虎皮全剥尽。	And flayed the ten tigers completely.
再拿虎肉做干巴，	He dried the tigers' meat,
虎心虎肝烧熟吃一顿。	And baked their hearts and livers to eat.
挑起干巴和虎皮，	With a shoulder pole, he carried the dried meat and hides gladly;
双双爬上悬岩顶。	They two climbed up to the top of the cliff happily.

蒙诗彩奏前边走，	Mengshi Caizou walked ahead,
扎董丕冉后面跟。	Followed by Zhadong Piran the lad.
有说有笑回家转，	On their way back home, they were talking and smiling;
顺着山路结伴行。	In her company, along the mountain path, he was walking.
走了一程又一程，	League after league, for home they were heading;
忽然天上起乌云。	Suddenly, in the sky, dark clouds were gathering.
蒙诗彩奏越走越缓慢，	Mengshi Caizou walked slower and slower;

嘴皮发紫脸发青。	Her lips were turning purple, her face green in color.
泪水不住往下淌，	Here tears were streaming down ceaselessly,
点点滴滴湿衣襟。	Drop by drop, wetting the front of her clothes completely.
扎董丕冉问她为哪样，	Zhadong Piran asked her why she was weeping,
她只是叹气不出声。	But she just sighed and said nothing.
来到扎董丕冉睡觉处，	Arriving at where Zhadong Piran had had a sound sleep,
她的双脚再也迈不起。	She couldn't take a single step.
啪地昏倒在地上，	With a bang, she fainted and fell on the ground;
口吐白沫四肢冷。	She foamed at the mouth, her four limbs cold.
扎董丕冉心焦急，	Zhadong Piran felt so anxious
将她抱进草丛中。	That he lifted her and put her on the grass.
又是嚎哭又是喊，	He shouted and cried,
再哭再喊也不应。	But she didn't respond whatever he tried.
一会她才睁开眼，	After a while, opening her eyes, she looked ahead;
喘着粗气哼出声：	With great difficulty, she wheezed and said:

“我的阿哥哟，	“O, brother, my honey,
听我说原因。	Please, listen to me!
魔虎欺侮我，	The monster tigers bullied and humiliated me;
心中积仇恨。	In my heart, hatred grew like a bamboo tree.
身陷魔洞里，	I was stuck in the monsters' lair;
灾难无穷尽。	Disasters were endless like blowing air.
天天想念你，	I missed you every single day;
夜夜噩梦生。	Night after night, in my dreams did nightmare stay.

思念太过分，	I longed for you extremely,
早已成了病。	So illness has come to me already.
杀死十只虎，	You've killed the ten tigers thoroughly;
阿妹最高兴。	Your sister is only too happy.
本该得幸福，	We deserve the best life can offer,
共度好光景。	And should be entitled to a good time together thereafter.
回到家里去，	When we get back home to start a new life,
正好结婚姻。	It's the best time for us to become husband and wife.
可是如今我病重，	But now, I'm seriously ill,
难得跟你度光阴。	And it's hard for me to be with you as I will.
过了一难又一难，	Coming through disasters one after another,
患难夫妻又离分。	A couple out of adversity is parting from each other.
这时我心中最难过，	Now, I feel the most terrible inwardly;
眼睛发花头发晕。	My eyes blur and my head is dizzy.
恐怕难得过午时，	I'm afraid I can't live through the noon;
阿哥呀，	O, I'll die very soon, brother.
望你好自奔前程！”	I wish you a prosperous future!"

扎董丕冉放声哭：	Zhadong Piran burst out crying:
“我的阿妹呀，	"O, my sister, my darling!
怎能说跟我又离分！	How can you say you're parting from me!
为了你，	In order to rescue you, my honey,
我踏遍山和岭；	I climbed mountains and ridges tirelessly;
为了你，	In order to rescue you, my honey,

我历尽饥寒和苦辛；	I've gone through hunger and cold;
为了你，	In order to rescue you, my beloved,
我只身闯虎穴；	I broke into the tigers' cave;
为了你，	In order to rescue you, my love,
我九死又逢生。	By a hair's breadth, I escaped and managed to survive.
我俩的情意呀，	O, the affection between us, my honey,
比路长来比海深。	Is longer than the road and deeper than the sea.
如今要是没有你，	Now, if, without you, I have to live,
阿哥我也活不成！”	I, your brother, am not going to survive!"
蒙诗彩奏缓缓说，	Mengshi Caizou said slowly;
声音细得难听真：	Her voice thin, it was hard to hear clearly:
“我的阿哥哟，	"O, my brother!
如今你还正年轻。	You're still young and have a future.
一定不能为我死，	You mustn't die for me, my honey;
不要随便就轻生。	You shouldn't take your own life irresponsibly.
多看几回菜花黄，	Appreciate more the yellow vegetable flowers;
多瞧几次荞叶青；	Enjoy more the green buckwheat leaves;
多望几回蜂蝶舞，	Gaze more at the dancing bees and butterflies;
多听几次百鸟鸣；	Listen more to the chirping of all birds;
多吹几回芦笙调，	Play more the lusheng tones;
多爬几次花杆顶。	Climb more the flower pole in festivals.
人间快乐都享尽，	Enjoy worldly happiness as much as you can,
也才不枉这一生！	So, you won't waste your life and live in vain!

红花绿柳我都爱，
命到尽头爱不成。
眼看午时已快到，
分离就在这时辰！”

Red flowers and green willows I really adore,
But at the end of life, I can't love them anymore.
Very soon, the noon is coming,
And it's the time for our parting!"

“阿哥呀，
我本不愿离开你，
要想跟你度终生。
你若是棵常青树，
我愿做条小青藤，
青藤缠着常青树，
枝繁叶茂绿茵茵；
你若是个圆月亮，
我愿做颗小星星，
星星跟着月亮转，
天长地久不离分；
你若是汪池塘水，
我愿做片小浮萍，
浮萍漂在水面上，
追风逐浪紧相偎；
你若是只画眉鸟，
我愿做个小百灵，
百灵画眉共啼鸣，
一唱一和最动听。

"O, brother, my honey!
I didn't mean to leave you, really;
I just want to spend my whole life with you, truly.
If you're an evergreen tree,
A little green rattan I'm willing to be;
Around the evergreen tree the green rattan twines;
So flourishing are the twigs and green leaves.
If you're a full moon, my honey,
A little star I'm willing to be;
The star keeps the moon company;
Enduring as the universe, I'll never part from thee.
If you're a pond of water, my honey,
A piece of duckweed I'm willing to be.
Duckweed floats on the surface of the water;
Following the wind and chasing the waves, it sticks to the other.
If you're a song thrush, my honey,
A little lark I'm willing to be.
The lark and the song thrush sing together;

可是这些难如愿，
你阳我阴两离分。
我俩若要再团聚，
要看你心真不真。
你若真心爱着我，
将我埋在花丛中。
然后砍根小金竹，
插在我的墓门顶。
你就睡在墓旁边，
天天为我守坟茔。
若是金竹发新芽，
你就刨开我的坟。
将我轻轻扶起来，
连续将我喊几声。
你的喊声惊醒我，
我就重又得生命。

不管三年和五载，
还有指望成婚姻。
要是金竹枯死了，
我就永远不还魂。
你就干净忘记我，
另找姑娘去成亲。”

They are singing sweetly and echoing each other.
But these wishes are hard to be fulfilled;
You're in the mortal world, I the nether world.
If we two are to be reunited,
It all depends on whether your love is true, indeed.
If you love me from the heart,
Please, bury me in flowering shrubs, my sweetheart.
Then, cut down a small golden bamboo tree
And stick it into the earth at the head of my grave, honey.
Close to my grave, you then sleep and stay;
Right there, you keep my grave every day.
If the golden bamboo tree sprouts,
Just excavate my grave, and have no doubts.
Please, prop me up gently,
And call me several times continuously.
Your call will wake me up with a start,
And my life I'm going to restart.

Whether it is three years or five years,
To get married, we still have a chance.
If the golden bamboo tree withers and dies one day,
I can never revive from death, doomed to pass away.
Just forget me completely,
And look for a lass to get married happily."

蒙诗彩奏说完话，
躺在地上不出声。
扎董丕冉大声喊，
再喊她也不答应。
只听天空炸雷响，
大雨哗哗下不停。
蒙诗彩奏真的死掉了，
静静躺着任雨淋。
扎董丕冉拿起魔虎皮，
将她裹了一层又一层。
十张虎皮裹完了，
又拿藤子细细捆。
然后就在花丛中，
冒着大雨刨个坑。
将她埋进土坑里，
又用石头砌座坟。

Mengshi Caizou finished the last word,
Lay down on the ground and made no sound.
Zhadong Piran shouted loudly;
She was silent, though he tried desperately.
A clap of thunder was heard suddenly,
And it rained in torrents ceaselessly.
Mengshi Caizou was truly dead;
Quietly, she lay on the ground, rain pouring down overhead.
Zhadong Piran picked up the hide of each tiger,
And wrapped her up layer upon layer.
The ten hides were used up completely,
And with thin rattan, he bundled her up carefully.
Then, in the flowering shrubs, he,
Braving the rain, dug a pit quickly.
He buried in the pit his love,
And by laying stones, he built a grave.

砍根金竹插在坟头上，
守在坟边不离身。
这时他才放声哭，
山谷四面传悲音。
眼泪打湿坟边草，
山上岩石也伤心！

Cutting down a golden bamboo tree, he stuck it into the grave's head,
And by the side of the grave he stayed.
After that, he burst out crying,
And in mountains and valleys, voices of sadness were spreading.

His tears wetted the grass on the side of the grave,
And even the rocks in the mountains began to grieve!

三十四　XXXIV

守坟五个月，	For five months, he kept the grave hopefully;
干巴已吃完。	All the dried meat had been eaten up completely.
桃树开了花，	Peach flowers had come out,
金竹没发芽。	While the golden bamboo tree failed to sprout.
守坟一年多，	More than a year, he kept the grave hopefully;
野果已摘完。	All the wild fruits had been picked completely.
桃树又开花，	Peach flowers had again come out,
金竹没发芽。	While the golden bamboo tree failed to sprout.
守坟三年整，	For three whole years, he kept the grave hopefully;
草根已挖完。	All the grass roots had been dug up completely.
扎董丕冉看金竹，	Zhadong Piran looked at the golden bamboo tree;
金竹仍旧没发芽。	It still didn't sprout, though he had been waiting eagerly!
守了三年整，	He had kept the grave for three whole years,
尝尽苦与辣。	And tasted the bitterness of sorrow and tears.

太阳晒金竹，
他拿树叶遮；
大风刮金竹，
他拿衣裳拦；
大雪压金竹，
他忙抖雪花；
可是金竹不发芽……
扎董丕冉呀，
心痛如刀扎。

The sun shone upon the golden bamboo tree;
He shaded it with tree leaves carefully.
Strong winds blew against the golden bamboo tree;
He shielded it with his coat immediately.
Heavy snow pressured the golden bamboo tree;
He shook the snowflakes off it hurriedly.
However, the golden bamboo tree didn't sprout.
O, Zhadong Piran, the young loving heart,
Felt painful as if a knife had pierced his chest.

想起蒙诗彩奏赠手镯，
手捧金镯泪水如雨下，
本说二人结下百年好，
只落得你阴我阳不成家。
如今镯在人不在，
铁打的心肝也碎啦！
扎董丕冉好灰心，
他没心思吹金笛，
也无闲情采野花。

Recalling Mengshi Caizou presenting him with the gold bracelet,
Tears falling down like rain, in both hands he held it.
They had vowed to get married,
Yet, one was now in the nether world, the other in the mortal world.
Now, the bracelet was in his hands, while his love wasn't around;
Even an iron man would have felt broken-hearted!
Zhadong Piran felt so discouraged in his heart
That he wasn't in the mood to play the gold flute;
He had neither leisure nor wish to pick wild flowers around.

扎董丕冉正伤心，

When he was still feeling broken-hearted,

一对蜜蜂来传话：
“小米种在坡地上，
不到节令不结籽；
桃树栽在大路边，
不到时候不开花。
要叫金竹发新芽，
你要耐心侍护它。
金笛你要吹，
野花你要采。
诚心能使天睁眼，
再守十年也不怕！”

A pair of bees came to send him word:
“Millet seeds are sown in the slope field;
If out of season, they produce not a single seed.
Peach trees are planted on the side of the road;
If the right time doesn't come, they can't flower, indeed.
If you want the golden bamboo tree to sprout,
You have to patiently take care of it.
Play the gold flute as before;
Pick wild flowers you adore.
Sincerity can make the sky open its eyes;
Fear not even if you have to keep the grave for ten more years!”

扎董丕冉听完话，
摘把野花供坟前。
他又拿起金笛吹，
笛声悠悠四处传：

Having heard that, Zhadong Piran took heart,
Picking wild flowers and presenting them before his
sweetheart.
He then picked up the gold flute to play;
The sound of the flute spread slowly away:

“布哩布哩布哩噜，
吹起金笛把情诉。
守坟守了三年整，
金竹越来越干枯。
要到几时才发芽？
要到哪天叶才绿？

“Boo-lee-boo-lee-boo-lee-lu,
I play the gold flute to pour out my heart to you.
I've kept your grave for three whole years;
The golden bamboo tree gradually withers.
When will it sprout again?
Which day will its leaves become green?

蜜蜂使者来安慰，	The bee messengers came to comfort me when I was hopeless,
我才丢开悲和苦。	So I cast away my sadness and bitterness.
我要死守在坟前，	I'll keep your grave till I pass away;
誓跟阿妹共堆土。	I vow to be buried with you under the same clay.
活着不能在一起，	When alive, we can't be together;
死了也要埋一处。	After I die, I'll be buried with you forever.
哪怕地旋天倒转，	Even if the earth quakes and the sky spins the wrong way,
也要守到春色染金竹！”	Till spring turns the golden bamboo tree green, I'll stay!"

扎董丕冉刚吹完，	The moment Zhadong Piran finished playing,
云间传来木叶声：	From the clouds, leaf music was heard coming:
“布哩布哩布噜哩，	"Boo-lee-boo-lee-boo-lu-lee,
叫声阿哥莫焦急。	O, brother, don't behave so anxiously!
劝你仔细听我说，	Please, listen to me carefully;
我是山间凤凰女。	I'm a phoenix in the mountain and the valley.
见你勤劳又善良，	I saw that you were diligent and kind,
心中暗暗爱慕你。	So I adored you secretly in my mind.
知你上山来砍柴，	Knowing you were coming to the mountain to cut firewood,
走出树林来会你。	To meet you, I walked out of the wood.
不幸遇到大魔虎，	I ran into First monster tiger, unfortunately;
穷追猛扑将我欺。	It pursued me and pressed hard to bully me.
危急之中你救我，	In crisis, you saved me from being bullied by the brute,
我把金笛送给你。	And I presented you with the gold flute.
你在坡上种小米，	When you were sowing millet seeds in the slope field,

我又赶来帮助你。	I came to offer you my aid.
那年寨上踩花山，	That year, on the day of the Flower Hill Festival,
你我相会是良机。	It was an opportunity for you and me to meet as a couple.
可是我施仙家法，	However, I played magic arts,
变成三个小幺女。	And changed into three fair hearts.
将你拦在大路上，	On the main road, I stopped you,
三次纠缠考验你。	And pestered you thrice to test whether you were true.
考你三次有结果，	Having tested you thrice, I reached the conclusion:
知你果真有诚意。	You were really sincere and yielded not to temptation.
你只爱着蒙诗彩奏呀，	O, you loved only Mengshi Caizou!
眼不乱来心不迷！	Your heart didn't get confused; your eyes didn't glow.
我又变成蒙诗彩奏哟，	I then changed back into Mengshi Caizou;
你见了我多亲昵。	Seeing me, you became intimate and your eyes did glow.
我就跟你把情定，	I then pledged love to you from the heart,
拿只手镯送给你。	And presented you with a bracelet.
你把项圈送给我，	You gave me a neckband as a gift,
我的心中也欢喜。	And I also felt happy in my heart.
我俩合心又合意，	We two found each other congenial,
只愿到老不分离。	Hoping we would never be separated and remain loyal.
谁知你去学芦笙，	You left to learn to play the Lusheng unexpectedly;
魔虎又来将我逼。	The monster tigers came again to bully me.
魔虎实在太凶恶，	The monster tigers were really so ferocious
将我抢到山洞里。	That they took me to the cave by force.
你来追杀十只虎，	You chased the ten tigers and killed them successfully;

我俩终于得团聚。
哪知我忧心过了头，
又遭残害成了疾。
死在半路野坝中，
埋在路边花丛里。
你守坟守了三年整，
你的诚心动天地。
你对我的情意真，
我不忍心离开你。
这个地方你睡过，
地上还在有热气。
我俩的热气润金竹，
金竹发芽我喘息。
如今我已活转来，
听见你在吹金笛。
请你抬头看金竹，
青枝绿叶多稀奇。
请你快快刨开坟，
我俩回家成夫妻！”

We two reunited as we wished eventually.
Who would have thought I worried too much before you came;
I became ill because of all the harm and shame.
I died in a wild basin halfway,
And was buried in the roadside flowering shrubs without delay.
You have kept my grave for three whole years;
Your sincerity has moved the sky and the earth to tears.
Your love for me is true;
I don't have the heart to leave you.
You have slept in this place;
Right here, of the warmth of your breath there's still a trace.
Our warmth has infiltrated the golden bamboo tree;
The moment it sprouted, I regained my breath instantly.
Now, I have resurrected already,
And heard you playing the gold flute sadly.
Please, raise your head to look at the golden bamboo tree;
With its green twigs and leaves, it looks so strange, really.
Please, dig me up out of the grave quickly,
And we'll go back home to get married happily!"

三十五　　XXXV

扎董丕再听见木叶声，	The leaf music Zhadong Piran heard,
像从梦中醒过来。	And as if from a dream he awakened.
越听心里越高兴，	The more he listened, the happier he was;
眼前突然添异彩：	Before his eyes suddenly there came radiant colors.
山更青呀水更绿，	The mountains were greener, the water bluer;
青山绿水更可爱。	Green mountains and blue water were lovelier.
抬起头来看金竹，	Raising his head to look at the golden bamboo tree,
一看不禁喜心怀。	In his heart, he couldn't help feeling happy.
金竹果然发新芽，	The golden bamboo tree sprouted, really;
绿叶丛丛像伞盖。	Green leaves clumped together like a canopy.
他一下扑到坟头上，	All at once, he threw himself onto the grave mound;
将层层黄土全刨开。	Layer by layer, he dug all the clay up from the ground.
虎皮已经沤烂了，	The tigers' hides had rotted and decomposed;
化成一摊细土块。	They had become blocks of clay, indeed.
他开口高声喊阿妹，	Opening his mouth, he called his honey loudly,
又将她轻轻抬出来。	And then he lifted her up from the cave gently.
睁大眼睛看阿妹，	Eyes wide open, he looked at his honey;

一看他就发了呆。
头发更比原来长，
牙齿更比原来白，
眉毛更比原来弯，
眼睛更加有光彩。
阿妹变得更漂亮，
叫他越看越喜爱。

蒙诗彩奏伸伸腰，
打个呵欠站起来。
她像刚刚才睡醒，
抖抖长裙摸摸腮。
哭泣变成了欢笑呀，
幸福撵走了悲哀！
扎董丕冉拉着她，
翩翩起舞好自在。
一边跳舞一边唱，
歌声传到青山外。
树木听了齐叫好，
小河听了也喝彩。
沿着小路转回家，
翻山越岭多轻快。

Just one sight, he felt surprised, but pleasantly.
Her hair grew longer;
Her teeth were whiter;
Her eyebrows were more curved;
Her eyes were more brightly colored.
His honey had become more beautiful;
The more he looked, the more he felt joyful.

Mengshi Caizou straightened herself up, her smile sweet;
She yawned and rose to her feet.
As if from a sleep she had awakened newly,
She shook her long skirt and touched her cheeks gently.
Crying had changed into laughing already;
Happiness had driven away sadness thoroughly!
Zhadong Piran held her hands lovingly,
And danced lightly and freely.
Happily, they were dancing and singing,
To the mountains beyond, the sound of their singing spreading.
Hearing their singing, trees applauded;
Hearing their singing, rivers cheered.
Along mountain paths, they were returning home happily;
Climbing mountains and crossing ridges, they walked briskly.

来到彝家山，	They came to the Yi people's mountain,
找到老佑保，	And found the elder Yi man again.
扎董丕冉说：	In a soft voice said Zhadong Piran:
“我杀死魔虎来见你，	“I've killed the tigers and come to pay you a visit;
三年前的话我没忘记！”	What I had said three years before I didn't forget!”
来到瑶家山，	They came to the Yao people's mountain,
找着咪尼娇。	And found the little Yao kid again.
扎董丕冉说：	In a soft voice said Zhadong Piran:
“我杀死魔虎来见你，	“I've killed the tigers and come to pay you a visit;
三年前的话我没忘掉！”	What I had said three years before I didn't forget!”
来到壮家大河边，	They came to the Zhuang people's riverside,
又去找彩伊。	And again, the Zhuang lass he found.
扎董丕冉说：	In a soft voice, Zhadong Piran said:
“我杀死魔虎来见你，	“I've killed the tigers and come to pay you a visit;
三年前的话我牢记在心底！”	What I said three years ago is buried deep in my heart!”
三年的时光多漫长，	So long was the three years' time
像是隔了千万代；	As if thousands of generations were between them;
阴间阳间离得远，	The nether world and the mortal world were far from
隔着两个大世界。	each other;
扎董丕冉最真诚，	Between them there were two big worlds altogether.
含辛茹苦守坟台。	Zhadong Piran was the sincerest, undoubtedly;

沉沉黑夜过去了，
东方发白天地开。

Enduring all the hardships, he kept the grave whole-heartedly.
The long, long dark night was gone;
The sky whitening, here came the dawn.

第十一章　悲去喜来

Canto 11　Sadness Passing, Happiness Came in

三十六

XXXVI

蒙诗彩奏前边走，	Mengshi Caizou walked ahead;
扎董丕冉后面跟。	Zhadong Piran followed behind.
不觉来到寨子边，	Before they knew it, outside the stockade village they stood;
忽听寨里起闹声。	Suddenly, they heard noises rising inside.
他俩走进寨子里，	They went into the stockade village at once,
看见房前站满人。	And saw crowds of people standing before the house.
家里打响牛皮鼓，	Inside, someone was beating the cowhide drum,
屋里吹响大芦笙。	The big lusheng was being played in the room.
为啥要打牛皮鼓？	Why beat the cowhide drum?
为啥要吹大芦笙？	Why play the big lusheng at home?
大鼓咚咚能传话，	The drum's sound "boom-boom" could convey meaning;
芦笙呜呜能传情。	The lusheng's voice "wooo-wooo" could express feeling.
扎董丕冉最懂事，	Zhadong Piran was the most intelligent;
蒙诗彩奏也聪明。	Mengshi Caizou was also very smart.
知道大鼓传话召亲戚，	They knew the drum was calling relatives together,
明白芦笙传情唤寨邻。	And the lusheng neighbors to come over.
亲戚朋友一齐来，	Relatives and friends had come to the house together;
正在办丧悼亲人。	They were mourning and making funeral arrangements

together.

你看吧——	Look, please—
那边有人擤鼻涕，	Over there, one was blowing his nose;
这边有人擦眼睛。	Right here, one was wiping her eyes.
哭哭啼啼真凄惨，	Crying and sobbing, they looked so miserable;
嘘嘘叹叹好伤心。	Whining and sighing, they appeared sorrowful.
扎董丕冉很奇怪，	Zhadong Piran felt very amazed;
蒙诗彩奏也吃惊。	Mengshi Caizou was also surprised.
心想莫非阿支过了世？	They thought: can it be that Pop has departed from the world?
又想莫非阿奈归了阴？	They also thought: can it be that Mom has died?
二人不禁心酸难忍耐，	Both of them couldn't help feeling grieved;
哇地一下哭出声。	Each of them burst out crying like a child.
呼天唤地肝肠断，	They cried to heaven and earth as if their hearts would break,
串串珠泪往下滚。	Beads of tears streaming down to make a lake.

扎董丕冉拉阿妹，	Zhadong Piran held his honey's hand,
一步一步往前行。	And one step after another, they moved ahead.
上前没有走几步，	Just a few steps they walked forward
又见场上挤满人。	Before they saw on the square a large crowd.
有的跳芦笙，	Some were playing the lusheng and dancing;
有的招魂灵，	Someone was conjuring;

有的刮牛头，	A bull head someone was scraping;
有的剁牛筋，	Sinews someone was chopping;
有的切牛肉，	Beef some were slicing;
有的抱柴薪，	Firewood some were carrying;
有的忙接客，	Guests some were receiving;
有的搬桌凳。	Tables and benches some were carrying.
闹闹嚷嚷好排场，	The square was extravagant and noisy;
烟雾腾腾好阴森。	Full of smoke, the place was foggy and ghostly.
二人抬头往前看，	Raising their eyes, they tried to see what was happening;
墙脚又有巡逻人。	Along the wall, some villagers were patrolling.
有的吹牛角，	An ox horn someone was blowing;
有的拿弯弓，	A machete someone was holding;
有的提大刀，	A broadsword someone was carrying;
有的喊出声：	Someone was shouting:
“我们在为死者巡逻呀，	“We're patrolling for the deceased
要让死者能安心。	To help make the dead feel at rest.
白天巡逻三回得清静，	Patrolling thrice during the day will make them quiet;
夜晚巡逻三次得太平！”	Patrolling thrice at night will make them peaceful at last!”
到底死了什么人？	Who on earth died?
二人心里更纳闷。	Both of them felt more puzzled.
扎董丕冉带阿妹，	Zhadong Piran, together with his honey,
两步跨进自家门。	Stepped inside his family's house quickly.

堂前不见大棺材，	In the front of the central room, they saw no caskets,
只有两个大簸箕在屋厅。	But on the floor, there were two large bamboo winnowing baskets.
簸箕上面插篾圈，	On the baskets, two thin bamboo strip effigies were standing;
看着篾圈好吓人！	The bamboo effigies were so frightening!
一个篾圈在左边，	One effigy was standing on the left;
套着男人新衣裤；	In a man's new clothes it was dressed.
一个篾圈在右边，	Another effigy was standing on the right;
套着女人新褶裙。	In a woman's new pleated skirt it was dressed.
还有两对小竹卦，	There were also two pairs of bamboo divination sticks;
合拢放在簸箕中。	They were put side by side in the winnowing baskets.
堂中栽根大竹竿，	A big bamboo post was inserted into the floor of the central room;
大鼓挂在竹竿顶。	On the top of the bamboo post hung a big drum.
一人站着打大鼓，	A man was standing nearby, beating it;
一人绕竿吹芦笙。	Another man was playing the lusheng around the post.
鼓点伴着芦笙曲，	The drumbeats went with the lusheng melody;
曲曲调调撕人心。	Each tune and each tone were tearing people's hearts ruthlessly.
满屋的人在啼哭，	A roomful of people were crying,
眼睛哭得红彤彤。	Their eyes red and glowing.
他们一边揩眼泪，	While they were wiping their tears,
一边忙着做事情。	They were busy doing things.
有的忙烧香，	Incense someone was burning;
有的忙念经，	Sutras someone was reciting;
有的忙磕头，	
有的忙烧灵，	

有的忙把丧歌唱，
有的忙着收礼金。
只见么公拿着小竹卦，
丢在地上问吉凶。
反复丢了好几次，
直到竹卦一翻一扑手才停。
这卦是个吉利卦，
表示死者活者都安宁。

么公提起一只公鸡来，
对着篾圈念几声。
然后活活捏死那公鸡，
剖开鸡肚取鸡心。
再把鸡心拿到火上烤，
烤得满屋香喷喷。
一个鸡心分两半，
放在两个簸箕中。
接着倒了两杯酒，
一边一杯摆得正。
口里唱起“指路歌”，
慢声慢气听得清：

Some were kowtowing;
Offerings some were burning;
Funerals songs some were singing;
Condolence money some were collecting.
A shaman held a small bamboo divination stick,
And threw it on the floor to foretell good or bad luck.
Several times the action he repeated;
He didn't stop till the obverse and the reverse sides appeared.
That divination was really lucky,
Indicating both the dead and the living enjoyed serenity.

The shaman picked up a rooster;
Facing the bamboo effigies, he began to murmur.
Then, he pinched the rooster and killed it;
Cutting open the rooster's belly, he took its heart out.
He then put the heart to the fire to roast;
Everywhere in the room, the smell was really sweet.
He halved the rooster's heart,
And put respectively one piece into each winnowing basket.
Then, two cups of liquor he poured,
And put each of them straight on one side.
He began to sing the Way-showing Song feelingly;
In a mild and slow tone, he could be heard clearly:

“鸡是人的伴，	“The chicken is a companion of man;
人和鸡同心。	Man’s heart looks the same as that of the chicken.
你们吃了这鸡心，	You two, please eat the rooster’s heart;
跟这公鸡结伴行。	Travel with the rooster and never part.
然后再喝一杯酒，	Then, drink a cup of liquor;
路行千里有精神。	You’ll be energetic on the road you’ll cover.
你们骑在鸡背上，	You two, on the rooster’s back, please ride;
走起路来快如风。	On the road, you’ll be as quick as the wind.
太阳出来天气热，	When the sun comes out, it will be hot;
翅膀底下好躲荫；	Under its wings, you can take shelter from the heat.
要是老天下大雨，	If it rains hard,
尾巴下面好藏身。	Under its tail you can hide.
走到毛虫坡，	When you arrive at the Caterpillar Slope,
鸡会啄完小毛虫；	All the caterpillars the rooster will eat up.
遇到大灰狼，	If you run into a wolf accidentally,
鸡会啄瞎狼眼睛；	The rooster will peck its eyes and blind it mercilessly.
走到岔路口，	If you come to a fork in the road in a place far away,
公鸡自会辨西东。	The rooster will show you the way.
你们的鸡叫起来，	If your rooster begins to crow,
人家的鸡不打鸣，	While a family’s rooster does not follow,
那就不是你们的亲奶爷，	It means its owner is not your grandparents,
你们不要去相认；	And you shouldn’t claim yourself to be their descendants.
你们的鸡叫起来，	If your rooster crows,
人家的鸡也答应，	And a family’s rooster also follows,

那才是你们的亲奶爷，	It means its owner is your grandparents,
你们就要去相认。	And you should claim yourself to be their descendants.
我劝你们莫着急，	However, I advise you to be more patient, dear;
我还有话要说明：	There are some words I want to make clear:
要是奶爷出来看你们，	If the grandparents come out to see you at once,
只是站在远处看，	But they stand far away from your place,
那是别家的奶爷，	They then are another family's grandparents,
你们不要去相认；	And you shouldn't claim to be their descendants;
要是奶爷出来看你们，	If the grandparents come out to see you at once,
站在近处看，	But they just stand close to your place,
那是你们的堂奶爷，	They then are your granduncle and grandaunt,
你们可以喊一声；	And you can call them to make a salute.
要是奶爷跑过来，	If the grandparents come out of their house,
伸开双手搂你们，	And stretch out their hands to hug you at once,
那才是你们的亲奶爷，	They then are your real grandparents,
你们就要去相认。	You should claim to be their descendants.
奶爷住在浑水河那边，	Your grandparents live near the Muddy River, and
有田有地好耕种。	They have a very good paddy field and dry land.
牛也杀给你们了，	A bull has been killed for your future work;
你们安心带着牛去种庄稼；	You can feel at ease to lead the bull to do farm work.
狗也杀给你们了，	A dog has also been killed for your future use;
你们好好领着狗去看家门。	You can bring the dog with you to keep guard over the house.
我的‘指路歌’，	
句句唱得清。	I'm singing the "Way-showing Song" for you currently,

顺着我指的大路走，
回到老家找先人！”

And I sing each word and each sentence clearly.
Walk along the main road I showed you, and
Look for the ancestors in the ancestral land!”

扎董丕冉听罢更伤情，
心想家里定是死了两个人。
莫非阿支阿奈双双去世了？
可又不见棺材停在堂屋中。
只有左边篾圈套的男人衣，
还有右边篾圈套的女人裙。
到底死了什么人？
可要细细问分明。
扎董丕冉刚想问，
吹师又吹起芦笙来招魂。
扎董丕冉一边抹眼泪，
一边又侧耳仔细听。
听出曲曲芦笙调，
吹的都是自己的事情：

Hearing that, Zhadong Piran felt sadder inwardly,
Thinking two people must have died in the family.
Could it be that both Pop and Mom had passed away?
Yet, there weren't any coffins in the central room, anyway.
He saw only, on the left, over the bamboo effigy, a man's coat
And on the right, over the bamboo effigy, a woman's skirt.
Who on earth had passed away?
He needed to check it out, anyway.
Zhadong Piran was about to ask what had happened
When a lusheng master played to recall the spirit of the dead.
While Zhadong Piran was wiping away his tears sadly,
He was listening to the lusheng music attentively.
He figured out each tune of the lusheng music,
Knowing that Zhadong Piran himself was the only topic:

“嘀啦哒，嘀啦哒，
啦哒伦罗啦嘀啦，
啦哒伦罗啦嘀伦，

“Dee-la-da, dee-la-da,
La-da-lun-luo-la-dee-la,
La-da-lun-luo-la-dee-lun,

嘀罗伦啦嘀罗啦。	Dee-luo-lun-la-dee-luo-la.
太阳已经落了山，	The sun has set behind the mountain from the sky's dome;
亲人远去不回家。	The dear ones have gone far away, never coming back home.
月亮出来没有光，	The moon comes out without any luster;
亲友个个把泪洒。	Relatives and friends shed tears like a shower.
不幸的人儿遭灾难，	Unfortunate people have suffered a great disaster;
山水也在闪泪花。	Even the tears in the eyes of mountains and rivers glitter.
'蒙嘎祝' '蒙嘎老' ①，	'Menggazhu', 'Menggalao', ①
哭丧的调子不断吹，	One after another, tunes of mourning are played;
吹得人心乱如麻。	They make people utterly confused and disconcerted.
悲悲戚戚来办丧，	Plaintive and mournful, we come to conduct a funeral,
不是祭奠爹和妈。	But we aren't here to mourn Pop and Mom, the old couple.
只因扎董丕冉到远方，	Just because Zhadong Piran has gone far away,
为救妻子去把虎追杀。	And to rescue his wife, he chased tigers along the way.
蒙诗彩奏救不回，	Mengshi Caizou hasn't been rescued;
他俩反被虎糟蹋。	They two have been killed by tigers, instead.
扎董丕冉变成魔虎屎，	Zhadong Piran has changed into the tigers' waste,
早被屙进山旮旯，	And has been excreted in the mountain corners as shit.
蒙诗彩奏变成魔虎尿，	Mengshi Caizou has turned into the tigers' urine,
也被撒在山垭巴。	And has been urinated at the saddle back of the mountain.
他俩双双把命丧，	Both of them have been killed by the monster tigers tragically;
寨邻亲友来超拔。	

① 蒙嘎祝、蒙嘎老：苗语，老人为儿女办丧事时吹的芦笙调。

① (Hmong language) Names of lusheng tones played when parents conduct their children's funerals.

男人眼泪像水淌，
女人眼泪如雨下。”

Neighbors, relatives and friends are releasing their souls
from purgatory.
Men's tears are streaming down like a river;
Women's tears are pouring down like a shower."

“嘀啦哒，嘀啦哒，
啦哒伦罗啦嘀啦。
哭声阵阵不停息，
哭得头昏眼发花；
丧歌声声不间断，
唱得心痛如刀扎。
芦笙吹出‘招魂调’，
大香烧了好几把，
纸钱化了好几捆，
要将他俩的魂魄招回家。
不幸的扎董丕冉呀，
可怜的蒙诗彩奏呀，
路头路脑莫停留，
三魂七魄回来吧！
山间莫摘果，
岭上莫采花，
林里莫打鸟，
水边莫捞虾。”

"Dee-la-da, dee-la-da,
La-da-lun-luo-la-dee-la.
Mournful people are crying continuously,
And their eyes are blurring, their heads dizzy.
Songs of mourning are sung ceaselessly,
And their hearts hurt as if pierced by knives mercilessly.
Out of the lusheng flows the 'Tune of Calling the Soul of the Dead';
Quite a few bunches of large incense sticks have been burned;
Quite a few bundles of spirit money have been burned
to ashes;
We are here to recall their souls.
O, Zhadong Piran, an unfortunate man,
O, Mengshi Caizou, a pathetic woman,
At road junctions, don't stop to stay;
Souls and spirits, come back home from far away!
In mountains, don't pick fruits, please;
On mountain ridges, don't pick flowers;
In forests, don't shoot birds;
Near rivers, don't catch prawns."

"回来啦，回来啦，	"Back home, back home,
三魂七魄回来啦！	The young couple's souls, don't roam!
蛇缠就拿竹鞭抽，	If a snake stops you, hit it with a bamboo whip;
豹撵就用铁猫夹，	If a leopard chases you, prevent it with an iron animal trap;
蜂叮就拿火烟熏，	If bees try to sting you, drive them away with fire and smoke;
狗咬给它吃粑粑。"	If a dog tries to bite you, throw it a pancake."
"回来啦，回来啦，	"Back home, back home,
三魂七魄回来啦！	The young couple's souls, don't roam!
撑起花伞遮太阳，	Open colorful umbrellas to shelter from the sun, and
披起蓑衣挡风沙，	Put on palm-bark capes to keep out wind and sand;
缠起裹腿脚不疼，	Wrap puttees and your feet won't hurt on the journey;
穿起草鞋路不滑。"	Put on straw shoes and the road won't be slippery."
"回来啦，回来啦，	"Back home, back home,
三魂七魄回来啦！	The young couple's souls, don't roam!
跌倒赶紧爬起来，	If you fall down, rise to your feet quickly;
淌汗就拿花帕擦，	If you sweat, wipe it away with a flowery handkerchief instantly;
渴了就喝山泉水，	If you are thirsty, drink some spring water;
饿了就吃荞疙瘩。"	If you are hungry, eat buckwheat rice to ease your hunger."
"回来啦，回来啦，	"Back home, back home,

三魂七魄回来啦！	The young couple's souls, don't roam!
我吹'招魂调'，	'Tune of Recalling the Soul of the Dead' I'm playing;
吹得嘴发麻。	So numb is my mouth becoming.
吹了好几回，	I've played it many a time
要催你们转回家。	To urge you to come back home.
不让你们受孤苦，	I do this to keep you from hardship and loneliness,
魂魄落在荒山和野坝。	In case your souls wander in mountains and wilderness.
你们回到家里来，	When you have come back home,
立刻拜见爹和妈。	Hurry to pay your respects to Pop and Mom.
顺着公公指的路，	Walk along the way I showed you, and
赶快回老家！	Go back quickly to the ancestral land.
回到老家见祖先，	There, pay your respects to the ancestors promptly
祖先定会乐哈哈。"	And they will definitely be happy."
"公公在唱'指路歌'，	"'Way-showing Song' I'm singing;
唱得嗓子哑。	So hoarse my voice is becoming.
路已指明白，	I've shown you the way clearly,
一点也不差。	And my direction is precise, undoubtedly.
就等你们来，	We're waiting for you to come back home eagerly,
骑马上路啦。"	So you can ride on horses and start your journey."
"回来吧，回来吧，	"Back home, back home,
三魂七魄回来吧！	The young couple's souls, don't roam!
嘀啦哒，嘀啦哒，	Dee-la-da, dee-la-da,

啦哒伦罗啦嘀啦，	La-da-lun-luo-la-dee-la,
啦哒伦罗啦嘀伦，	La-da-lun-luo-la-dee-lun,
嘀罗伦啦嘀罗啦……”	Dee-luo-lun-la-dee-luo-la…”

三十七 XXXVII

扎董丕冉听完了，	Zhadong Piran finished listening to the lusheng master;
哭笑不得难回答。	Not knowing whether to laugh or cry, he found it hard to answer.
原来是为这回事，	The reason was finally uncovered;
解开一个大疙瘩。	The puzzle in his heart was completely solved.
事到此时真相明，	Not until then, did the whole truth come out;
顿时心里乐开花。	Suddenly, in his heart he felt cheerful and buoyant.
转悲为喜热泪滚，	His sorrow turning to joy, his eyes brimmed with tears;
对着吹师忙说话：	He hurried to speak to the lusheng master with smiling eyes:

“你的芦笙吹得妙，	“You played the lusheng really wonderfully;
婉转悠扬真热闹。	The music was mild, melodious and lively.
招魂调子动人心，	The ‘Tune of Recalling the Soul of the Dead’ is touching,
将我吹得心欢笑。	And it made me burst out laughing.
我看你已吹累了，	I think you are now very tired;

让我替你吹一调。”	Let me replace you and play one tune, instead.”
吹师一听怔住了，	Hearing him, the lusheng master felt stunned,
不知这是什么话？	Not knowing what had actually happened.
个个痛哭他发笑，	People around were crying, while he was laughing;
莫非他是疯了吗？	Could it be that he was mad or something?
看他吹的什么调，	The lusheng master wanted to see what tune he would play,
且把芦笙交给他。	So the master handed the lusheng to him, anyway.
扎董丕冉接过芦笙来，	Zhadong Piran took the lusheng instantly,
吹出一番真情话：	And played a tune of his true feelings immediately:
“嘀啦哒，嘀啦哒，	“Dee-la-da, dee-la-da,
啦哒伦罗啦嘀啦，	La-da-lun-luo-la-dee-la,
啦哒伦罗啦嘀伦，	La-da-lun-luo-la-dee-lun,
嘀罗伦啦嘀罗啦。	Dee-luo-lun-la-dee-luo-la
西边太阳映晚霞，	The sun shines on evening clouds in the west;
东边月亮往上爬。	The moon rises upward in the east.
亲戚呀，朋友呀，	Friends and relatives,
大家莫把眼泪洒。	Please, don’t shed tears.
吹哪曲，唱哪调？	Which song to play, which tune to sing?
哭调悲调不吹它。	I won’t play tunes of sadness or crying.
吹起一曲团圆调，	I will play a tune of reunion;
哥弟姐妹来玩耍！”	Brothers and sisters, come to play and have fun!”

“嘀啦哒，嘀啦哒，	“Dee-la-da, dee-la-da,
啦哒伦罗啦嘀啦。	La-da-lun-luo-la-dee-la,
那个扎董丕冉呀，	O, Zhadong Piran, for whom you feel sad,
为救妻子走天涯。	To save his wife, went to the end of the world.
历尽千难和万险，	He has gone through thousands of difficulties and dangers,
终于把那魔虎杀。	And finally killed all the monster tigers.
扎董丕冉没有死，	Zhadong Piran didn't die, fortunately,
如今他已回到家！”	He has now come back home safely!”
“嘀啦哒，嘀啦哒，	“Dee-la-da, dee-la-da,
啦哒伦罗啦嘀啦。	La-da-lun-luo-la-dee-la.
蒙诗彩奏没喂虎，	Mengshi Caizou was not killed by tigers;
堂屋里面就是她。	Now, standing in the central room she is.
快把簸箕收起来，	Remove the bamboo winnowing baskets quickly,
快把大鼓也放下！”	And also put down the big drum promptly!”
“嘀啦哒，嘀啦嘀，	“Dee-la-da, dee-la-dee,
啦嘀伦罗嘀啦嘀。	La-dee-lun-luo-dee-la-dee.
扎董丕冉还活着，	Zhadong Piran is still alive, really;
他已站在堂屋里。	He's been in the central room already.
快把香火扫出去，	Hurry to sweep away the incense ashes;
快把灵堂也收起！”	Hurry to put away the mourning hall and offerings!”
“嘀啦哒，嘀啦嘀，	“Dee-la-da, dee-la-dee,

啦嘀伦罗嘀啦嘀。	La-dee-lun-luo-dee-la-dee.
寨邻亲友莫悲伤，	Don't be sad, neighbors, friends and relatives;
哥弟姐妹莫哭泣。	Don't cry, brothers and sisters.
远方亲人已归家，	The dear ones have come back home from the faraway place;
快把衣裙都藏起。	Hurry to hide the coat and the skirt someplace.
要是他们真死了，	If they have already been sent to Eternity!"
你再超拔也无益！”	It's useless for you to release their souls from purgatory!"
扎董丕冉吹的欢乐调，	A tune of happiness Zhadong Piran had played,
吹师觉得很惊奇。	And the lusheng master felt greatly surprised.
唱出扎董丕冉已归家，	The tune said Zhadong Piran had already come back home,
又唱蒙诗彩奏在屋里。	And it also said Mengshi Caizou had been in the room.
个个高兴又心疼，	Each of them felt happy and relieved;
人人将信又将疑。	Each of them was not quite convinced.
“扎董丕冉在哪里？	"O, Zhadong Piran! Where is he?
蒙诗彩奏在哪里？”	O, Mengshi Caizou! Where is she?"
人们纷纷来询问，	People came to ask him one after another,
都想搞清这秘密。	And all of them expected a straight answer.
扎董丕冉微微笑，	Zhadong Piran smiled a little;
忙向大家作个揖：	With hands folded in front, he hurriedly bowed to all people:
“扎董丕冉就是我，	"Zhadong Piran is me;
莫非你们已忘记？”	Can it be that you've forgotten me completely?"

蒙诗彩奏扯扯裙，	Mengshi Caizou straightened her skirt,
忙向大家行个礼：	And hurriedly bowed to all people to show them respect:
“蒙诗彩奏就是我，	“Mengshi Caizou is me;
我是头回来这里！”	It’s the first time for me to be here, everybody!”
人们一齐围拢来，	All the people gathered around;
老人使劲往前挤：	To push to the front old people struggled:
“扎董丕冉出门已多年，	“Zhadong Piran has been away for many years;
变了模样难记忆。	He has changed, of whom they have only vague memories.
胡子长了没有刮，	His beard becoming long, he didn’t shave it;
头发长了没有剃，	His hair becoming long, he didn’t have it cut;
衣裳烂了没有补，	His clothes worn out, he didn’t have them mended;
裤子脏了没有洗。	His trousers dirty, he didn’t have them washed.
好像变成两个人，	He is totally different from the one he was;
哪里还能记得起？	How can they remember him after so many years?
如今见面不相识，	Meeting again, they can’t recognize him, though in sight;
莫怪乡亲不讲礼！”	Don’t blame the village folks for being impolite!”
扎董丕冉唱起歌，	Zhadong Piran began to sing;
亲亲热热答亲戚：	Warm-heartedly and affectionately, he was answering:
“乡邻亲友我不怪，	“Neighbors, friends and relatives, I blame you not;
只怪魔虎施奸计。	The tigers are only to blame for their evil plot.
害我离乡好几年，	For quite a few years, I’ve been forced to leave the village;

春去冬来无归期，	Seasons changing, there was no possibility of returning home.
如今大害已除尽，	Now, the evil monsters have been eliminated;
亲人才能得团聚！”	The dear ones could finally be reunited!”

屋里屋外是欢歌，	Inside and outside the room, there were happy songs;
房前房后是笑语。	Before and behind the house, there were cheerful voices.
阿支躲在竹楼上，	Inside the bamboo house, Pop was hiding upstairs;
伤伤心心在哭泣。	Broken-hearted, he was crying and shedding tears.
听说儿子回到家，	Hearing that his son had come back home,
揩干眼泪下楼梯。	He dried his eyes and went downstairs to see him.

阿奈坐在墙角落，	Mom was sitting in a corner;
哭得腰也直不起。	She couldn't straighten herself, and her cry was so bitter.
听说媳妇也来了，	Hearing that her daughter-in-law had also returned safely,
抹把眼泪笑嘻嘻。	She wiped her eyes and smiled broadly.

三十八　XXXVIII

阿支阿奈欢笑着，	Pop and Mom smiled happily,
跑到儿子的身边。	And ran to their son quickly.
摸着他的宽肩膀，	Touching his broad shoulder lovingly,

从头到脚仔细看：

From head to toe, they surveyed him carefully.

“孩儿呀，
都说你们被虎吃，
早已离开人世间。
今天办丧来超度，
希望你们早升天。
如今你们回来了，
莫非是在梦里见？”

“O, my children, my beloved!
You have been eaten by tigers, people said,
And have already left the mortal world.
Conducting a funeral to release your souls from purgatory,
We hope you can go up to Heaven early.
Now, you have come back home;
Can it be that we're meeting in a dream?”

扎董丕冉微微笑，
蒙诗彩奏眨眨眼。
双双站在爹面前，
双双站在妈面前，
向着爹妈躬躬腰，
异口同声齐开言：

Zhadong Piran smiled faintly;
Mengshi Caizou blinked sweetly.
In couple, they stood before their father;
In couple, they stood before their mother;
They bowed before their parents,
And began to speak with one voice:

“阿支阿奈在家里，
挂儿挂媳好几年。
如今我们回来了，
从此全家得团圆！
叫声阿支和阿奈，
莫难过呀莫心酸！”

“Staying at home, Pop and Mom, in tears,
Worried about us for quite a few years.
Now, we have come back home safely;
From now on, the whole family will live together happily!
Pop and Mom, our beloved!
Don't be sad! Don't feel grieved!”

管事寨老一声喊，
人们一起拥上前。
放下牛皮鼓，
拔去长竹竿，
取走篾圈和衣裙，
扫尽香火和纸钱，
收起簸箕和灵堂，
撕掉祭幛和挽联。
重新换上喜酒席，
丧事转成喜事办。

The village chief shouted out loud;
Together, people thronged forward.
They put down the cowhide drum immediately,
And removed the long bamboo post quickly.
Taking away bamboo effigies, the skirt and all the clothes,
Sweeping away spirit money and incense ashes,
Putting away the mourning offerings and the winnowing baskets,
Tearing away the funeral condolence cloth and elegiac couplets,
They put things anew for a wedding feast quickly;
Funeral arrangements had changed into a wedding ceremony.

管事提调各套人，
点起红烛和油灯，
贴上纸花和喜对，
摆好碗碟和果品，
布置新房和新床，
唱起喜歌来迎亲。

The village chief assigned villagers different duties;
They lit oil lamps and red candles;
They pasted paper-cut flowers and wedding couplets;
They put on tables bowls, plates and fruits;
They arranged the honeymoon room and the wedding bed;
They sang happy songs to escort the bride.

蒙诗彩奏巧梳妆，
活像一个仙女样：
长裙轻轻在摇摆，
手镯闪闪在发亮，
双颊微微在泛红，

Mengshi Caizou adorned herself and dressed smartly;
She looked like a beautiful fairy:
Her long skirt swung gently;
Her bracelets shone brightly;
Her cheeks reddened slightly;

两眼熠熠在生光。	Her eyes glittered beautifully.
扎董丕冉细穿戴，	Zhadong Piran dressed delicately;
活像一个王子样：	He looked like a prince, so stately;
布褂软软贴着身，	The cloth jacket clung to his body;
腰带悠悠在飘荡，	At his waist, a sash waved gently;
金笛横插在腰间，	Into the sash, the gold flute was inserted at an angle handsomely;
长刀斜挎在肩上。	Over his shoulder, the long machete was slung awesomely.
寨中一位老婆婆，	An old stockade village granny,
抱着一只大公鸡，	Holding a big rooster in her arms tightly,
领着新郎出门去，	Led the groom outside,
带着新娘出门去。	Followed by the bride.
新郎身后有陪宾，	Behind the groom was a groomsman;
新娘身后有福女[①]。	Behind the bride was the lucky woman.[①]
吹吹打打往前走，	Trumpets blowing, drums beating, they walked
一直走到树林里。	Until they went into the forest.

① 福女：苗族接亲时，要选择一个子女齐全的妇女参加，负责照料新娘，表示吉利。这个女子叫福女。

① The lucky woman: According to Hmong custom, when the groom goes to meet his bride at her home before escorting her back to his own home for the wedding, a woman who has both sons and daughters should be invited to take care of the bride on the way, which can bring good luck. The woman is called the lucky woman.

大家坐在树荫下，
说笑唱歌表情意。
生火烤肉吃晌午[1]，
边吃边闹多有趣。

They sat in the shade of a tree;
Chatting and singing, they expressed their feelings
affectionately.
They made a fire to have a barbecue for the midday meal[1];
Eating and bantering, they laughed a great deal.

新郎夹起一块肉，
放进新娘饭碗里；
新娘夹起一块肉，
放进新郎饭碗里。
肉香饭热吃得甜，
你敬我让多亲密。

The groom picked up a piece of meat,
And into the bowl of the bride he put it;
The bride picked up a piece of meat,
And into the bowl of the groom she put it.
The meat good and the rice warm, they felt life was sweet;
Respect and cherishing made them more intimate.

陪宾夹起一块肉，
举在面前笑嘻嘻：
“我这块肉烤得香，
要叫新郎新娘一起吃！
你们吃了这块吉祥肉，

The groomsman picked up a piece of meat,
Put it before his eyes and laughed:
“This piece of meat smells good;
The groom should eat it together with the bride!
If you two eat this piece of lucky meat,

---

① 生火烤肉吃晌午：苗族接亲时，不管男方家和女方家相隔多远，都要到山里走一遭，黄昏时才能归男方家。途中必须在山里吃一顿午饭，而且必须吃饱。表示婚后夫妻有饭吃，不会受饥饿。

① To make a fire to have a barbecue for the midday meal: When a Hmong groom goes to meet his bride at her home before escorting her back to his own home for the wedding, no matter how far their families are from each other, they have to go to the mountains, and can't go to the groom's family until dusk. On the way, they have to have lunch in the mountains, and they also have to eat their fill, which means that after marriage, the couple will lead a well-off life and will never suffer from hunger.

永远得过好日子。”	You'll live forever a life so sweet."
新郎对着新娘眨眨眼，	The groom winked at the bride tenderly,
慢慢把嘴凑过去；	And his mouth moved closer to her slowly;
新娘对着新郎点点头，	The bride nodded at the groom bashfully,
轻轻把嘴凑过去。	And her mouth moved closer to him gently.
两人同时咬断那块肉，	They bit off the meat simultaneously,
嘴唇相碰在一起。	And their lips came together lovingly.
逗得众人哈哈笑，	The others laughed heartily,
雀鸟也跟着叫叽叽。	And birds also chirped happily.
新郎激动得手发抖，	The groom felt excited and his hands trembled;
新娘害羞得把头低。	The bride felt so shy that she lowered her head.
闹一阵又笑一阵，	They bantered and laughed;
不觉太阳已偏西。	Before they knew it, the sun began to set.
大家顺着寨子绕一圈，	They walked around the stockade village once,
要让整个山寨添喜气。	And wanted to add to the village's happiness.
又叫新郎新娘肩挨肩，	They then asked, shoulder to shoulder, the bride and groom
双双走进堂屋里。	To walk as a couple up to the central room,
表示迎接新人进家来，	Which conveyed that the bride and groom were ushered home;
说是这样才吉利。	It was believed that by doing that, good luck would come.
福女拿起一把伞，	The lucky woman picked up an umbrella, and

罩住新郎和新娘。	Held it high above the bride and groom.
老婆婆抱起大公鸡，	The old granny took the big rooster, and
举到新娘头顶上，	Held it over the bride's head;
转去转来绕三圈①。	She spun the rooster thrice① quickly;
然后夫妻才拜堂。	The bride and groom then performed the marriage ceremony.
先拜天和地，	They kowtowed to Heaven and Earth, firstly;
再拜众先人，	They kowtowed to all the ancestors, secondly;
又拜爹和妈，	They kowtowed to Pop and Mom, thirdly;
还拜亲友和寨邻。	They kowtowed then to relatives, friends and neighbors, respectively;
亲疏远近都拜过，	They kowtowed to relations close and distant;
夫妻互拜最真诚。	The kowtow between the husband and wife was the most important.
临时又找四个老公公，	Just before the ceremony, four old grandpas
换上新衣做媒人。	Were invited to put on new clothes as matchmakers.
四位媒公坐上席，	The four matchmakers sat in seats of honor;

① 转去转来绕三圈：苗族婚俗，新郎将新娘接进家后，福女拿伞将他们罩住，再由那个老年妇女将那只活公鸡拿到新娘头上绕三圈，表示“捉魂”。通过“捉魂”，新娘便正式成为新郎家的成员，再也不能离开男方家。

① To spin the rooster thrice: According to Hmong marriage custom, after the groom escorts the bride back his home, the lucky woman shelters them with the umbrella, and then the old granny spins the living rooster thrice above the bride's head, which means "to catch the soul". After "catching the soul", the bride becomes formally a member of the groom's family and she can never leave the groom's family in her lifetime.

饮酒对歌来贺喜。
你一杯呀我一盏，
一杯一盏甜如蜜：
“他们二人自相爱，
历尽艰险成夫妻。
有情的人得幸福，
我们做媒也欢喜。”

Drinking and singing responsively, congratulations they did offer.
One cup after another, they drank happily;
One cup after another, the liquor tasted as sweet as honey:
“They fell in love of their own accord;
Having gone through hardships and dangers, they got married.
Lovers have gotten happiness;
As matchmakers, we also feel joyous.”

“我们做的现成媒，
没费口舌没出力。
定要多喝一碗酒，
不怕酒醉爬不起！”

As matchmakers, we didn’t do anything;
They have spared us all the talking.
We’ll certainly drink one more bowl of liquor;
We aren’t afraid of getting drunk as a fiddler!”

大家唱起“祝酒歌”，
喝一口酒唱一句。
酒香歌甜心里乐，
三杯两碗醉如泥。

The four matchmakers began to sing “Songs for Toasts”;
They took a gulp and sang a sentence.
Fragrant liquor and sweet songs made them more delighted;
With three cups or two bowls, each was as drunk as a lord.

四位接亲老长辈，
喜上心头笑在眉。
夸赞新娘人品好，
跟这新郎正相配：

Four bride-escorting elders
Felt jubilant and were all smiles.
They praised the bride for her good character,
Saying she and the groom were meant to be together:

“看这新娘懂礼节，
又像天仙一样美。
扎董丕冉跟她在一起，
就像一对鸳鸯比翼飞。”

“The bride has good manners and behaves politely,
And she is as beautiful as a fairy.
Zhadong Piran marries and lives with her;
They are like a pair of mandarin ducks flying together.”

“今天迎亲日子好，
愿他俩情意如同长流水，
来年生个胖娃娃，
像金竹一样越长越青翠！”

“Today’s a great day for a wedding;
Wish their love lasts like a river, ever flowing.
Hope that in the coming year, they’ll have a chubby baby;
It’ll grow increasingly fresh and green as a golden bamboo tree!”

他们高唱“迎亲调”，
唱了一回又一回。
歌声入耳酒入心，
喝酒不多也会醉。

They sang “Song of Escorting the Bride” loudly,
And they sang it repeatedly.
The song was pleasant to the ears, the liquor sweet to the heart;
One didn’t have to drink much to get buzzed.

陪郎阿哥最爱玩，
拉着新郎跳得欢。
姑娘一齐来伴唱，
跳通了地呀唱翻了天！

The groomsmen liked to have fun;
Taking the groom by the hand, they danced, filled with elation.
Lasses came together to sing songs for them cheeringly;
They danced whole-heartedly and sang heartily!

陪嫁姑娘了不起，
唱起山歌醉倒你。
伴着新娘唱主角，
歌声传遍几十里。

The bridesmaid was really fantastic;
When she sang, people would get drunk.
She sang along with the bride;
Dozens of miles away their singing spread.

姑娘小伙肩挨肩，
围成几个大圈圈。
圈圈转去又转来，
轻歌曼舞乐无边。
腰带飘飞裙子摆，
犹如身临彩云间。

Shoulder to shoulder, lads and lasses
Sang and danced in several big circles.
The circles moved around and around joyously;
Singing merrily and dancing gracefully, they were only too happy.
Sashes flew in the air, skirts swinging;
They seemed to be in the clouds, singing and dancing.

帮忙的人不简单，
抱柴挑水当厨倌。
烧火煮饭磨豆腐，
摆碗理筷抬盘盘。
来来往往如穿梭，
脚不停歇手不闲。

Those helpers were really helpful in arranging the wedding;
They carried firewood and water, and did cooking.
They lit fires, made bean curd and cooked rice;
They carried plates and prepared bowls and chopsticks.
Back and forth, they were shuttling;
They were busy preparing a banquet for the wedding.

桌椅碗筷摆满场，
宾客欢笑聚一堂。
桌桌都有八碗菜，
旁边还有牛肉汤。

Tables, chairs, bowls and chopsticks had been prepared;
Chatting and laughing, guests gathered around.
On each table, there were eight bowls of food;
A wooden bucket of beef bouillon was by the tableside.

一缸喜酒放桌下，	Under the table was a jug of wedding liquor;
满场尽是米酒香。	The whole place was filled with the rice liquor's fragrance.

三十九　XXXIX

蒙诗彩奏抬金碗，	In her hands, a gold bowl Mengshi Caizou raised.
扎董丕冉抱酒缸。	In his arms, a liquor vat Zhadong Piran carried.
挨一挨二来敬酒，	One by one, they proposed a toast.
喜气盈门心欢畅。	Happiness filling the room, they beamed with delight.
一碗喜酒喝下肚，	They drank a bowl of wedding liquor,
调子唱得更响亮。	And sang tunes much louder.

新郎唱起“谢媒歌”，	The groom sang “Appreciative Songs for the Matchmakers”.
字字句句表衷肠：	Each word and each sentence expressed their inner feelings:
“多谢媒公来操持，	“For the matchmakers we are deeply thankful;
我俩才得结成双。	With your great help, we can finally become a couple.
敬请媒公多喝一杯酒，	Please, drink one more cup of liquor, ye;
祝你们添福添寿永安康！”	I wish all of you happiness, health and longevity!”

新娘唱起“谢厨调”，	The bride sang “Appreciative Tunes for the Cooks”, and
感谢厨师来帮忙：	She thanked all of them for giving the family a hand:
“多亏厨师手艺巧，	“Thanks to the cooks' great expertise,

喜酒席上饭菜香。
恭请厨师多喝一杯酒，
愿你们油盐满罐米满缸！”

We can enjoy the delicious flavor of food and steamed rice.
Please, drink one more cup of liquor;
I wish all of you a wealthy life hereafter!”

阿支笑得坐不稳，
阿奈笑得热泪淌。
夸赞媳妇情意深，
魔虎越逼越刚强；
又夸儿子最勇敢，
将那魔虎全杀光。
堂屋里面更欢乐，
姑娘小伙心花放。
男女各分两边坐，
饮酒对歌庆吉祥。
酒歌情歌尽情唱，
罚酒罚歌闹洋洋。

Pop laughed heartily and couldn't sit steadily;
Mom laughed heartily and tears streamed down happily.
They praised their daughter-in-law for being faithful;
However hard the tigers pushed her, she didn't yield to the evil.
They also praised their son for being the bravest man,
And having killed all the monster tigers alone.
The central room was more joyous;
Lasses and lads beamed with happiness.
Men and women sat opposite each other in the central room, respectively;
Celebrating the auspicious day, they drank and sang responsively.
They sang toast and love songs heartily;
Forfeit drinking and singing filled the room with gaiety.

蜜蜂蝴蝶齐飞来，
祝贺新郎和新娘：
“祝你俩白头共到老，
贺你俩夫妻和睦日子旺！”

Bees and butterflies flew together to them
To congratulate the bride and groom:
“May you two live and grow old together!
Wish you two harmonious and prosperous lives hereafter!”

通宵达旦来祝贺，	Guests came to congratulate them all through the night;
一直闹到太阳出东方……	They had fun drinking and singing till the sun rose in the east...

About the Translator

Yin Shaodong is a lecturer of English in the School of Foreign Languages and Literature at Yunnan Normal University. His recent publications include one translation: *A Study of the Sadu Language* (American Academic Press, 2015. Co-translator), two textbooks: *Comprehensive English Students' Book 4 & Teachers' Book 4* (China Renmin University Press, 2017. Co-compiler), and more than ten articles on translation strategies, English rhetoric, linguistics, and English teaching. His research interests focus on literary translation, English rhetoric and cognitive linguistics.